FINDING MASLOW

A Novel

Susan Lee Walberg

Copyright

ISBN: 1517175216
ISBN 13: 9781517175214

DEDICATION

To all of the dedicated people who worked so tirelessly at St. John's Episcopal Hospital through Hurricane Sandy and beyond. Your commitment and perseverance are truly an inspiration.

CHAPTER ONE

A s she stepped off the train in Long Beach, New York, Justina had absolutely no idea what was coming her way. The salty breeze whipped her straight hair across her face, tangling it in her lip gloss. With one hand Justina twisted the long strands away from her face as she wrestled her bag of law books with the other. The deserted platform, populated by only a few dry leaves that skittered in circles around her, sent a ripple of inexplicable unease down her body.

Justina frowned, realizing there were no taxis lined up in the usual place. Her eyes darted over to the parking garage, which also appeared abandoned except for a flickering light above. "I guess I'm walking," she said to herself—it really wasn't too far. The streets were quiet. She thought sadly about the summer that had ended and the upcoming fall. Jack-o-lantern pumpkins dotted several porches—glowing orange and gold in the moonlight—and windows were decorated with ghostly Halloween decals. Another chilly gust of wind whipped across her face and she quickened her pace.

When she got home, the Gonzalez house sat quiet and dark. Justina fought a rush of anxiety as she let herself in. Noting the eerie shadows of half-naked branches dancing across the living room wall, she switched on the lights, locking the door behind her. She dumped her bag of books in the marble foyer and went around turning on light after light and closing all the blinds. Justina wondered if she should have stayed in the city to study, then reprimanded herself for being jumpy for no reason. She turned on some music to dispel her sense of solitude.

Then, stomach growling, she headed to the kitchen to find something to eat. There she spotted a note her father had written for the housekeeper, Celeste, at some unknown point in time. Apparently her father would be out of town for at least two weeks and had instructed Celeste to throw out any perishable food and not to clean the house while he was away. Justina opened the refrigerator, and surveyed the barren shelves. Salsa, jelly, mayonnaise, and mustard could not constitute a dinner. She did find a frozen pizza in the freezer from the last time she was home. At least her father owned an extensive wine collection, to which she promptly helped herself.

Justina brought her law books and laptop into the dining room to do a little reading before bed. She stuck to her resolution not to watch television when she was supposed to be studying, but still found it hard to concentrate. A branch scratched at the window above the table and in her peripheral vision she could see the shadows moving around the house. She tried calling her father, but he didn't answer. He had been difficult to reach over the past couple of weeks; she wondered what he was doing and where he had gone. Usually they were better at keeping in touch than that. She left him a message that she was at home, then texted her roommate in the city, but didn't get a response. Giving up on the Family Law cases for the day, Justina piled the books on the corner of the table with a sigh. They'd still be there tomorrow.

Going to bed in an empty house always struck her as the creepiest aspect of being alone. She left several lights on as she headed to bed, and flicked on a few more as she went up the stairs. As she flipped on the hall light, she caught sight of her parent's wedding picture. There it hung in the center of the hallway photo gallery. It still made her so sad. Every time she looked at that photograph it reminded her not just of her mother, but of her father too—how her father used to be. She turned away and went to her room, not wanting to dwell on those losses or trigger another bout of nightmares. She was already anxious, and she struggled to keep it under control. She had no intention of going back into therapy, no desire to take more anti-anxiety medication. It was better to not think about it at all.

As much as she tried, she found it difficult to sleep that night. The little noises and odd shadows cast upon the walls could not be ignored—she obsessed about them until she was wide-awake. She finally got up, took a Xanax, and brought one of her casebooks to bed with her. Nothing like a law book and an anti-anxiety pill to knock her out, she reasoned, shaking her head with a smile of dismay.

The next morning she awoke with a start, a branch from the tall oak outside her window was banging on the pane. The wind had picked up considerably and she recalled hearing there was going to be a hurricane along the coast. Apparently their neighborhood was getting the spillover effect from that. She knew hurricanes didn't usually hit New York so she wasn't worried, but hoped there would be no thunder or lightening. Thunder and lightning really freaked her out.

She went downstairs to the kitchen and for breakfast she finished off a box of stale cereal she found in the pantry. Suddenly, the sound of hammering right outside the door set her heart racing once again. Justina wavered—she didn't want to look out the window and get caught peeking, but she needed to see what was happening to her house.

She thought to herself, *Why is Dad not home?* Justina went to the living room and parted the drapes just a few inches to peek out, but discovered that everything was dark. The view was blocked by something. She couldn't see anything, but it sounded like the pounding was right outside. Confused, she decided she had to open the door. She stepped partway out onto the porch.

And that's when she discovered a puzzling sight—over the top of the Yew tree she could see a man's broad shoulders and curly blonde hair. He was busy at work, hammering a big piece of plywood over the living room window. *That explains the darkness,* she thought to herself. Unsure of the right way to handle it, Justina cleared her throat awkwardly, hoping he'd turn her way. And he did, saying, "Oh, hello. I'm sorry, did I wake you up?"

It was then that she realized she still had on her pink flannel pajamas with the teddy bears all over them. She promptly retreated back into the house, embarrassed.

"No" she replied, peeking around the door. "Who are you, and why are you putting wood on my windows?" It occurred to her that maybe he was confused, maybe someone else needed to board up their house and he had the wrong address.

He smiled a wide, easy grin and said, "I'm Daniel. You're Justina, right? Your Dad asked me to cover up the windows. I do stuff around here for him sometimes. You do know there's a storm coming, right?" He paused, and then added, "He didn't tell me you would be here—I thought the house was empty. Sorry if I scared you." He held his hand out and she took it, noting the size and roughness of his hands. Otherwise, he didn't resemble any handyman she had ever seen—with his bright blue eyes and easy way of speaking.

She shrugged, "You did scare me a little—I'm not exactly expecting someone hammering on my house! I haven't talked to my Dad in a while, I couldn't reach him yesterday to tell him that I was coming. It was kind of last minute. Anyway, as for the storm,

I thought it was no big deal. Hurricanes don't come to New York, right?" Just as she said that, a wild gust of wind blew in her face, making her pull back even more behind the door.

He shook his head. "It's gotten worse. We're supposed to get hit with a lot of wind and rain. You're in law school, right? Don't you spend your free time watching CNN? It's all over the news, that's how your dad knew and called me. They might be over-reacting—you know how that goes. We don't get those storms here, but they're stopping trains today because the tracks could be impacted if the waters rise too much. Especially here—think about it."

"Are you kidding me? I left the city and now I'm trapped here?" She felt herself starting to panic, but tried to keep her voice steady. The wind began picking up and the clouds were turning dark and angry. Daniel looked up at the tree branches whipping back and forth.

"I need to get this done, it's getting worse. I promised your Dad." The branches of nearby trees dipped and swayed. "You're probably right about the hurricane, but I don't want to let him down, in case it does get rough." By the looks of things now, Justina thought, it could very well get rough. She didn't like it. He continued, "You don't want a branch breaking one of these windows. That would totally suck and your Dad would kick my butt. You should go inside, I'll check in with you before I leave, okay?"

"Okay. Thanks," she said, thinking of the branch on her bedroom window a short time ago.

She shut the door and headed back to her room. Justina quickly threw on a pair of jeans and a sweatshirt, and then turned on the television to see what was happening with the storm. Sure enough, the news channels were talking about it and nothing else. Hurricane Sandy was coming and would hit in the evening. *How did I miss this?* She thought to herself, *I guess that's what happens when you have your head in law books all day.* The ticker at the bottom of the screen scrolled by, residents with houses on the water were ordered to evacuate, and people should do whatever they needed to secure their homes and have supplies on hand. She checked her phone and found two messages from her father telling her about the storm and advising her to stay in the city. Too late, she thought. She tried calling him back, but again he didn't answer. She left a message letting him know she was at the house alone and that the handyman had come to put up the plywood.

She watched various reports from further down the east coast showing the impact of Sandy. She just couldn't wrap her brain around the fact that her house, the house that held all her child-hood memories, might end up like the homes on the news. House after house flashed on the screen—battered and flooded by fierce waves and wild wind. She watched as the wind blew the report-ers sideways and they braced themselves, holding onto light poles and fence posts while they shouted their broadcast over the violent storm.

After trying to absorb the news for a few minutes, Justina real-ized with alarm that she had no food in the house and that she'd have to go out in the storm. She thought for a minute about at-tempting to get back to the city before Sandy hit, but truly believed that the house was secure. It wasn't on the water and it was well-built. Despite her general anxiety, she felt safe in the house—it was home. *I better go while I still can*, she thought. So she found a jacket and gave Daniel a quick explanation before she headed out.

The scene at the store was unlike anything she'd witnessed be-fore. People packed the aisles, filling shopping carts with bread, canned goods, crackers—anything that did not require cooking or refrigeration. She found a couple gallon-jugs of water—all that re-mained in the bottled water section—and an errant bag of hoagie rolls someone had left on a shelf in the canned goods aisle. There were no actual loaves of bread to be had, or any baked goods at all. The tall wheeled racks in the bakery section had clearly been full at some point, but they now stood empty. She also got a jar of peanut butter, tuna, two bags of chips, and a box of crackers. She threw some canned soups and things that wouldn't need to be refrigerated in her cart. She went looking for a flashlight and batteries, but they were completely sold out already. The lines wound through the aisles with each person's cart piled high. *Wow*, she thought, *these people are really going overboard with this storm thing.* She couldn't fathom more than a day or two without power—it had never happened in her experience. She thought everyone in Long Beach was overreacting to Sandy—it was like the response to a snow forecast on steroids, where the whole town panicked and bought enough food for a year. *Ridiculous*, she thought to herself.

Justina listened to everyone in the checkout lines talking about Sandy. Apparently some people had left Long Beach—many of those living right on the beach were taking the warnings seriously. Judging by the amount of people in the long snaking lines, the remaining friends and neighbors all seemed to be at the grocery store, comparing forecasts and predictions. Many people were skeptical about the severity of the coming storm—they had heard it all the prior year with Irene. They weren't about to leave their homes only to then be unable to get back if the parkways were closed. They would take their chances, thank you very much. The other popular topic of conversation was storm preparation and the shortage of supplies. They were complaining about the long wait at the gas station and how the hardware stores had run out of small generators, lanterns, tarps, and crank radios. They were also talking about filling up bathtubs, sinks, and buckets with water to have something safe to drink, which puzzled Justina a little. She wasn't quite sure how rain and wind could contaminate water, but then she hadn't been through anything like the storm being predicted. After listening in for half an hour, Justina was getting nervous again. She was so glad she decided to go to the store—typically she didn't think of those things. Usually if she got hungry and there wasn't anything in the house, she just ordered out.

When she got home Daniel was nowhere to be seen, but the windows were boarded up tight. The sky was dark now, the winds more intense. It all seemed ominous, almost threatening. She unloaded her groceries and went around back to look for Daniel, wondering if he had left. She found him piling firewood at the back door. Rain started to fall in large, pelting drops that had soaked him through his waterproof coat. The wind blew the rain at an angle so it was impossible not to get saturated. When he saw her he said, "We need to get this wood inside, it'll get soaked out here! You don't want to be coming out here to get it during this storm. Can you get the door for me, and I'll bring it in?" Seeing her puzzled face, he added, "For when the power goes out." She was overwhelmed by all this preparation, but held open the door nonetheless. Daniel's preparation skills were impressive—she would never have known how to ready for the storm. She was pleased with herself just for going to the store! But he knew exactly what to do and did it. She felt so grateful and realized, as he passed her bringing in the firewood, how freaked out she would be without him there. Without Daniel, she would not have turned on the news or gone to get food. She would have been sleeping in with stale cereal and law books as her only supplies.

He continued to carry in the wood, armload by armload, stacking it on either side of the oversized rock fireplace in the living room. When he appeared to be done, she asked him, "Are you ready for a cup of coffee? Or would you like something to eat? I just got some soup, crackers, and stuff like that. You must be starved."

He peeled off his dripping wet jacket. "Sure, if you can tell me where to hang this nasty wet thing. I don't want to wreck your floors." She took his coat, hung it on the kitchen hook, and put the coffee on. She took a quick glance in the pantry, thinking there might be something interesting for lunch. Finding nothing, she grabbed a couple cans of soup and some crackers from the supplies she'd just brought home.

Daniel said, "Thanks for doing this. I'm starving! When your dad called, I hurried right over. I wasn't sure how long it would take me to get this done and didn't want to be doing it during the middle of the storm." He raked back his wet hair and went over to the sink to wash his hands. Justina watched him, noticing the way his soaked t-shirt and jeans clung to him, before she realized that he had to be uncomfortable.

"Do you want to dry those clothes? You could borrow some of my dad's clothes to wear while they dry. You must be miserable in those wet jeans."

He smiled, "Sure, that would be nice. Are you sure it's okay?"

She nodded, "Of course! I'm sure Dad won't mind after everything you did for us today. I'll find something for you to wear, then I'll get the soup warmed up while you change." She found him a pair of her father's running pants and a sweatshirt, and showed him where the dryer was, so he could throw his wet things in there while she got lunch started. She put the soup on the stove, then poured it into an old tureen they'd had forever—a shade of deep indigo blue that stood out against the dark granite counter. Taking the crackers out of their sleeve, Justina arranged them in concentric circles on a plate. She grabbed some bowls, spoons, and napkins, and laid it all out on the kitchen island. She didn't like eating in the dining room, never had. It just felt too formal.

Daniel emerged wearing his ill-fitting borrowed clothes and they both had a laugh at his ankles sticking out from the pants.

As they ate, Justina asked him, "Daniel, what do you do? I mean, are you in school? Or working?" She was curious about him: he didn't fit any type she had encountered. He seemed very intelligent, but also looked like someone who worked outside and certainly appeared competent from what she'd see so far.

He was quiet for a minute before answering. "I've been going to school studying civil engineering, at the University of Maryland, but I dropped out last year when my mom got sick, and I needed to take care of her." He was eating the soup quickly, obviously hungry.

"Are you going back? Is your mom better now?"

He smiled, a sad, resigned smile that didn't reach his eyes. "My mom died last year. She had cancer. I guess I will go back to school eventually." He shrugged.

Justina wasn't sure how to respond. "I am so sorry to hear that. And I shouldn't have asked, I didn't mean to pry. I can't imagine going through that. Do you have any brothers or sisters?"

"I have a brother, but he moved to California a couple years ago. He's living near our father. My brother always blamed my mother for their divorce, so as soon as he had a chance he relocated. When Mom got sick, he said he couldn't get away from work. But I think the truth is he just didn't want to deal with it and didn't care that it was left to me. So…that's life, right? I haven't spoken to him much since then—I don't have anything to say to him. You find out how people are when bad things happen, you know?"

"Yes, you do." She really didn't know, she was lucky in that respect, and she knew it. Compared to what Daniel had been through, she felt like her petty little problems were pretty ridiculous. She would be ashamed to even tell him the things that she considered her problems. There was one thing they had in common, though. She didn't know if she should bring it up, especially since she felt guilty for prying into his life. His situation wasn't her business—she barely knew him. And now she had made him revisit something so painful.

"My mom was killed in a plane crash when I was eight," she volunteered. "She went to Guatemala to visit her mother who was sick. Her plane crashed in the mountains on the way back. I'll never quit missing her. And my father has never been the same."

"I'm sorry to hear that, I didn't know. Your dad seems great, very on top of his game—you'd never guess he's carrying around all that grief. I guess we all have our tragedies, right?" They were both silent for a few moments, and Daniel focused his attention on the soup. Justina broke the silence.

"I'm sorry I got us into such a sad conversation. And I just met you. You must think I am a horrible downer."

"Not at all," he said, a kind smile spreading on his face.

"Let's change the subject. The storm is really picking up, is there anything else we should be doing?"

Daniel followed her cue. "Well, do you have any candles or flash-lights? Matches? We should get all that stuff down here, handy, in case you need it."

"Oh, good point. I do think we have some," she replied.

"They'll be hard to find in the dark, after you lose power." He picked up the nearly empty bowl of soup and tipped it to his lips to get the last drops.

Justina considered for a minute. "I mean, I know we have them, I just don't know where they might be. The cleaning lady puts stuff away, she knows where things are better than Papa or me. You want to help me check in the closets? There are probably matches in the kitchen drawer here, but the other stuff—I'm not sure." Daniel agreed, relieved to have something to do. Justina took the upstairs, Daniel took the downstairs, and he found the candles in a clos-et full of cleaning supplies and towels. "Bingo!" he yelled up the stairs, "got candles!"

Justina emerged from the stairwell with a hurricane lamp that held a candle. "I think we're set," she said. Daniel looked it over, and said, "Maybe I should check the garage, there might be some flashlights or lanterns out there."

She thought about what the people at the store were saying about water. "Daniel," she said, "I heard at the store that we should fill up bathtubs and sinks with water, do you think we need to do that? I'm not really sure why we would…"

Daniel nodded. "Yes, good idea, I hadn't thought of that. If the sewers get backed up with flooding, it can get pretty nasty and water can be contaminated. Better fill up whatever you can, just in case. It can't hurt."

Justina nodded. "Okay, I'll go do that." She went upstairs and filled both tubs and the bathroom sinks, then filled the kitchen sink as well as some pitchers and bowls. It still seemed like overkill but, as Daniel had said, it wouldn't hurt to be prepared just in case.

Meanwhile, the rain and wind continued to pick up, heavy enough that the noise could be heard from inside the solid brick house. Justina found it very eerie to have the windows boarded up so there was no way to see outside except by opening the door. She opened the door to check outside and even though the storm door was still closed, she could feel the wind and chill coming through. The trees were bowing back and forth and the wind was starting to howl. She thought to herself, *it hasn't even really hit yet.* Then she thought, *Oh my God.* She realized she didn't see a car in the drive. It hadn't even occurred to her how Daniel had got there. She went to the garage and found him going through the shelves. "Daniel, where's your car?"

"No car," he said. "I have a motorcycle, it's in the back."

She considered that for a moment, then said, "Do you need to leave?"

He cocked his head, considering.

"Because if not," she continued, "and you can stay here awhile, you should put your bike in the garage." She was hoping he wasn't going to leave, but she didn't know anything about his personal life, and didn't want to pry any more than she already had. She was terrified of being alone, but was trying hard to hide it. No way was she going to ask him to stay. He had already done more than she could have asked for.

"I'd like to ride out the storm here, if that's okay," he responded. She nodded in affirmation and tried not to show the rush of relief she felt. "I can put my bike inside, that's a good idea. It might wash away otherwise!" He handed her a flashlight he found on the shelf and pushed the button on the electric garage door. Neither of them expected what they saw when the door opened—the late afternoon sky was almost black and the rain came down in sheets. Small ponds had already formed in the yard around the drive-way, and the vicious wind blew right into the garage. The trees leaned precariously away from the wind, which howled through the branches. "Damn," Daniel muttered, as he pulled up the hood on his borrowed sweatshirt and raced out to get his bike.

He was only gone a couple minutes, but when he came back into the garage he was soaked through to the skin. "I guess I'm going to need another one of your dad's outfits, unless my clothes are dry," he commented as he stripped off the dripping sweatshirt. "I don't want to go in the house soaking wet like this." He hung the sweatshirt on a hook on the wall, so it could drip on the concrete floor to dry. "Could you grab my clothes for me, so I don't drip all through the house?"

Justina tried not to check out his strong chest, although it was hard not to notice. He was in great shape. "Of course, I'm sure they're dry, they've been in there forever. I'll go get them." She retrieved his warm clothes and then scurried out of the garage so he could change. She was embarrassed about having a partially unclothed stranger in her house, even though the circumstances were unusual. She wondered what her father would say—he was so overprotective. Not that it mattered. Her dad should be grateful to have a nice guy like Daniel looking out for her. Anyway, her dad must trust him to have him helping around the house. She appre-ciated the twist of fate that brought him to her doorstep at just the right time.

Daniel found her in the family room next to the kitchen, glued to storm coverage on the news. They were showing areas where the brunt of Sandy was hitting. The reporter was standing on the beach with huge waves in the background threatening to swallow her while the wind pushed her sideways.

"What a job, huh?" Daniel commented, watching the poor reporter try to give an update. Rain splattered the camera lens, blurring the view, and the howl of the wind echoed in the audio system, forcing her to yell into her microphone.

"They are saying the center of the storm is still several hours away from New York," Justina told him incredulously. "What's going to happen? I've never seen anything like this." She twirled her hair around her fingers, her eyes were wide, and she was chewing on her lip. She looked to Daniel for answers, for reassurance.

"I don't know," he responded, "but really, this house is probably one of the best built homes around here. And it's pretty elevated—we're not on the water. The windows are boarded up. I think the worst we'll get is flooding and maybe some tree branches will come down. Just thank God your dad didn't buy a beachfront home!" She smiled at that—a small, nervous smile—but she did feel a little better. What he said about the house was true.

"Well," she said, "it looks like we'll be hanging out for a while. Should we break into my dad's wine collection?"

Daniel laughed. "Sure, I can think of worse ways to ride out a storm. Pick something out and I'll open it. Meanwhile, I will keep an eye on this reporter to see if she gets washed away!"

Justina returned in short order with a bottle in each hand and a corkscrew sticking out of her jeans pocket. "We have choices!" She announced with a flourish. "And guess what I have? Even better than wine—champagne!" She set down a bottle of champagne and a bottle of red wine. "In case you prefer the red wine over champagne," she explained. "If we are going to be stuck here in a storm, let's make the best of it." She had decided it would be preferable to try to make this into a little party rather than sitting in front of the TV and getting freaked out, and she was so relieved to have him there that she did kind of feel like celebrating. "Do you want a snack?" She asked and then retreated to the kitchen without waiting for a response. She returned with cheese and more of the crackers left over from lunch. "Now we can relax. Nothing else we need for a while."

"Okay. Here we go!" Daniel grabbed the champagne and worked the wires off the top. The bottle opened with a loud pop—the cork was carefully aimed toward the door, which it bounced off and then disappeared.

And that's when the power went out.

CHAPTER TWO

Justina gasped, suddenly remembering the storm and feeling surprised at being plunged into total darkness. "It's okay," Daniel's voice came through the blackness. "Let's light some candles. The power might only be out for a little while, maybe it will come and go." He felt around for the flashlight, which fortunately was close by, and flicked it on. "Okay, now where are the matches?" She handed him the matches that she'd found in the kitchen drawer and he lit two candles. "Okay, better now?" She nodded, but warily surveyed the room where weird shadows were moving around in the candlelight.

"It's kind of creepy in here, don't you think? Like a cave or something." The sound of the storm pummeling the house was much clearer without the competing noise from the television. In the candlelight their faces were in planes and shadows. The rest of the room faded into the background with only the barest flickering light.

"Yeah, it feels like we are all alone in the world, doesn't it?" Daniel asked. It did feel that way with the ferocity of the storm outside and the lack of lighting inside. The rest of the world seemed very far away. "Are you okay?" he asked.

"Sure, I'm okay. We knew the power would probably go out, I just wasn't really expecting it or thinking about it at that moment— it startled me. I'm okay. And yes, it does feel like there is nobody else on the planet. It feels very isolated." She paused for a moment, and then added, "I have to admit, I'm really glad you are here. I would be so flipped out if I were alone. Thank you."

"No problem," he said easily. "If I was at home I would be sitting all alone in a dark house too. And I don't have a wine collection to fall back on!"

She laughed at that and said, "Oh, that's right—the champagne. Now that it's open we have to drink it! Can't waste Papa's good stuff! Oh wait—we need glasses. Hang on." She took a candle and went to the kitchen, returning with two champagne flutes. "May as well do it right."

He smiled and shook his head. "You and I sure do have different lives. If I even happened to have a bottle of champagne I'd be drinking it out of a coffee cup or a souvenir glass from a ballgame or something." He laughed.

"Really?" she asked.

"I think my mom maybe had a couple wine glasses, but I'm pretty sure she didn't have special champagne glasses! And I know I've never bought anything like that. Although I do have some decent beer glasses!"

She laughed, "Of course you do, that's a guy thing!"

"Well, speaking of guy things, we should get some heat going in here before it gets too cold. I think the best plan is to stay in here and use the woodstove rather than the fireplace in the living room. That room is much bigger and draftier. What do you think?"

"Sounds good," she agreed, realizing that she was a little chilly. She held the flashlight while he brought some wood in from the living room and got the fire going. "Good thing you thought of that earlier," she said. "There's no way we'd want to go out there in this weather and get the wood—and it would be soaked. So we would be freezing. I feel sorry for the people with no heat. You see those stories on the news—towns where there is a big snowstorm or something and the power is out for weeks. Can you imagine? What a nightmare. In the past, ours has only gone out for a couple hours at the most. We've been lucky."

He agreed, "Power outages really suck, especially if it goes on too long. And people always get sick, especially old people. I suspect there will be some massive outages from this storm—it's a monster. Hopefully it won't last long here, though!" he smiled.

She nodded, and they munched on the snacks and drank the champagne, listening to the violent wind and rain outside, punctuated by car alarms going off. It sounded like they were in a war zone. After a few moments of silence between them, Daniel asked her, "Tell me about your plans—what exactly do you want to do when you get out of law school?"

Justina took a big gulp of champagne and gave a little shrug. "I'm not exactly sure yet. Of course my father would be thrilled if I got involved in something related to politics as that's his passion. But I'm not really feeling the love there. I want to do something meaningful, you know? It sounds corny, but I'm still trying to figure out what that looks like for me. I don't know. I'm hoping at some point it will hit me and I'll know what I want to do. Right now I am just kind of drifting through school."

"Did you go to law school because that's what your father wanted you to do?" He asked.

"Kind of," she admitted. "I really didn't know what I wanted so I thought I might as well do what would make him happy. I'm sure I will find some way to use that degree that I feel good about. It's hard, you know, because I'm all he has. I try to do the things that really matter to him. He wanted a big family—instead he lost his wife, never had more kids, and now he only has me. We both do the best we can."

"That's kind of a lot on you, though. It doesn't seem like you are able to do what you want. That's not right at your age"

The look of regret appeared on his face as soon as the words were out of his mouth, but she just laughed. "I hear what you're saying. It's really not like that. We take care of each other. Now that I'm older I can cook his favorite meal now and then or go with him to a charity dinner. Doing things like that doesn't hurt me and it makes him happy, so it makes me happy too. It's not so different from what you went through—you were there for your mom when she needed you and nobody else was. Family is family. That's a good thing." She was starting to feel the champagne and was getting a little sentimental and talkative.

"What about you?" she asked. "What do you think you will end up doing?"

"I need to go back to school. I just haven't really gotten myself motivated to do it. The last year has been hard. But I can't go on delivering bagels and doing odd jobs, that's not what I want out of life." He reached over and grabbed the bottle of red wine and the corkscrew. Justina was glad to see he was getting more relaxed with her, at first he had clearly been uncomfortable.

"You deliver bagels!" She exclaimed, "From which place?" There was nothing she loved more than a fresh, warm everything bagel. She started thinking about how good one would be right then—right when she knew she couldn't have one.

"You know the place on Beech Street?" he asked. She knew it, of course, and they discussed the merits of various bagel shops in the area. She told him that her favorite place was on Park, but then she went back to the original discussion.

"You said you were studying civil engineering—what exactly does that mean? What do you want to do? And how did you get interested in that?" He poured some wine for each of them before responding.

"I worked construction jobs for my girlfriend's dad during the summer in high school. I really enjoyed the building and developing process, and I love to be outdoors. But what I really like is the designing of buildings and the science of it. A civil engineer is the one who can make sure that buildings are designed in such a way that they will stand up structurally—they will maintain their safety and integrity during, say, a really bad storm!" he laughed.

"Well, that's relevant," she smiled back.

He continued, "Or just through normal wear and tear, over time. For me it made sense because I don't want to be stuck in an office, but do like the mental aspect of building. So I think this gives me the best of both worlds." He spoke with a lot of energy, and then paused. "I just have to get back to school. Maybe next quarter, I don't know," he trailed off.

Justina enjoyed the passion in his voice when he explained his goals, but was distracted by the girlfriend reference. She wondered if the girlfriend was still in the picture. She wouldn't normally be bold enough to ask, but with the drinks in her she didn't show her usual restraint. "Do you still have that girlfriend?" she asked.

He smiled at her question. "We are still friends," he said. "We live in the same neighborhood and have known each other forever. We hang out sometimes, but we're not dating."

She pondered that for a moment and then asked, "Are you hungry? I am, all of a sudden. There's not a whole lot here, but we could do some sandwiches or something like that. Something cold unfortunately." She thought about her trip to the store and realized that there weren't too many desirable food choices in the house and the food in the refrigerator wouldn't stay good anyhow. "I guess we should start with checking the fridge and freezer—that stuff won't keep. Who knows how long we won't have power."

They ended up with tuna and cheese sandwiches with ice cream for dessert. She figured there was no point in letting it melt in the freezer. It wasn't the best meal either of them had ever had, but after all the champagne and wine it didn't seem to matter.

Justina began to wonder about the storm. "Daniel, let's go see what's happening outside," she suggested. "Maybe it's starting to ease up. It's hard to tell from in here, you know?"

"Sure," Daniel responded, standing and stretching. "Back or front?"

"Front's good," she said, and led the way to the living room.

As she opened the door, the wind caught it and jerked it out of her grasp, slamming it open all the way.

"Whoa!" Daniel exclaimed, grabbing the door and pulling it partway back. He stood over Justina and they peered into the black night.

As soon as their eyes adjusted and they could see what was happening they pulled back reflexively. The big full moon lit up the black water that swirled around the steps, inches from the threshold of the front door. "Oh my God!" Justina gasped. "Daniel, it's going to come in! What do we do?"

Daniel shut the door hard, and looked around before answering.

"Let's put some towels under the doors," he answered. "Front and back." Justina looked at him for a second, hearing uncertainty in his voice for the first time.

"Okay, I'll go get them," she said and rushed off.

They rolled up bath towels and stuffed them around the doors and stood back for a minute, watching to see if any water would come through.

"Daniel, do you know how long this will last? I mean, is it going to stop soon?" her speech was shaky and her eyes were wide and frantic, the glow from the wine and champagne long gone. "Do you realize we are underwater? The whole island. We are at the center, probably the highest point. If our house is going underwater, all of Long Beach is too. That water is all the way up our stairs, and this house is high up. It must be coming at us from both sides of the island!" Her voice was rising, and she felt tears stinging her eyes. "What if it comes in? What will we do? We're trapped!" She desperately wanted Daniel to have the answers, but she saw on his face that he was overwhelmed as well.

"Hopefully it won't come in, but if it does we'll go upstairs. It's getting late, I think high tide is like around 10..." he trailed off, glancing around for a clock.

Justina looked over his shoulder at the clock behind him. "It's well past 10," she said, relief in her voice. "Do you think the water will go down soon? It is still so stormy," she fretted, a frown creasing her brow.

"I can't tell you what will happen. I haven't been through anything like this either. The last one was Irene and it wasn't this bad... but if this is high tide I would think this is as bad as it will get. But I really don't know how those storm surges go, if high tide really matters...I just can't say." He looked at the door, waiting for water to come through, but it appeared to be watertight. "I'm going to check the back door," he said, and headed to the kitchen. Justina followed close on his heels—not wanting to be left alone, even in her own house.

When they got into the kitchen they saw dirty brown water coming under the door. "Get some more towels," Daniel instructed before Justina could say a word. He tried to mop up the water with the towels. As they were saturated he handed them off to her and took a fresh armload. Justina took the filthy dripping towels and threw them into a pile in the corner, watching Daniel attempt to block the bottom of the door with the fresh towels. Dark, smelly water came pushing through on one side as he started plugging the other side.

"I don't know, Justina," Daniel said, standing back and eyeing the door. "If it's high tide now, we can only hope this is it. But you might want to bring down some more towels."

Justin grabbed the flashlight to go retrieve more towels from the upstairs bathrooms. She piled them on the kitchen counter alongside the collection of pitchers and bowls of water and they watched and waited. No more water came through so after a half hour they went back to the family room, mentally exhausted.

Daniel drained what was left in his wine glass. "Did you notice how nasty that water was, Justina?" he asked, and then added, "I think we probably already have a contaminated water issue. That smelled like sewage."

She frowned. "I guess it's a good thing we filled up those tubs, then. I hope this doesn't go on too long…"

"Yeah, me too. At least it looks like we won't have any more water coming in here, may as well get some rest."

Justina nodded, found some bedding in the closet, and they settled in for the night. Justina curled up on the couch and Daniel stretched out on the floor in front of the woodstove while the wind and rain continued pummeling the house.

CHAPTER THREE

The next morning, Daniel awoke first. He noticed how chilly it was and how silent. The storm had finally moved on. He tried to be quiet as he put a couple more pieces of wood in the woodstove and worked on building the fire back up. Justina was sound asleep, curled up in a ball with her long hair hanging down over her face. He thought how cute she was, nothing like what he would have expected from a politician's law school daughter for sure. She had such a small frame, such delicate features, and she seemed so hesitant, her manner almost nervous. He couldn't picture her in law school, much less doing battle in a courtroom. She appeared so young, so naive, as though she had never experienced anything of the real world. And yet she lost her mother so young—he knew that had a profound effect. He wondered what her future would be—her gentle nature seemed at odds with her career path.

He recalled the night before—the expensive champagne and wine, the lousy dinner, and then the scare of the storm water coming into the house. Justina was very sweet and pretty he decided, but he wouldn't want to have to depend on her in a crisis. He was glad he had been there, in part because he couldn't imagine a girl like that alone in the storm, but also because he knew his house surely fared much worse. Despite the storm drama, he had enjoyed most of the previous night. He realized that it wasn't the drinks or the fancy home that made the night so pleasurable, it was having company—someone to talk to. Such a wonderful change from the way he had been living since his mother died, scraping by with odd jobs and coming home to an empty house that held nothing but heart-breaking memories.

With the fire in the woodstove finally roaring hot, Daniel tiptoed to the kitchen to peek out the back door.

Everything was awash in piles of smelly, wet sand—the staircase halfway buried up to the door. He looked out across the backyard, and saw that a tree at the neighbor's home had split in two. One half had fallen across the house, ripping off the gutter and leaving a gaping hole in the roof, the other half had fallen across the front yard. That explained some of the horrible noises they'd heard in the dark, along with blown transformers and car alarms. Chunks of roofing material were scattered around where the street had been. Everything he saw was completely covered with muddy sand and debris. Electrical poles and trees lay about haphazardly and cars were bunched up like bumper cars at an amusement park— having been tossed around by the sheer force of the storm. Daniel stood dazed, trying to comprehend the new reality that was Long Beach.

Finally he went to look out the front door, dreading what he would see. It appeared even worse because that side of the house faced the closest beach. Even though the beach was a couple blocks away, the tide had wreaked havoc on everything in the neighborhood, leaving complete devastation—like a scene from a disaster movie. Porches, roofs, and cars were torn up and thrown around. Some houses, like the Gonzalez home, seemed relatively intact, but older homes or those not as well built stood in shambles. All the houses had water lines on them and Daniel could tell that they must be flooded inside, given the proximity of the front doors to the ground. He watched a couple of people wading through the sand and rubbish in their yards, presumably to retrieve something displaced by the water, but many didn't leave their doorways. The horror and grief was evident on their faces as they surveyed their decimated homes, yards, and neighborhood. Nobody had really believed what this storm would do and he felt paralyzed by disbelief.

His next thought was of Justina. He realized that she would be terrified—a girl who was traumatized by thunder and lightning would fall apart when she saw her home in the middle of a disaster zone. He went inside to see if she was awake and found her sitting up on the couch rubbing her eyes. "Good morning!" he greeted her.

"Good morning. Have you been up long?"

"Just a bit. Did you sleep well?" He wasn't sure how to tell her the news about her destroyed neighborhood and the fact that the entire island of Long Beach was most likely devastated as well.

"I slept pretty well. I woke up a lot with all the noise of the storm, till it calmed down. I'm starving. Do you think the power is back on at the bagel place yet? A hot breakfast bagel sandwich sounds *so* good. That tuna sandwich last night didn't really cut it."

He hesitated a moment. "I doubt the power is on yet and, I have to tell you, it's a mess outside. We probably aren't going anywhere right away. It's pretty bad out there."

She frowned. "Really? I would have thought the water would be down and things would get back to normal, let me see." She stood up and finger-combed her hair back, out of her face, before padding to the back door to look out. Once she took in the scene, she stood in silence for a moment. Finally she murmured "Oh my God." She didn't move, just stood staring out. Finally she looked up at Daniel. "What do we do? I've never seen anything like this.

Oh my God," she repeated, her eyes as huge and panicked as a cornered animal.

Daniel wasn't sure what to say either. He shook his head. "I don't know. I guess we wait and see how soon the city gets the road clear and the power back on. We are real lucky the house is intact and we have food and firewood. We can make do for a little while and then I'm sure the city will get things up and running. It could be worse, look over there." He pointed to a house on the side street. The owners had prepared for the storm by putting tape over their windows instead of shutters or wood. The windows in the front had shattered, probably from the debris flying around. A balding middle-aged man stood on the porch in a t-shirt and boxer shorts, absorbing the damage to his neighborhood and his home. A woman in a fuzzy red bathrobe came outside and joined him, holding a crying baby, and Daniel could see that she was sobbing. The man shook his head and went back into the house, the crying woman right behind him.

"This is so awful!" Justina exclaimed. "You're right, we are lucky. Thank God my father called you. I can't even imagine." Her voice rose as the shock of their reality began setting in. "Do you realize," she began, "that I would not have known this was coming if you hadn't come? I don't turn the TV or radio on when I'm studying, I get too distracted, and I'm such an idiot. So I would have been here with no food, no covers on the windows, no heat, all by myself. Oh my God," She said again. Daniel could tell that she was trying not to cry and the more she pondered their situation, the more shaken she was. "Last night," she began, "we were drinking champagne! Sitting here living the good life while this whole neighborhood washed away! I had no idea . . . if you hadn't been here . . . I don't even know what would have happened to me, oh my God!" The tears started flowing in earnest now and Daniel finally put his arms around her awkwardly and tried to soothe her.

"It's okay, we're fine, and the house is fine. And we still have plenty of tuna and wine, we got no problems, right?" He said, trying to lighten the mood.

She gave him a teary smile. "You're right. But I just can't believe this. This is a nightmare. I can't even imagine how many people's homes are wrecked or even how many people got hurt. And there's nothing we can do about it. This is so horrible."

"I know, I know. I don't have any idea what I will find at my house. It's not much, but it's all I got. And it looks like I won't be there for a while. It's going to take some time to clean up."

"Oh my God," she said again. "I am so sorry—I didn't even think about your house, you must be so worried. Where is your house? Is it near the water?" She looked mortified that she had completely forgotten about his house.

"It's not too far from the water, in Far Rockaway. Maybe twenty minutes from here. But it's all beach along there too, so I imagine the flooding was similar to Long Beach. I had shutters on my house, but it's made of wood, not brick, and it's an older house. So I am pretty sure I will have damage to deal with. It's okay. I'm sure it was flooded there too, not much I could be doing right now anyhow." He wanted to reassure her, but he was worried. His neighborhood was low-lying and he thought it had probably flooded far worse that what had happened to the Gonzalez house. The homes in Long Beach looked very bad, but Justina's house was in good shape by comparison.

"So I guess this means we're not going out for breakfast bagels?" Justina made her own attempt at forced humor, sniffling and wiping her eyes.

Daniel appreciated that she was trying to be a good sport. "Let's check out the rest of the house to make sure everything is in order." He was just glad the house was so elevated—he figured many homes had water inside, his own included. It looked like the water on Long Beach was at least five feet deep, judging by the water line on the stairs outside, so people whose homes were level with the ground had certainly flooded.

They went through the house and found no problems. There had been a lot of water in the garage, not surprisingly, and everything was coated in muck. Once they determined that the house was more or less intact they went back to the kitchen to find something to eat, which ended up being rolls and peanut butter and jelly. Justina was clearly upset still, but trying hard to put on a good face. Daniel was getting restless—he felt that he should be doing something. He found it difficult to sit around, particularly when there was obviously so much that needed be accomplished. He decided to start with the windows because the house was still dark like a cave and the storm had obviously passed. He figured he should at least remove a couple of them, so the house wouldn't be so dim and depressing. He told Justina his plan, put his boots on, and went out to remove the boards on the windows.

As he pulled the boards down he wondered how long it would take for the power to be restored so people could start repairing the damage to their homes. He pried off the boards over the windows in the front, and then headed toward the back of the house, wading carefully through the sand and debris that covered everything he could see. It was difficult walking through muddy sand without knowing what debris might be underneath. He took his time, stepping carefully.

All of a sudden he heard a pitiful mewing sound. He looked around to find the source. It sounded like a frightened cat, but he couldn't see anything. He continued around the house until he found it—a very small, wet, grey cat up in one of the Gonzalez's trees. It was peering down at him with its little mouth wide open crying, its soft ears laid back, and its whole body shaking. He went over to the tree, but the cat was too high up so he grabbed a large branch and managed to get a toehold on the trunk, pulling himself up. As he reached for the cat it tried to back away from him, terrified, but he was quick enough to get one hand around its scrawny body before it could climb further up. Carefully holding the trembling cat, he dropped to the ground, falling backwards into the wet sand.

"Hey little buddy," he said to the cat. "Justina is going to love you!" He didn't think the cat belonged to the Gonzalez household—he couldn't imagine them having any pets with their schedules and the house was pristine. He also knew for sure that Justina would have said something about missing a pet. The cat looked up at him with huge gold eyes and mewed, still shaking. Daniel tucked it inside his jacket to provide some warmth and headed back to the house to present Justina with his find. "I guess the rest of the windows can wait," he told his little shivering bundle.

"Justina," he called as he entered the house, "I found something outside. Maybe it's yours?" He knew it wasn't the Gonzalez' cat, but was eager to see her face when she saw it.

She came out, "What is it?" She had obviously made an attempt to clean herself up—she had combed her hair and changed her clothes while he was outside. Daniel was momentarily distracted when he saw her, she looked so beautiful even though she was just wearing a soft aqua sweatshirt and jeans, nothing fancy. He regained his composure quickly, though, and recalled his mission.

He pulled the cat out of his jacket, "Does this belong to you?"

"Oh my God, the poor little kitty!" She immediately reached out and took the little cat. "Oh, baby, you are so cold and wet," she crooned, snuggling it against her sweatshirt. "You must be so hungry!" She looked at Daniel, "Where did you find it?"

He told her the story with his attention mainly directed at her back as she carried the cat to the kitchen. As he took off his filthy boots he could hear her telling the cat, "Looks like I have to share my tuna, doesn't it? You poor little baby." Daniel wondered briefly how much tuna they had, what other food there was, and when the stores would be open. But he didn't blame her for feeding the cat—he would do the same.

"Daniel, come here and look," she called. "The kitty is so happy, he's purring!" Her delight was childlike and unrestrained and he thought again how cute she was. She looked like a little girl in her oversized sweatshirt, fawning over the cat. "Look at him, he's so small. I've never seen him around this neighborhood. I wonder how far he came?" The cat was purring loudly while he ate. Of course, his face was buried in a bowl of tuna.

"You called it a *him*, are you sure it's a boy kitty?"

She looked up at him with an embarrassed smile on her face. "Yeah, I'm pretty sure. I think we should call him Hercules—he survived such a storm and maybe the name would give him some confidence!"

"We need to make sure he doesn't have a home," Daniel reminded her. "Once things are back to normal, we need to post notices that we found him. People have lost so much already, you don't want to cause someone to lose their pet, too."

"I know," she admitted, "but I've never had a kitty and I've always wanted one. At least it will be nice to have a little fur-ball to snuggle with for a bit. Look at him, he's so sweet." She scratched the cat's neck as he continued licking the bowl, purring ferociously and arching his back.

The rest of the day was spent getting things in order for the evening. Daniel brought in more firewood from the living room and nurtured the fire in the woodstove to stave off the chill in the air. Then they went through the kitchen to see what they had to eat. Daniel was relieved to find a case of bottled water in the garage, since the water coming out of the faucet sputtered and smelled bad, and he knew they shouldn't use it. He pointed out that they could use the woodstove to heat things up, which gave them more eating options since there was a variety of canned food in the house. He warned her that the pots might not be quite the same after they were used on the woodstove, but they both understood that keeping the pans pristine wasn't a big deal compared with going hungry. Daniel was relieved to have the woodstove to cook on as he suspected their furry little friend would be getting first dibs on the tuna and the package of rolls was nearly gone.

That night for dinner they warmed up some canned chili and washed it down with more of Victor's wine. Daniel didn't know much about wine, but the bottles Justina produced looked expensive—they didn't resemble the $4.99 bottles Daniel saw at the end of the aisles at the liquor store. As they were sipping wine and watching the cat chase a ball of paper across the floor he said, "Tell me about your dad. He seems like an interesting guy, but I don't know him all that well. What exactly does he do?"

She gave a little shrug. "He works as an advisor for Senator Goldberg—he helps with public relations and foreign affairs. He's pretty much the Senator's right-hand guy. The Senator is thinking about running for President. My Dad is helping him build all those relationships he will need in order to run." She wrinkled her nose. "Politics. That's what he does. You know, getting the Latino vote and the relations with Latin American countries are important. My father helps him understand what he needs to do to keep on good terms with that group."

"Wow," Daniel said, impressed. "Does he have a girlfriend? I mean, since you're mom?"

Justina gave a snort. "No, no girlfriend. He dates, if you can call it that. He thinks I don't know about his lady friends, but I'm not stupid. Women love my father. He travels constantly and they are always chasing him. I see it when I go to events with him. But I think, since my mom died, he doesn't want anyone. He lives for his work, and to take care of me. Maybe someday he'll meet someone. I think he is afraid I would be upset, but I wouldn't.

He doesn't need to protect me. I'm not a little girl anymore." She said the last part almost with defiance, as if expecting Daniel to challenge her on it.

Daniel smiled, "Well, it sounds like he has a really full life. It must be interesting—all the people he meets and places he goes. Are you sure you don't want to get involved in politics? Seems like you would have a leg up, you know?"

She shook her head. "No, I don't like all the schmoozing and lobbying that goes on. It's all about who has money or influence and I don't agree with that part of it. I like the idea of making the world a better place, but it seems that politics get in the way of real progress. I don't know what I want to do, but I'm pretty sure that isn't it." She shrugged and threw a paper ball for Hercules, watching him bat it across the floor until it went under the couch. "Look at him, he's so funny!" she exclaimed, as the little cat lay on his side, reaching under the couch with one paw to get the paper. "I never realized how entertaining a kitten could be!"

"He is a cutie," he replied. He watched with amusement as she got on her hands and knees, helping Hercules to retrieve the ball, and tossing it for him to chase.

CHAPTER FOUR

The next day, when they looked outside they could see more people out and about. Daniel was eager to get outside, he hated being cooped up indoors when there was so much to do. Justina said she didn't want to be left alone in the house, and she was getting restless too. They put on their boots and went out the front to the street, surveying the homes in the neighborhood. A few of the houses were in similar condition to the Gonzalez home, but many were badly damaged with broken windows or torn up roofs. There was debris everywhere and cars were bunched up at odd angles, all flooded. It wasn't like a typical windstorm where you had to go grab your empty garbage can that blew into the neighbor's yard. Daniel couldn't imagine where to begin a cleanup when you have a soggy home with a hole in the roof, shattered windows, no power, and an upside-down car full of water. He knew he most likely would be facing a similar situation at his house and was not looking forward to dealing with it.

A number of people had their garage doors open and were hauling soaked and stained furniture and carpeting to the sand-covered area that used to be the curb. Bag after bag of debris was being deposited there as well. It was obvious that in those homes there was major destruction to the first floor and everything was being hauled out. Some homes, however, were still closed up with no signs of life. Presumably those people evacuated before the storm. Daniel wondered if they had any idea how their homes had fared.

He wanted to get out and get a better sense of the damage. He didn't really think he could make it to his home in Far Rockaway yet, but perhaps he might at least get down the main streets of Long Beach and see how things looked. He figured he could navigate any downed trees or displaced cars on his bike. When he told Justina his plan, she wanted to go. "I'm tired of being in this house, too." She whined. "And maybe something is open, a store or restaurant. Don't those places have generators? You never know . . . think about it . . . pizza! And we need cat food!"

He doubted any stores or restaurants would be open, but agreed to let her come. "It may be a short trip," he warned her. "If it's dangerous, we go home." She nodded, and he realized that she would have agreed to anything at that point. It was odd that it had only been a couple days, but it was as though they had been trapped forever. He understood how she felt. The possibility of good take-out food was hard to resist, even if they knew it was an unlikely find.

His motorcycle had seen a little water, even in the garage, and everything was covered in dried muck from being flooded with the sewage-laden water. Fortunately Daniel was able to get it started and Justina climbed on the back of the motorcycle, hanging onto Daniel tightly. "Have you ever been on a motorcycle?" He asked, although he was certain he knew the answer.

"Are you kidding? With my dad? He would kill me if I did something so *foolish and dangerous!*" she laughed, "This storm has been so horrible, but even so it seems like we are living in a different world now. Like anything goes because everything is so screwed up.

You know?" her voice had a reckless tone and Daniel realized she was probably feeling some freedom she had never really known, now that some of the shock from the storm had started to wear off. Like a bird in a gilded cage finally being released.

They headed to one of the main streets in Long Beach, which was somewhat passable on the bike. At first glance it looked like almost everything was boarded up. There was sand washed up everywhere, piled in drifts. The sidewalks and road were covered in it and cars and electrical poles littered the roads and sidewalks. There was more activity here than there had been in the neighborhood. People were removing boards from their windows and doing what they could to start restoring their places. Power was still out though and, with all the sand and cars everywhere, it was obvious that *normal* was a still a long way off. Debris and wreckage was piled everywhere, waiting for a trash collector to come haul away the remains of the life before Sandy.

People who were not working on their homes or businesses walked along looking like survivors in a war zone, kind of glazed and aimless, appearing to have no idea where to go or what to do. Some just sat on porches, waiting for someone to come find them or for things to somehow improve. Phones weren't working and cars had been destroyed, creating a sense of isolation for many on Long Beach. Members of the National Guard and Long Beach Police patrolled the city, apparently watching for looters or looking to render assistance if necessary.

"Daniel," Justina called out over the sound of the engine, "Can we go check out the beach?"

"We can try," he said, and turned left on a street that looked relatively clear.

As they approached the beach, they began to comprehend the fury of the storm they had just survived. The devastation of the homes near the water was horrifying with fences flattened and pulled loose, decks hanging off houses, and mountains of sand

and wrecked cars everywhere. Trees had been toppled, smashing homes and cars, and power lines hung uselessly from uprooted poles. Daniel pulled to a stop when they came to a mountain of sand with what appeared to be a section of the boardwalk sticking out. "We need to walk," Daniel said, "this sand is too deep."

They headed toward the beach on foot, seeing up close the destroyed homes, giant piles of debris, and cars scattered about haphazardly—like toys in a child's room after a violent tantrum. Most homes were still boarded up with no signs of life, undoubtedly evacuated.

When they got to the beach, they confronted a painful scene that made the devastation of the storm very real and personal for them both. The famous Long Beach boardwalk, which had been in place for at least 75 years, was virtually destroyed. There were huge areas where it looked as though a giant sea monster punched through from beneath, the boards broken and jutting upwards. In other places, large sections had been ripped out or broken off.

"Oh my God, Daniel, look at this!" Justina said with despair in her voice. "Do you know how many hours I have spent on this boardwalk, how many summers? And it's just gone. I used to come down here and go for a run in the morning, when it was just getting light outside, and it was so peaceful. Or at night, when I needed to get out of the house, I would sit on one of the benches and watch the sunset. I can't believe it." She tucked her hand into the crook of Daniel's arm absently as she looked on at remnants of the beloved boardwalk with grief on her face.

Daniel covered her hand with his. "I know, I used to come over here in the summers and play volleyball, right near here. This beach was always so packed, so much going on, I always loved it here. Unbelievable," he said, shaking his head. They stood silent, surveying what used to be a favorite place. "I remember," Daniel began, "coming here in the summer, and having to get here early in the morning to get a decent parking place. Especially when they had something going on at the beach, like a surfing competition. Remember that?" he asked, smiling at the memory with sadness in his eyes.

Justina nodded, her eyes full of tears and her face sorrowful.

Although Daniel was horrified by the condition of the boardwalk and the homes in Long Beach, he was also thinking again of his own neighborhood and wondering how bad things were there. He figured maybe in the next day he could try to make it over the bridge and find out. He almost didn't want to know—it couldn't be good.

As they looped around to head back to the house, they saw a large cluster of people on the corner at one of the cross streets to the main road. Daniel pulled the bike over to see what was going on. It was a miracle! A little market with a deli and a bakery had managed to open its doors. Apparently the owner had a generator and wanted to be there for the neighbors. Justina squealed when they saw the place open. Daniel had to stop the bike for fear that she would jump off while they were moving.

There was, of course, a line, but the owner and his family were trying valiantly to provide fresh bread and other basics to the people who showed up. Justina assigned Daniel to get in the bread line while she went to find anything useful that might be left in the grocery. The store was pretty much picked clean, although she did find some canned cat food which she snatched up.

She held it up to him in victory, with a smile.

"Oh, good," Daniel said, "At least Hercules won't get our dinner tonight!"

They only bought one loaf of bread and the cat food, because other people were lined up and they still had canned food at home. The warm bread smelled delicious. Daniel found it fascinating how much something like that mattered after only a couple of days, particularly when they still had food in the house. Just knowing it wasn't possible to get something made it that much more desirable.

Nobody in the store seemed to know how long the power and water would be out or what was happening to restore Long Beach. The anxiety and uncertainty of the people in the store was unsettling, and they were both quiet on the way home.

When they got back to the house, Hercules greeted them at the door, mewing and winding around their legs, as if he knew they had treats for him. Daniel thought how nice it was, like coming home after a hard day of work and not being alone. He hadn't thought much about how his solitary existence bothered him, but being with Justina showed him how much he enjoyed having someone to spend time with. He wished that instead of a temporary scenario, borne out of an emergency, this was a life that was his to keep. Soon he would have to face going back to his solitary home and he probably wouldn't even see Justina again. He reminded himself not to get used to this life, just to enjoy it for now. It struck him that he was crazy to be finding enjoyment in this awful situation and felt a flash of guilt knowing how many people had lost everything—probably him included.

They dove into the fresh bread as soon as they got in the house. It was so good! As he'd done before, Daniel built up a fire in the woodstove and they ate warm soup and bread. Hercules dined on Friskies Tuna and Salmon Feast, which suited him very well.

As they drank yet another bottle of Victor's wine, Daniel told her, "I think I'm going to head over to Far Rockaway tomorrow morning. I need to check out my house and see how much damage is there."

"I want to go too. Can I come with you?"

He had expected her to say that and, in fact, he would prefer to have her with him, but he didn't know what he might find when he got there. He felt like he needed to face it alone. His home held so many memories for him and he suspected it might be seriously damaged, given the proximity to the water and the low level of the land.

"I don't know if it's safe," he responded. "How about this? I will go tomorrow morning and check it out, but I'll come back after. This is something I feel like I need to do alone, okay? Maybe the next day we'll both go."

He could tell by her face that she understood, but she pouted anyhow. "Okay, I get it, but you do realize that I want to go. I hate being trapped here! Just do me a favor and keep an eye out for open stores, okay? If you see any place that's open, bring home something good!"

He smiled and agreed, relieved that she hadn't made a fuss. He figured she was accustomed to getting what she wanted and she would easily make that happen in a normal situation. She could be very charming and indeed he found himself charmed by her, wanting to please. But in this case he needed to take care of his own business alone. He wanted to face his challenges without worrying about her. He also knew that his neighborhood was not up to her normal standards, even before the storm, and he didn't know how well she would handle that. Although Far Rockaway was close by, it wasn't Long Beach, or Manhattan, or anywhere else that she frequented with her father. He wasn't ashamed of his neighborhood, but he wasn't ready to bring her into his world—at least until he'd evaluated the situation.

They spent another pleasant evening with an unsatisfying dinner but plenty of wine and went to sleep with a warm fire burning in the woodstove. Hercules nestled with Justina on the couch, keeping her even warmer.

CHAPTER FIVE

D aniel left early the next morning to check out his home and neighborhood. Justina stood, hunched up in a thick grey sweatshirt, watching as the bike kicked up small fountains of sand in its wake and disappeared out of sight.

After he left, Justina sat on the couch wrapped in a blanket for a long time. She wasn't nervous being alone but, after having Daniel around, the house seemed empty. Although it had only been a few days since she met him, it seemed like she had known him forever. She felt so safe with Daniel. She knew she could trust him and was convinced he could handle anything. She didn't know his opinion of her, though. He treated her like a little sister—someone to be protected. She realized that, compared to him, she had not suffered many hardships in her life and her father continuously sheltered her from many of life's difficulties. Losing her mother had been awful, and the loss was still with her, but it was many years ago.

She remembered how life was when her mother was still alive. A few memories always came to her mind and she let her thoughts wander.

Mama was in the kitchen, cooking something that smelled delicious— onions and some type of meat simmered on the stove. Salsa music was playing, turned up loud, and Mama spun me around, dancing with me while we waited for Papa to get home. I spun too hard and got dizzy, falling down, giggling. Mama picked me up and held me with one arm, over her hip, and continued swaying with the music. The front door opened and Papa called, "where are my girls?" Mama answered, "We are in the kitchen, mi amore, waiting for you!" Papa came in and scooped me off of Mama, giving her a kiss. "Come on, mija, let's go pick out some wine!" He loosened his tie as he took me into the pantry and asked me which wine they should have with dinner. I pointed to a bottle of champagne with the brightly colored foil top. Papa laughed at me, "Okay, we drink champagne tonight, just for you!" Mama laughed when she saw my choice and giggled as Papa set me down and spun her around to the music.

And the summers. Summers were always spent down on the beach and I rode high on Papa's shoulders. The beach was full of people and the boardwalk was bustling. Papa walked out into the surf, threatening to dunk me, with Mama splashing us or taking pictures. We would go home hot, covered with sand, and Mama would start dinner while Papa taught me a card game or how to draw some imaginary sea creature. I always asked why we didn't see those creatures at the aquarium or if we could catch one and have it as a pet in a fish tank. Papa told me they were very rare, very shy animals and hard to find. . . for years I believed him.

Justina smiled at the memories, and even though they made her sad, she was grateful to have them. She realized how different her father had been then and pondered how events in life can change a person, for better or worse.

Daniel was alone taking care of his mother as she died. Justina could not imagine how awful that must have been. It obviously hit him hard, hard enough that he couldn't face going back to school and doing something he clearly cared about.

From what she knew of Daniel so far, it made sense that Daniel had taken care of her through the storm.

He was a person who takes care of other people and wasn't used to being taken care of. She had welcomed him doing it, in part because she was scared, but also because it's what she was accustomed to. It made her take a closer look at herself. *It's time for me to grow up*, she realized. *I don't want to spend my life like some pampered pet!* With that thought, she decided she would do some things around the house before Daniel returned.

She brought in some firewood and stacked it by the woodstove, then gathered up the various cans, food wrappers, and wine bottles and put it all out in the garbage. She folded up the blankets and pillows, stacking them on a chair. At least the place should be pleasant for him to return to, especially if he found serious problems at his own house.

As she surveyed the food and water supplies, Justina wondered if the grocery store might be open so she could find something more desirable to eat. She decided to take a walk up the street. Putting on her boots and jacket, she headed to Waldbaums. As she neared the store she saw a line of people and other people gathered in clumps, although the store appeared dark. As she got closer, she realized the people were lined up at a Red Cross truck that was handing out supplies and police were patrolling.

She approached the line of people to find out what was being handed out and what the situation was. So far they hadn't really heard any news about the neighborhood or when the power and water would be restored. The last man in line was a tall, grey-haired man with a small blonde girl holding his hand, her blue eyes wide under her fuzzy pink hat.

"Excuse me," Justina said to him, "Do you know what's going on? I haven't heard anything. How long is the power supposed to be out?"

He shook his head. "I'm not sure, miss. I think at least a week or two. Nothing is working. They are saying folks should leave here until it's back in order. Lots of us here aren't going anywhere, though, so they are handing out some food and water."

Justina processed this latest information, frowning, as the little girl tugged on the man to move forward in the line.

She stepped forward automatically, too, and then asked, "Where are people supposed to go? And how, with so many cars wrecked?"

"They have been loading people onto buses, taking them to shelters. Me, I'd rather stick it out, my house isn't as bad as some. I don't want to take my grandkids to a shelter, anyhow. I can't see how that's any better. You see on the news how well people live in those shelters and I want to keep an eye on my house. Lord knows what might happen otherwise." He shook his head in disgust at the idea and stepped forward to get some packages of food and bottled water. Justina got some bottled water too, but didn't take any food. She could see many people lined up behind her and knew she still had plenty to eat at home. Other people might not have as much and the supplies could run out.

As she walked home she wished she could reach Daniel to tell him what the situation was. She realized she should try to reach her father too, but the cell phones were not working. He always worried about her and she wondered when he would be home. He must have been held up with something important or perhaps travel was difficult after the storm. He would have come home otherwise, she was certain. She was a little bit glad he hadn't and it was just as well she couldn't reach him, given how bad the situation was. He would be more concerned than he would need to be. *He would probably tell me to go to a shelter or a hotel,* she thought. She would also have to tell him about Daniel staying there and wasn't sure how he would handle that. Better to wait for that discussion. He would probably be fine, she told herself. She also worried about the cat. That would be a tricky conversation as well. But she would deal with that later. Perhaps Hercules' owners would claim him anyhow—although she selfishly hoped not. She realized how much her life had changed in the past few days and wondered how it would all sort out, and when. Her whole world was upside down and it wasn't altogether a bad thing.

Once she got home and settled in, she surveyed the wine rack, and found some wines for dinner. Daniel might be happy to have a glass of wine when he got back from his house.

CHAPTER SIX

Daniel was eager to go home, but dreading what he would find in Far Rockaway. Justina clearly still hadn't been happy to see him leave, but she put on a good face. He reminded her that he'd be back and he'd try to locate something more appealing to eat for dinner.

He found that there were no problems getting across the parkway. It helped that he had the motorcycle because he could skirt the various mounds of debris and cars that blocked the street. *So far so good*, he thought hopefully, as he navigated an electrical pole that lay across the sand-covered roadway coming off the bridge.

However, his optimism was short-lived. As he approached Far Rockaway he discovered large piles of sand and rubble nearly obliterating the road. As he slowly navigated his way toward his neighborhood, he found the familiar streets looking like a war zone from a third-world country that might be featured on the news. Houses were battered, some beyond recognition, and some completely gone or broken in pieces, falling off their foundations. Piled-up cars lay on top of each other, half buried in mounds of sand and debris.

People had begun dealing with their own tragedies—the contents of their homes stacked outside waiting for a trash collector who most likely wouldn't be coming anytime soon. Just like in Long Beach, mountains of filthy, saturated furniture were out in front of homes. Broken tables, stained curtains, chairs, and televisions, tires, bumpers, broken pieces of windows, gutters, and roofs, all piled up one after another in a never-ending mountain of wreckage. Chunks of stained and waterlogged sheetrock and insulation were piled up in front of a couple homes where the residents had started gutting the inside of the house. Piles of sand and muck covered everything and stunk like sewage.

Despair showed on the faces of the people in Far Rockaway. Daniel guessed that many didn't have insurance or the resources to go stay in a hotel so, unless they had family or friends to stay with, they would be stuck. The power was off here, too, and the people in the streets wore filthy clothes and grim expressions. Children covered in muck played in the piles of debris, parents sitting and watching them blankly. An air of hopelessness permeated everything—as though the people here understood that their condition would not improve any time soon.

Daniel's heart ached for them. He wanted to help, but he suspected that his own problems were comparable.

As Daniel rounded the corner to his house, he understood that his luck was no better than anyone else's. Although he had shuttered his windows and no trees had gone through his roof, the watermark ran halfway up the outside wall and the sand piled up over the top of his front steps. As he pushed aside the sand and opened the door, the smell immediately hit him in the face—stale salt water and sewage. His furniture looked similar to the furniture he had seen piled outside. It was saturated and soiled beyond recognition. Everything in the living room had been knocked about and was covered in brown stinking muck. A watermark circled the room, memorializing the tide level in his home. He gagged as he surveyed the first floor, lifting his sweatshirt up to cover his mouth and nose. The air in the house was already on its way to being toxic.

He went up the stairs to see if he could salvage clothes and other furniture. The upstairs appeared fine, although the stench of sewage permeated the whole house. He realized a couple things right away. For one thing, the amount of work needed was enormous. It wasn't something he could do in an afternoon. He would need to gut the house, just like his neighbors. Secondly, it was not healthy to be in the contaminated house, breathing the air. He knew the longer it took to repair it, the worse the mold and mildew would get. Everything would have to be ripped out, but not today.

Going through his room, he gathered up some things that he could manage to carry on the bike. He collected a bag of clothes and ran across the charger for his phone, grabbing it in the hopes that Long Beach would have power soon. Downstairs in the kitchen he found canned goods on the top shelf and took a few cans, even though they weren't very appealing.

He opened a few windows in the futile hope that the air quality would improve before he came back to clean it out. As he stepped out of the house and locked up, he wondered why he bothered. He doubted any of the neighbors would break in and steal his ruined stuff. They all had their own ruined stuff. In situations like this there were always looters, though. It was only a matter of time. He thought wryly that it was maybe a good thing he owned nothing worth stealing. He started thinking about insurance and wondered what kind of relief the city or state would provide; surely this would qualify as a disaster area.

He figured once he got his phone charged up he'd start trying to sort it out. He knew it would take forever to get any help, particularly with everyone on the East Coast having similar issues. The magnitude of things to be done was overwhelming and he wondered how he would manage. Sure, he was fine for the moment, staying at Justina and Victor's house, but he couldn't do that forever and he needed to get busy with repairs.

He suspected that even when the power came back his heating and electrical systems would require expensive repairs or replacement that shouldn't be put off with winter coming. *And how exactly am I supposed to do that?* He wondered, since the life insurance money from his mom was running low. He could make it for a while if he lived modestly, as he normally did, but it was not sufficient to rebuild a house.

He felt a headache coming on, probably a combination of stress and the toxic air he'd been breathing. He was grateful to be heading back to Long Beach and Justina—a happy place compared to his reality. It was a good thing that he hadn't brought her with him. *No need for that.* The damage in Long Beach was horrific, to be sure, but in Rockaway some homes had completely disappeared, leaving only foundations. Many of those remaining were not well-built and had not withstood the onslaught of Sandy as well as their Long Beach neighbors had. Any way you looked at it, there was nothing here to feel good about. He wondered how long his neighbors would be cold and hungry and how they could live.

The one bright spot came as he headed back to Justina's house and saw that one of the Chinese take-out places was actually open! He knew how excited Justina would be about having hot food, so he picked up an assortment of entrees with rice for dinner. He was impressed with the owners of the restaurant. They had cleaned up and powered up in record time, better than almost anyone else in Long Beach. And it was obviously appreciated by the residents who were lined up for a hot meal. He was surprised about the number of police and National Guard members patrolling the town, and was even more surprised to learn of a curfew at night. It was reassuring, in one way, to know that the town was being looked after while it recovered, but unnerving to know that people had to stay in their homes at night. Daniel felt like the neighborhood had become a police-state overnight and wondered if there were problems with looters. He thought of Justina, home alone, and picked up his speed and best he could.

When he got back to the Gonzalez house, Justina had opened the wine and poured him a glass. "Well?" She asked. "How bad is the damage?"

He raised an eyebrow. "Let's just say I'm going to be here for a while. My neighborhood is a disaster area. I hope that's okay. But I do have a hot dinner!"

CHAPTER SEVEN

Although she didn't wish for Daniel's house to be destroyed, Justina was disproportionately happy at his announcement. She was becoming very comfortable with their little domestic situation, albeit a temporary one. She knew it was selfish, but she wanted him there. She had been afraid he might decide to go back home if things in Far Rockaway weren't too serious. She knew that he had no obligation to stay at her house, except that he was a good guy and seemed to have taken on that responsibility. She did need to tell him about her trip to the store and what she had learned.

"Daniel, they are saying that people should evacuate because there is no water or power. They are taking the residents in busses to a shelter. Quite a few people are staying, though, and they have facilities set up to keep us supplied with water and food. They said it might be a week or more before they get everything back up and running. I don't want to go to a shelter—I think we are fine here. What do you think?" She pulled some silverware out of the drawer and handed him a couple of white paper plates that she had found in the back of a cabinet.

"Wow. Yeah, I agree, I don't really want to go to a shelter either. You could go to a hotel, though. Then you would have clean water and a shower. And better food. I can stay at my house—it's a mess, but I can do it." He said resolutely as he dished up the Chinese food and handed her a plate.

She shook her head. "No, I don't want to go to a hotel. I'm sure there aren't any nearby that are even open. I'm sure the Allegria is closed, you know they had to be flooded too," she said, referring to the local hotel on the beach. "Besides, I want to stay here. This is my home and we can make do. Tell me about your house."

As they ate their take-out dinner, Daniel shared with her the condition of his house and neighborhood. He explained to her the problems with the sewage and the mold and mildew that were certain to follow. He told her he would have to completely empty out his house, sooner rather than later, and that it was a nasty job he would probably have to do himself. It would be challenging to find help when everyone else would be tied up doing the same thing in their own home or their family's home.

"What about insurance?" She asked. "Don't they have to come and inspect it before they pay?"

He finished chewing his mouthful of cashew chicken before answering. "Probably. I need to call them. I've never had to do this before, so I don't know the process." He tried to imagine how long before an insurance person would come check out his house. Months he imagined. And he wasn't even sure what the policy covered; he had never actually read it.

She attempted to be helpful. "Do you think you should talk to some of your neighbors? Maybe they have already spoken with someone and can give you advice?"

He got a stricken expression on his face. "Oh my God." He said. "Willie. I forgot my neighbor Willie. I should have checked on her today."

Seeing Justina's questioning look, he elaborated. "I have a neighbor, an old lady, across the street who lives alone. I doubt she left before the storm. She doesn't get around too well and I didn't even think to check on her today. She's not very healthy. Damn. I was so worried about my own problems, I forgot all about her." He was obviously furious with himself and Justina had nothing to say to make it any better.

"I'm going back in the morning," he announced. "I can't leave her like that."

Justina nodded. She wouldn't expect anything different from him. But this time, she was going to go. "Let me come with you," she said, in an insistent voice. "I might be able to help. I don't know how, but I want to help. There is no reason for me to sit in this house when I might be able to make a difference some way. Please."

He hesitated, then said, "Justina, it is such a mess over there. I really don't think. . . ." He stopped as he saw her face—her mouth was tightening.

"Daniel, don't you treat me like my father does! I do not want to be protected from the real world any more. I don't want to spend my life being useless. I want to go with you!" Her voice had a sharp edge to it and her eyes flashed with intensity. He looked at her, appearing stunned by the outburst. She knew that he did not want to drag her into that disaster, but she was not going to give in gracefully this time.

"All right," he conceded. "But I warned you how unpleasant it is over there. It's a mess. You'll need to wear your oldest boots and jeans and you are not going to enjoy it, I promise you."

She nodded, and simply said, "Okay."

The next morning they set off on the bike towards Far Rockaway, dressed in worn clothing that couldn't be harmed much by the dirty conditions they would be facing. They brought two scarves, at Daniel's insistence, to wrap around their faces. Justina appeared skeptical about needing a scarf, but it was Daniel's turn to be unrelenting.

Justina was gripped by horror at the devastation in Daniel's neighborhood and she understood why he had not wanted to bring her here. It was even more bleak and depressing than Long Beach, if that was possible. She wondered how this area would ever rebuild—she couldn't even imagine how people would go about doing that.

They wound around the various obstacles in the road and down the side street toward Daniel's house. He pointed out his home as he pulled into the driveway of Willie's house across the road. He dismounted as soon as he came to a stop, his attention focused on the well being of his neighbor.

Justina said, "I will wait here unless you need me." He nodded as he strode toward the house.

Daniel got up the front stairs as fast as possible while pushing sand and muck aside to secure a good foothold on each step. Pounding on the door, he called "Willie! Willie! Are you in there?" After hearing no answer, he moved to the back door, navigating several garbage cans and other debris tossed haphazardly against the house by the storm.

He knocked and called out again. This time he got a faint response through the door. "Daniel? Is that you? Come in, the door is not locked."

As he entered the house, he was struck by the same smells as in his house, but in addition there was a sour odor of illness and old cooking grease. He could tell that water had been inside the house—the brown shag carpet in the living room was still damp and coated with muck and the walls had a water line all around. The living room, which wasn't much in the first place, was a shambles. He found Willie at her kitchen table with her legs propped up on the chair opposite her. Her dark skin had an unhealthy grey tint to it and she had a blanket wrapped over what appeared to be a grimy housedress or nightgown. Her large legs were swollen and the skin discolored. Daniel flinched when he saw them.

"What happened?" he asked. "Are you hurt?"

"No, I ain't hurt, but I am in sore need of my heart medication. I ran out a day or two ago and got no way to get over to St. John's. My car's dun gone—it floated away. I can't go nowhere. Water was bad here, I had to sit up on the stairs all night, couldn't quite get myself upstairs to the bed. I sat and watched it come up through the floor-boards there," she said, motioning toward the hallway. "You know I ain't scared of much, I been through a lot in this life, but that nasty ole water coming right up through the floor. . . seemed like it was never gonna stop coming. Thought it might take my whole house away, and me with it!" She shifted her bulk in the chair and gri-maced with the effort. "I don't even know if St. John's is still stand-ing, that old storm took apart everything. No power, no nothing left, don't know what folks are supposed to do. Got my little radio here, but batteries up and died on me so I don't know what help is coming."

Daniel pondered this for a moment, then said, "I think the first thing is for me to see if the hospital is open. I don't know if they evacuated or what happened. I haven't been here since before the storm. I was over at Long Beach dealing with stuff there. Have you had anything to eat or drink?"

She made a face. "I've been living on those canned milkshakes that are supposed to be a meal. Let me tell you, those ain't like any meal I ever wanted! Doctor told me to get some 'cause I need to lose weight. Turns out a good thing I had those and hadn't been doing right by drinking them, most everything else got ruined with all that water coming in and the power out. I still got a couple left. So I'm good an' hungry, but I suppose I'm surviving okay. Maybe lost some of that weight the doctor got on me about." She smiled with one of her gold teeth shining right in front, but Daniel noticed her hands were shaking.

"Let me go see if the hospital's open, okay? If it is, we'll bring you there and get your medicine and get those legs checked out. I'll be back in a little bit, it might take awhile—the roads are all messed up."

"Oh, I know you're right about that!" she said with feeling. "I 'preciate your help, honey—not everyone remembers a sick old woman. You're a good boy, your momma raised you right, God rest her soul."

Daniel smiled and patted her arm, saying again, "I'll be back as soon as I can."

Justina was waiting by the bike, still looking a little shell-shocked. "Ready to go for a ride?" Daniel asked.

"Where are we going? How is your friend?"

"We're going to check out the hospital, see if it's open. Willie needs her heart medication—she's out and her legs are swollen up like sausages. I don't think she's doing well. She should see a doctor, but she's a tough old bird—I'll give her that." They had to take a circuitous route to the hospital and as they got closer to it they saw people milling around everywhere. They were still a block away from the hospital at St. Mary's Church. The whole property was set up as a relief station with people being served meals of some sort in one area and on the other side there were piles of supplies—basic things like diapers, toilet paper, food staples, and baby food. The people hanging around the tent looked cold, dirty, and grief-stricken—especially those with babies and small children who were crying or coughing.

As they neared St. John's it appeared that the hospital was open, based on the gaggle of people near the Emergency Room doors. Justina asked, "Do you want me to make sure it's open? Just so we know for a fact?"

Daniel agreed, so she hopped off the bike and walked up to the Emergency Room entrance. She soon discovered that St. John's was open, but the reason for the crowd outside was that it was full to capacity. Justina asked a thin blonde woman who was holding a coughing little girl of about two if the hospital was open and seeing patients. The woman sighed and looked at Justina with weary blue eyes. "It's open, all right, but good luck getting in. I think all the Rockaways are here and there just aren't enough doctors for everyone." With that she broke off in a coughing fit—a deep, barking cough that sounded painful. "Some of us are here because we have no place else to go. Houses are trashed or gone and nothing is open. At least here they have heat from the generators, but there is no space. The hospital doesn't have enough room or food to take care of this whole area for sure. They say help is coming, so far I've just seen the stuff over at St. Mary's. Dunno." She stroked her daughter's stringy blonde hair as the girl coughed again. "It's bad times here, miss. If you know anywhere else we can go, please tell me. We are in trouble here."

"I'm sorry. I wish I had some advice. I'm trying to figure this out myself. I hope you get in quickly to see a doctor. Hopefully more help will come soon—this situation can't go on like this. Hang in there, okay?" Justina felt so inadequate, and desperately wished she could help the poor woman.

She headed back to the bike. "Hospital's open," she told Daniel. "But it's not pretty. Not enough doctors or even space for the people who need it. Some of them are here just because they have nowhere else to go but, from what I heard, there's no other option so I guess we bring your friend in? We can't just leave her in her house without her medication."

"Right. But I can't put her on my bike. I will have to try to get my truck out. I haven't even looked to see if that's possible. Let's go check." He paused. "I wonder how much stuff washed up behind the garage. This might be a challenge."

They were relieved to discover that, although plenty of debris had washed up around the garage, none of it was too big to move. They both set to work moving the pieces of cars, houses, furniture,

garbage cans, and other assorted relics of other people's lives, so
they could get the truck out. Everything was wet and coated in
sand and sewage. "Aren't you glad you left your Gucci at home?"
He teased her as he surveyed their filthy clothes and hands. He
was impressed with how Justina had pitched in and helped like a
trooper.

She laughed. "Yeah, sure, now let's go get Willie to the hospital."

They were able to start the truck and drive around the block
to pull up in front of Willie's house, which was a miracle given the
depth of sand and piles of trash everywhere. Daniel mentally re-
viewed their trip to the hospital, wondering how hard it would be
to navigate to St. Johns in the truck. He thought he knew a way to
make it work.

He warned Justina, "Willie is a character, but she's not well.
And she's a big lady, it might take both of us to help her out of the
house with her legs like they are. Are you okay with that?" Justina
nodded, "Of course."

"Also, be prepared for the smell of the house, when I first went
into my place it gagged me. If you put that scarf around your face
it will help. Up to you, but it's awful, I'm warning you. It might be
just me—I am really sensitive to smells—but I don't think so. It's
pretty disgusting."

She grimaced. "I don't want to offend her by covering my nose!
That seems so rude!"

"Trust me, it's not, and I'm sure she knows how nasty it is. She's
living in it. She won't take it personal and she has bigger issues,
right? She's grateful for the help—she has no family or anyone else
to care for her. I just want you to know what you are walking into.
It was a shock to me at first."

Justina compromised by wrapping the scarf around her neck,
so she could use it if necessary.

Although Daniel had warned her, Justina still wasn't prepared
for the sights and smells that greeted her. The most important

thing, she reminded herself, was to help Daniel's neighbor get to see a doctor and get her medicine. Daniel greeted Willie, "Okay, Willie, it's time to go. The hospital is open, but it's crowded, there will be a wait. I have mom's truck out front—can you walk? I brought my friend here with me—this is Justina. We're gonna help you get to the hospital, okay?"

"Bless you, Daniel. And aren't you the cutest little thing?" she said to Justina. "Thank you for helping an old lady! I think I can walk jus' fine." Willie braced herself with each arm of her chair, slowly getting up.

Justina noticed Willie's filthy slippers. "Do you want to put on some shoes?" she asked. "Your feet will get wet in those slippers."

Willie looked at her ragged slippers and sighed. "Girl, I can't get these old swollen things in no shoes. I gotta go like this. I do need my pocketbook though. It's in the living room, would you fetch it for me?"

Daniel motioned toward the living room and Justina went to collect the purse. She looked around at the damp disarray and wondered how the woman had managed to exist for days in this house. The smell of sewage was strongest in that room, most likely because of the wet carpet. Justina wrapped the scarf around her face and located the old grey handbag.

As they started out of the house it became obvious that Willie couldn't make it, so she put an arm around each of their shoulders and they made their way painstakingly down the creaky stairs.

As they arrived at St. John's Hospital the line outside was no better, but they moved Willie past the group and into the Emergency Department. People of every description packed the hospital—old and young, black and white, and everything in between. There was a cacophony of languages, babies crying, and persistent coughing. Elderly people in wheelchairs were parked along the walls and people with oxygen tanks clustered around electric outlets where they plugged in.

Daniel and Justina finally got to talk to someone about Willie, an intake person who didn't appear much healthier than the patients. She had deep circles under her dark eyes with vague traces of makeup smudged at the sides.

"It's going to be several hours, at least," the woman said, sighing.

Justina and Daniel exchanged glances.

The nurse went on: "Our doctors have been working for 24 hours or more. We are supposed to get a couple more coming soon from the city to help, but you can see there are too many people here."

She said to Daniel, "Try to find her a place to sit down. You may have to scour the hospital for an empty chair. At this point use whatever you can find, okay?"

She looked past them. "Next?" She said, to the old black man who limped up behind them.

Daniel went off to locate a chair for Willie whose swollen legs didn't look like they could hold her body up for much longer. After a lengthy search he found an open storage closet and liberated the last remaining wheelchair. They parked her in a corner and settled in to wait.

As they waited, they watched the human dramas playing out around them. The conversations ranged from comparisons of ailments to discussions about lost or damaged homes; cold, hungry children; and anxiety over what would happen next. The most prevalent topic of conversation was the lack of power and food.

A family huddled together next to Justina. Based on their accents it sounded as if they were from somewhere in Africa. They were trying to fill out hospital paperwork, but they didn't understand what they needed to do. They noticed Justina listening to them and the young man in the group asked her, "Please miss. Can you help us with these paperworks? We don't understand." His melodious voice was tinged with anxiety as he struggled to find the right words. His wife or girlfriend beside him sat on the floor, back against the wall, rubbing her pregnant belly. An older woman, most likely a soon-to-be grandmother, crouched by her side. She occasionally murmured to the girl in their native tongue.

Justina took the paperwork and looked at them—application papers for medical assistance. She read through them and did her best to explain what the forms required, line-by-line. It was a slow process as the man tried to explain to his wife and the soon-to-be grandmother what they needed. Fortunately, in New York there wasn't much required by way of residency documentation, since they had almost nothing for identification. The minimal paperwork they had was in the girl's tiny beaded purse, but it was sufficient and they got the papers filled out as best they could.

As Justina gave the forms one last review, an Indian woman in scrubs came up to her. "Are you from the Hospital Association?" She asked.

Justina looked at her with a slightly puzzled frown. "Hospital association? No. . . ."

The woman explained, "The Hospital Association said they would send one or two social workers from the city to help patients with Medicaid and financial assistance apps. I hoped maybe that was you. Never mind."

Justina replied, "No, I am just here with a friend, waiting, but these people needed help understanding the forms. You don't have staff here to do that?" She wondered how the woman could have thought she was from the Hospital Association, given her grubby attire, but she decided that everyone looked rough so it had become the new normal.

"No, no," she responded. "I am the clinic manager, but I'm helping with triage in the Emergency room, registration, and everything else. We have not been able to find our social worker since the storm—we cannot reach her. Lots of our staff is missing. We have so many patients here and nobody to help them with this.

We need to get as many people as possible signed up for Medicaid. We have no way to cover our costs as it is."

Justina shrugged. "I can do it if it's what I just did—helping people fill out forms. I'm in law school, I suspect I can handle it! And I would like to do something."

"Thank you, thank you, right now we need any help we can get. My name is Priya, by the way. You know we can't pay you? I'm sorry. This is just such a desperate time here. We normally have a process for training and background checks. . ." she trailed off as a large Samoan couple jostled by her.

"No, it's fine," Justina assured her. "Tell me where to start!"

She had barely gotten to the triage area when a slender young black man came in carrying an older woman. He was sweating through his faded black t-shirt, despite the cold, and his eyes were frantic. Although her new job was to assist patients with their paperwork, the expression on his face made her go to him and ask if he needed help.

"Yes, yes," he said. "Please help me. I found my Aunt trapped in those apartments by the beach. She lives on the eighteenth floor and there is no power for elevators. I went to go check on her and she was like this." The woman was not unconscious, but almost. The man continued, "She is diabetic. There is no elevator because of the power, so I went up the stairs to check on her and had to carry her down. There wasn't any insulin in her apartment. I think she has been without it for days. She needs a doctor, right away. I don't know if she can make it."

Justina fought her own panic over not knowing what to do and reassured the man that she would get help, hoping her anxiety didn't show on her face. She ran to find Priya, or a nurse, or anyone who could handle this situation. The first person she found was a young woman whose badge identified her as a resident named Kathy.

Kathy went with Justina and started immediately taking the woman's vitals. "She's going to be okay," the resident advised Justina. "But we need to get her stable right away. It's a good thing they got here when they did." Kathy then took the patient's nephew by the elbow and guided him back to a treatment room. Justina, suddenly alone, took a deep breath. She wondered what she was doing here when she was unqualified to do anything.

I guess I will learn, she told herself, and headed to her assigned station.

CHAPTER EIGHT

Meanwhile, Willie finally managed to see a doctor after several hours of waiting and was able to get her medication, although the doctor expressed a concern that the hospital could run out of many medications before long. With no other hospitals open nearby, everyone was coming to St. John's.

Daniel located Justina after Willie was released. "Hey, are you ready to go?"

She looked at the mass of people lining the hallway and overflowing out of the Emergency Department doors. "Yeah, I guess so. I feel guilty going. Do you think you could bring me back tomorrow? Oh, and I have to tell Priya that I'm leaving."

"Sure," he responded. "I think it would be a good idea for me to keep an eye on Willie anyhow, in case she has any more problems. I'll start gutting my house if this is what you want to do. I need to do the same thing for Willie, too. It's very nice, by the way, what you're doing. These people really need the help." He saw how pleased she was with his comment. She had a flush on her cheeks as she smiled.

"Thanks," she said. "I am enjoying it actually. It's nice to be useful."

They got Willie settled at her house after picking up bottled water, a packet of sandwiches, and crackers for her at the relief station down the street. When they got home, Justina asked Daniel to get the fire going so she could boil a pot of water for a sponge bath. She was glad she had picked up extra bottled water the day before, she could see they were going to be using it. The water in the tub wasn't going to last very long at this rate.

"I really need to wash up after today!" She said. She took the warm water into the bathroom and gave herself a modified bath. As she came out, she told him, "That's the worst part of this for me. Especially if we are going to be out here getting dirty. I just can't stand going without a bath and shampoo! Cold food is bad enough. We are luckier than most people. I get that. I'm so glad we can heat things up. I hate being chilly all the time. How awful."

He laughed at her. "I see the princess is still there!" She made a face at him, but didn't try to deny it.

They got into a routine in the days that followed. Daniel dropped her at the hospital and brought food for Willie, now that one of the nearby grocery stores was finally open for business and getting restocked. Justina discovered she could take a warm shower at St. John's, which was what many of the staff had to do. The community did its best to take care of the local residents, providing supplies and food at St. Mary's, and the hospital took care of the people who continued to need help. Being at the hospital also helped Justina and Daniel conserve their dwindling supply of firewood, since the weather was definitely getting colder.

Then things got worse. The weather reports were forecasting a nor'easter to hit the New York area, packing snow and wind to a region already struggling to recover power and heat. Many people were being advised, once again, to evacuate their homes and places where power had been restored were again in jeopardy. Justina heard about it at the hospital and told Daniel when they got back to Long Beach one night.

Daniel stopped in the middle of taking off his coat and frowned at her like she was crazy. "Are you kidding me? A nor'easter in early November, right after a hurricane? How are people supposed to deal with all this? And speaking of that, we don't have that much firewood either. This has got to stop!" He flung his coat on the coach and raked his fingers through his hair in agitation.

Justina looked at him with wide eyes, surprised by his outburst. "Are we going to be okay, Daniel? Don't we have enough wood to last a while longer?" He was usually the calm one who could handle anything. *This is really getting to him*, she thought. *He seems about ready to snap*!

Daniel let out a deep breath. "Yeah, I'm sorry. We will be fine. It's just so hard hearing all the stories and problems in my neighborhood, and so many people can't come back to their homes. Now this. I don't know how much more this area can take."

"I know, but you scared me! Maybe we should go get some takeout tonight, in case we can't get out for a day or two. It's supposed to start snowing tonight and I'm already cold. Warm food sounds good, don't you think?"

Daniel agreed and, after starting a fire in the woodstove, he left to pick up some Chinese food from their new favorite place. Justina got wine and paper plates out and put on an extra sweater to combat the chill that had invaded the house. She worried about the coming storm and what would happen to all the people who already had too many challenges. She also fretted about her own lack of heat and power, she was getting tired of camping in her own home—even though she was grateful for what she had. *Almost everyone else has it worse*, she reminded herself. *You need to suck it up and not complain.*

Despite all of that, Justina was feeling happier than she had in a very long time. She realized that she had been lonely and pretty much living just for herself. Seeing how Daniel took care of everyone and never complained made her take a look at herself, and how she was feeling when she was with him.

She loved having him there; she could almost pretend that this was her life. *Don't get too used to it*, she thought. *Pretty soon Papa will be home and the party will be over!* She knew that Daniel would go back to his house and she would go back to school. She almost felt like she couldn't face that.

There was also the issue of work at the hospital. It gave her a purpose like she had never experienced, she was doing something that actually mattered. She had been struggling with that while she was in school—what was she going to do once she was done? She still didn't know exactly, but at least this gave her a taste of being out in the real world and making a difference.

Rain had begun turning to snow soon after Daniel returned with the take-out. He built up the fire in the woodstove and they ate a big dinner with plenty of wine. The wind picked up outside, blowing heavy, wet snowflakes sideways. Justina wrapped up in a blanket and watched the snow pile up outside the window.

"I can't believe winter is already here," she commented. "It's barely November. Look at this wind! We will never get power back."

"We will get power back, this won't last. Come on over by the fire and get warm, and finish your wine!"

She smiled, appreciating his attempt to distract her from the scene outside the window. She returned to the couch and picked up Hercules to cuddle with and snuggled up to Daniel. He put his arm around her and she nestled in, feeling as content as the cat with a bowl of tuna. "Daniel, what's going to happen?" she asked. "I mean, all of this has been so awful and yet it's so nice at the same time. I'm going to miss this...."

He stroked her hair thoughtfully before answering. "I don't know, exactly. You have to go back to school, even though they are giving everyone a delay due to the storm. I have to get my house in order as soon as I can. It's not like your dad is going to want us living here, at least he won't want *me* living here! And I really need to get my life back on track—I need to finish school as well. Seeing all the people without homes helps me feel motivated to finish. I would be more useful to people if I had my education."

"Am I going to see you?" she couldn't help but ask.

"Do you want to?"

"I do! We've been through all this together and I have really appreciated everything you've done and who you are. I like being with you," she finished simply.

"I like being with you, too," he responded. "But you and I live in different worlds. I'm more comfortable wearing blue jeans and holding a hammer. You are living in the world of politicians, housekeepers, and charity dinners. There's not much overlap and I'm sure your father would be the first to tell you that." When he saw how crushed she looked he added, "I'm not saying we can't see each other. I'm just being realistic."

"It's not up to my father what I do, I'm an adult. I try to please him, but it's my choice. We haven't had any real disagreements like that. And he likes you!"

"He likes me doing chores in the yard or house. He doesn't really know me. That's not the same as hanging out with his one-and-only precious daughter. I'm just saying. I think I understand him—he is the padre, the man of the house. I get that. And you are his world. He won't be letting go easily, trust me." He could tell that she was getting upset, so he put both his arms around her and gave her a hug. "Don't worry about it, okay? Things work out how they are supposed to—no point in fussing over it."

Without warning, she looked up and kissed him. He kissed her back for a moment, but then gently broke away. "We shouldn't do this," he said.

"Why not? You don't like me enough?"

"It's not that. When your father comes home I want to be able to look him in the eye knowing that I haven't broken his trust. He would want me to make sure you are safe—anything more and he will think I took advantage. I would love to kiss you, okay? But for now it's not right." He seemed very firm in his resolve.

She hated what he said, but she respected how he felt and she knew he was right about her father. It would not do for him to find out that she and Daniel were messing around while Daniel was supposedly looking after her. And he would know—her father was like that. "Okay, I get it." She said and snuggled up with her head against his chest. She needed to be an adult about it, like he was, but that was so difficult.

They sat like that for quite a while, both quiet and lost in their own thoughts, when Justina's phone buzzed. "Oh!" She said. "I've forgotten what that sound is!" She looked at the phone and for a moment wished her cell phone was still out of commission. "It's my father. I have to answer it."

"Hola, Papa. How are you? I haven't talked to you in so long!" She forced her tone to be perky, despite the fact that the last thing she wanted was to talk to him at that moment.

"I am good. How are you, mija?" Her father said. "Is it snowing where you are? I saw on the news, it looks awful. I got your message, are you back in the City? Any problems with the house?"

"No, Papa, I am still at the house. It's snowing now. Classes are delayed. The storm was terrible everywhere in Long Island, although the house is fine. I went over to Far Rockaway with Daniel and I've been helping at the hospital with patient's paperwork. There are so many people sick and without homes!" She wanted him to know about the hospital work, she was very proud of it.

"That's good, Sweetheart, I'm glad you found something helpful to do. Is the power on now? Has Daniel been by to take care of things?"

"Yes, Papa, he has been wonderful. The power is still out, but we have the woodstove and take-out. Where are you?"

"I'm in California, but I'm wrapping up. There was a school shooting while we were here, so we couldn't really leave. These school shootings are becoming very political, and the Senator wanted to stay there so we could show support here. I am coming home tomorrow. I can't wait to see you! What an adventure you have had!" She looked at Daniel and cringed, wrinkling her brow.

"I can't wait to see you either! Have a safe trip. Love you!"

"Love you too, sleep well, I will see you tomorrow. Ciao."

She hung up and looked at Daniel sadly. "He's coming home tomorrow. I don't know what to say to him. I want you to stay here until your house is livable, and I know it might be a while. I think he will be okay with that, but I'm going to have to tell him you've been staying here because of how bad your house is. Also, I want to keep Hercules and I know he will disagree about that. I'm so not ready for this." She poured another glass of wine. "Last chance for drinking Papa's wine collection, too!"

She held her glass up for a toast, "Salut!" They clicked glasses and finished the contents.

CHAPTER NINE

Although she had made it a point to tell Daniel that she was sure her father would be fine with him staying there while his house was unlivable, she really wasn't sure at all how her father would react. She knew he was going to give her some trouble about everything that went on while he was gone. Even if he understood about the circumstances of the storm, he probably wouldn't be receptive to a continued living arrangement—especially if he was going to be going away again soon.

Justina had a hard time sleeping that night—she couldn't get comfortable. She bunched up the pillows and tried to find the magical position to send her to sleep, but nothing worked. She was anxious about facing her father. It was as if she had been a naughty little girl caught doing something very bad.

She was worried that Daniel would disappear from her life and she had become too attached to him, she knew that. She didn't feel like she could face not having him around, but she also knew Daniel was right about the issues with her father. Daniel wouldn't get into any debates with her father, she was pretty sure of that. She was frustrated at the injustice of it—she had always done what she was supposed to, but this was something that was so important to her and it seemed that everyone was going to let it just disappear. She was even worried about the cat. Daniel had put up a notice at the store several days earlier and there was no response, but she was afraid of her father's reaction. Maybe she could take Hercules to her apartment in the city—there weren't any other options that she could even contemplate.

She finally fell asleep—an inconsistent sleep full of brief, disturbing dreams that kept her from getting any rest.

The next morning she shuffled into to the kitchen, looking sloppy in baggy pajama bottoms and a big sweatshirt. The dark trenches under her eyes and her dull, flat hair revealed how rough the night had been for her. Daniel, on the other hand, looked like he had taken some form of bath. His curly hair was damp and his skin looked fresh and healthy. He had a pot of hot water that he had heated up on the woodstove. "Rough night?" He asked. "Too much wine maybe?" He grinned at her mischievously.

"I'm fine, I just didn't sleep well," she said. She didn't want to whine any more to him about her worries, particularly since he appeared so unconcerned.

"You'll feel better after some coffee. Here, I'll get you a cup." He gave her a hot cup of steaming coffee, the aroma enticing her. She found herself grateful for the cheap instant coffee that was in the pantry. Even bad coffee was better than no coffee. "Do you want to go to the hospital today?" Daniel asked, "Or be here when your Dad comes? Do you know when he's coming?"

She shrugged. "He didn't tell me what time. I would expect afternoon, he's coming from the west coast—that's a long flight and there's a time difference. But who knows. I think I will stay here, I'm tired and I don't feel like going out in the snow. I can straighten up the house. How bad is it out there? Are you going to work on your house?"

She hadn't even looked outside yet and, although she wanted him there, she kind of hoped he would go so she could deal with her father privately. God forbid he decided to go all macho-dad with Daniel there. That was all she needed.

"Yeah, I'm going over there. I want to start doing some work on Willie's house, too. And I want to check on things after all the snow and wind. I think I can get around in it. It looks pretty wet, so I don't think it will stick around long. Anyhow, that carpet of hers has to go, along with a lot of other stuff. Hey, give me a call if there's a problem with me staying here. I can always stay with some friends over there. I'm sure someone has a house that's livable, okay? I don't want to cause a problem. Even though I am getting spoiled being here!" He smiled again.

Her thoughts immediately flashed to his former girlfriend who he was still close with. She hoped he wouldn't want to go stay at her house!

"I'm sure it's fine," she said quickly, "but certainly I will let you know if there's any problem. I expect the biggest drama will be about the cat." She rolled her eyes for effect as she said it. "He has this thing where he will say he's allergic to cats, but he doesn't show any signs of it until he actually sees a cat and then he starts scratching. If a cat is right behind him and he doesn't see it—no problem! So I know it's in his head. But just watch, he will play that card."

Daniel laughed. "You are probably right! But don't worry, we will figure something out. I bet Willie would keep him for you until you go back to your apartment or something. We won't let you lose the kitty, okay?"

"Okay." That's what she liked so much about Daniel, he always seemed calm and ready to find a solution to any problem, whereas she always went off into a panicked frenzy over everything. She felt like he kept her from getting too freaked out over little things. He was so capable of handling anything that she didn't need to worry.

She sighed, thinking again that their special time was about over and it had meant so much to her.

"I guess I'll go up and get cleaned up," she said. "I'm a mess. My father would think I was in a train wreck!"

"All right, well, I'm going to head out. I just stoked up the fire and it should be fine for a while, but don't let it go out. Call me if there are any problems, okay?" He gave her a little hug and kissed her on the top of her messy head.

"Okay, be careful. I'll let you know when he's home and how it goes."

She was pleased at the affection from Daniel, especially after the night before. She knew she was being needy last night and wasn't sure how he would act toward her this morning. She wouldn't have blamed him if he had left as fast as possible.

It was mid-afternoon when she heard her father's car pull up. *Here we go,* she thought to herself. She met him at the door, happy to see him despite all her worries.

He looked impeccable, as always. His black hair with its sprinkling of white had been cut with precision, his face smoothly shaved, and his expensive suit unwrinkled—even after traveling all day. Although he wasn't a tall man, he had a very large presence and nobody was ever able to ignore him. He had a certainty that rendered most people unwilling to argue with him and his confidence seemed unshakeable. He was also known to have a passionate temper, which was the aspect of his nature that Justina really hoped to avoid in this instance.

After exchanging heartfelt hugs and pleasantries about the trip, they discussed the storm. Victor said, "This storm has been truly terrible. And now this snow! I kept seeing everything on the news and I was so worried about you. But I knew you were in our house and I thought you would be fine. But you must have been so scared, mija. I know how you are. I wished I had been here with you, to keep you safe. What a terrible thing you went through."

74

"No, Papa, it was actually fine. Daniel was here with me during the storm. He was worried for me. He was very helpful—he covered the windows, brought in firewood, and got everything prepared before the storm. I would not have known what to do. You should thank him, I already have. I am very glad you sent him over here. I don't know what would have happened to me otherwise. I would have been very cold and hungry and freaked out—I know that." She decided just to lay it out there, rather than try to dance around it. And really, there was nothing unreasonable in what had happened. The guilt was mostly in her mind.

"He stayed here? How long did he stay here?" She could hear the protective tone coming into his voice immediately, but he didn't sound angry.

She hesitated. *Here we go*, she thought again. But she couldn't lie to him.

"He has been staying here ever since the storm," she said. As she saw his eyes widen and his mouth open to respond she cut him off quickly, "Papa, his house has been ruined by the storm. He can't live there. You haven't seen how bad it is over in his area. It's worse than here. And it's awful here, as you can see. He has been going every day to take out all the ruined carpet, furniture, walls, and flooring, because it's all destroyed. The sewers backed up and everything there is covered with it. That's where he is right now, gutting his house and his neighbor's house. I told him I was sure it would be fine for him to stay here until his house is safe to live in. He has been a perfect gentleman," She spoke quickly so he wouldn't have a chance to say anything until she was done.

She found herself silently thanking Daniel for his restraint the night before. It was helpful to be able to say with truth that nothing went on. Otherwise her guilt probably would have shown on her face and her father would not have missed that. No way. He may have only had one child, but his instincts were as impeccable as his suit.

His features relaxed as he listened to her, the frown lines on his forehead softening—particularly toward the end of her speech. It was clear that he was relieved she had been taken care of, but he was still not totally comfortable with the means to that end.

"Justina, you know I worry about you. Daniel is a good boy—I know that. I don't mind him staying here while he fixes his house. I owe him that for taking care of you. I think Daniel knows his place and I would not expect him to bother you, but a father worries—you know that. Especially with such a bonita chica!"

She laughed in relief and began breathing again. She bit her lip for a second, hesitating. "Papa," she began. "One more thing."

"What is that, sweetheart?"

"I also took in a kitty. He was stuck in a tree and had almost drowned. Daniel rescued him. We put a notice up for the owners, but we don't know where he's from, and nobody has called for him. I named him Hercules. Please let me keep him until I go back to the city, I will take him with me. He's such a sweet kitty."

"Justina. . ." he began, but then he shook his head, "I can't tell you no when you look at me like that with those big eyes. But—" he held up his hand to stall her response. "—I would ask you to keep him out from under my feet. You know I am allergic to cats."

She giggled, "Yes, I know that's what you say. Okay, thank you Papa!"

He grabbed his bags, shaking his head, but smiling as he headed up to change his clothes and get comfortable. Justina quickly grabbed her phone. She texted Daniel, "It's all good here. Are you going to be here for dinner?"

He texted back, "Okay, be there soon. I will bring dinner."

As they ate, they brought Victor up to speed on things in Long Beach. Justina told him about the instructions to evacuate and the work she was doing at the hospital.

"Justina, why would you stay here when you were supposed to evacuate? They must not think it is safe to be here. You could go to the city, you have an apartment, or you could go to a hotel. Why would you stay here?" he asked, and then he looked at Daniel as if sensing the answer.

"We are fine, Papa. I want to keep working at the hospital. I want to do something to help the people there. Besides, they will have the power and water back any day now—it's not so bad. And I can eat and shower at the hospital—it's what everyone is doing."

Victor sighed and shook his head. "Mija, you are as stubborn as your father. If the power is not back on soon, we go to the city. Understood? These are not proper living conditions."

"Sure, we will see how it goes," Justina said, unwilling to commit to anything. Victor looked at her for a moment, considering, then returned his attention to the lo mein.

Justina felt odd having her father back in the house while Daniel was there, but her father seemed at ease with the situation—even with the lack of power. Her father didn't seem to mind the cold as much as Justina. She returned to sleeping in her room, knowing that he would not approve of her sleeping in the same space with Daniel. She made sure he was comfortable in the guest room and everyone settled in for the night, Hercules sleeping on Justina's feet.

CHAPTER TEN

The following day they went back to Far Rockaway. The hospital was in an even worse state of chaos than it had been before the nor'easter. Entire families huddled together, crowded into St. John's. Several nursing homes had evacuated again, this time for the snowstorm, so the elderly and disabled patients lined the hallways. The deep, barking cough resounded everywhere and people cumulatively appeared more drawn and resigned. Each day was another day without adequate food, hot showers, or even a warm place to sleep and now there was snow. Out of all the sad cases, the old people upset Justina the most. There were so many old, frail patients parked in wheelchairs and plugged in to keep oxygen tanks going. It seemed that most of them had no family and it broke her heart to think of them spending days and nights sitting in a wheelchair in a hallway with little hope for better any time soon.

She spent a few minutes talking to two little old ladies who were sharing an outlet for their oxygen tanks and got them something warm to drink. Seeing their gaunt faces and skin that looked as thin as paper, she wondered how they had ever survived not one storm—but two—and how they managed to get to the hospital. One of the ladies was pasty white, with thin snow-colored hair hanging in limp strands from her bony skull. Her skin was so thin that the blue of her veins was clearly visible. The other was an Indian woman with her head wrapped in a filthy crimson scarf and a matching shawl around her frail shoulders. When Justina gave them their hot drinks she noticed the bones in their shaky hands were prominent and it broke her heart to think of the ordeal they must have been through. Despite all of that, however, the two kept up a spirited conversation about the food at the nursing home compared to the hospital and Justina admired their spunk. She would have liked to spend some more time with the ladies—she suspected they had some interesting stories to tell-but she knew that others needed her help.

When Justina went to check in with Priya she found her talking to a tall black woman whose hair was all in braids and tied in a ponytail; giant gold hoops swayed from her ears. Based on her accent, she sounded like she was originally from Jamaica or somewhere in the Caribbean. Justina stood back, not wanting to interrupt, but Priya saw her and called her over.

"Justina, this is our Missing in Action social worker, Mona. She finally decided to come to work!" Priya said with a laugh, then "her house was wrecked. She's staying with a cousin now, up by Kennedy airport. We are so glad to have her back. You can work with her and help get all these people sorted out."

Mona laughed, a warm, resonant sound that was smooth as warm honey. "So you're the little angel that showed up here and helped save the day! Bless you, child. We can surely use the help."

She turned to Priya and said, "Now you just scoot, we got it covered here, okay?" Priya smiled and nodded, darting off to take care of all her other responsibilities.

Mona quickly organized a system for them to coordinate the patient load and Justina went to work. She was relieved to have a backup to go to if she got stuck. Some of the people there had problems that she had no idea how to address.

One patient she found particularly distressing. He was an older man in a wheelchair and when he called her over it was in very broken English with a heavy Russian or eastern European accent. The man slumped in his chair, a dirty beret askew atop his bony head. He was bundled up in a heavy coat and scarf and his wife beside him was similarly dressed.

"Please, Miss. Can you help? Do you work here?"

She shook her head no. "Maybe I can help you though. What do you need?" She could see the distress on his face and hoped his problem was one she could solve.

"I am supposed to get transplant. It is my kidney." He opened his shirt and coat, showing her a tube attached to his body. His skin was mottled and bruised and an unhealthy shade of greyish-white. "I need to get the new kidney. It is supposed to come yesterday, but I think there is problem because it come from overseas. There is problem at Customs or some government office—they say they cannot bring it. I think the paperwork is not there." His voice became more agitated and harder to understand. "Please help me to get it, I will not live." With that he broke out into the deep, painful cough that shook his body. His wife patted his arm and spoke softly to him in their native language, trying to soothe him. He reached for her with a gnarled, shaking hand and held onto her arm.

Oh my God, Justina thought, *what can I do?* The seriousness of the man's crisis was clear and he appeared to be quite ill.

"One moment," she said. "Wait here, I will find someone who can help figure this out." She darted off as quickly as she could, maneuvering between the gaggles of families crowding the floor.

Mona was not hard to find, as she towered over many of the men and stood out in her bright red sweater. She was dealing with a couple of young men, one was pale white with straggly red hair and a goatee to match, the other Latino, both wearing dirty work clothes and clearly intoxicated. Mona was telling them, "It's time for you to leave. You do not need to be in the hospital. You need to go sober up. There is no room for you in detox and you have been there too many times. You clearly don't really want to clean up. There are people here who really need medical care." She spoke sternly, towering over both of them.

The Latino guy grinned at her, showing a missing tooth. "Maybe we can come dry out at your house, sister. I bet you could take care of both of us!" He leered at her, swaying slightly against his friend, who laughed loudly and elbowed his buddy.

"Yeah, that's right. Why don't you take care of us! Sure enough you are woman enough for two!"

Mona gave them an unamused look. "You want me to get security for you again? Time to go." She made a move as if to grab a pager or phone from the pocket of her sweater.

"All right, all right," the white guy said. "You sure don't care much about us cold and hungry folks." But he snickered as he said it and they stumbled away toward the front entrance.

"Wow," Justina said. "That's what you have to deal with? Those guys were awful."

Mona shook her head. "That's what we get here, especially now. They have nowhere else to go. They want to get admitted to detox so they can get a warm bed and food for a couple days. Then they go right back out and do the same thing again. It's a scam and they get by with it quite a bit. But they're not going to get away with it now—not in my house. There are too many sick and desperate people here. No time for bullshit."

Justina smiled, thinking how much she liked Mona already, then she recalled why she was there. "I need your help. We got a guy who needs a transplant; his kidney is caught up at Customs or something. He says we need to help with paperwork or he's going to die. Can you talk to him? I have no idea what to do. I can't imagine how to solve this kind of problem." Her eyes were wide and her voice tense.

Mona frowned, puzzled. "We don't do transplants here and that doesn't make sense," She said. "He must be a patient from another hospital who got caught here because of the storm. Maybe he gets dialysis here. I'll talk to him and sort it out. I suspect he's a LIJ patient—Long Island Jewish Hospital. We can try to coordinate with them—they will have a transplant coordinator to help him. You go take care of other patients, okay? Where is this guy?"

Justina told her where he was and breathed a sigh of relief. She had no idea how difficult the issues here would be. It made her feel very inadequate—these people had such serious, life-or-death problems and she was so ill equipped to deal with them. But she realized that all she could do was her best and she could at least take care of the easy stuff, leaving Mona free for the real problems.

The rest of the morning was much easier to manage—no more life-or-death problems—and time went by faster than Justina could have imagined. When it was getting close to noon Mona came to find her so that they could get something to eat.

"Okay," Justina said, suddenly realizing that she was hungry, "Whatever happened to the transplant guy?"

"We got him taken care of. We found his facility and I spoke with his transplant coordinator. They are sorting out his paperwork and we had one of our security guys take him there in the hospital's van. So he should be all set. Thanks for helping him. If you weren't here it's hard saying how long he might have sat here without getting the help he needed." Mona patted her arm. "Now let's go eat!"

When Justina and Mona got to the lunchroom downstairs she saw that there were prepared sandwiches with bottled water and little bags of chips. They grabbed their food and found a corner to eat.

Justina looked at Mona with a frown, "How come this wasn't flooded? I thought all the basements were destroyed around here." The kitchen was functioning normally from what Justina could see.

"Remember Irene?" Mona asked. "She caused us to evacuate, but the hurricane ended up not being that bad. The hospital lost money on it anyhow, having to close down. But they put in a pump system here. This storm was worse, but they re-worked the flood zones so we had to stay open. Go figure. But at least we have pumps and generators. Good thing for all these people, I don't know what would've happened otherwise." Mona took a bite of her sandwich and licked a glob of mayonnaise off her fingers.

Justina watched as a continuous stream of people filed through to get food—patients and hospital workers alike. Some of the workers appeared to be getting food for the wheelchair-bound patients as they came in and out, getting multiple packets of food. Justina thought again of all the old folks in wheelchairs that seemed to be everywhere. She asked Mona about it, because it certainly looked like every old person in New York was in that hospital.

"Don't you know that Far Rockaway is the Grand Central Station for old folks?" she asked with a smile. "Nursing homes here are like Starbucks in Seattle, there is one on every corner. I don't know why. But that's the truth. All those places evacuated and guess where those poor old folks got sent? Good ole St. John's. Got nowhere else to send 'em." Mona said in a matter-of-fact manner and took another bite of her sandwich. "We got the generators running, so they can stay warm and keep their oxygen or whatever going, keep their meds coming. . .at least till the hospital runs out of money. Folks on the radio are telling people to come for shelter here, but nobody is sending any money to pay for it."

"What do you mean?" Justina asked, horrified. "Isn't the government or somebody paying for this? I mean, aren't there disaster relief agencies or something?" She couldn't believe that there was nobody to help keep this place going, and to help these people, through this disaster.

"I'm sure the Good Lord will watch out for us all, somehow. Don't worry about that. We just need to keep these people alive and as comfortable as we can for now." Mona ripped open her little bag of Fritos. "Don't forget," she added, "There are places all up and down the coast probably just like us here. There is only so much money to go around. Who do you think is gonna get taken care of first—Far Rockaway or Wall Street? Just tryin' to keep it real, we gotta take care of ourselves as much as we can. That's how it is. Not sure we ever got our money for Irene even, that's above my pay grade," she added.

Justina mulled that over for a minute. "I will talk to my Dad. Maybe he can help."

Mona looked at her, eyebrows raised. "Who is your Daddy, he owns the World Bank or something?"

"No, he works with Senator Goldberg. He is kind of his right-hand guy. The Senator listens to my dad—he is very good with politics. So I will tell my dad, you never know." She had no idea what her father could do, really, but it seemed like something should be done.

"Wow, I am impressed. You tell your daddy we need some help here for sure. But for now, we should move on out of here."

Justin surveyed the lunches. There seemed to be plenty there. She thought about Daniel and Willie and felt certain that they would appreciate the lunch too.

She told Mona, hoping she could get a quick ride over to Daniel's to surprise him with the treat.

"Oh, you can use my car, no problem," Mona said immediately. She fished around in the pocket of her oversized red sweater. "Here you go, here's the keys. It's the crappy little silver Honda parked across from the side entrance. It's not locked, no reason to be. You can't miss it—there are a bunch of Mardi Gras beads hanging off the mirror. You take that boy something to eat, and his neighbor too. We all need to take care of each other these days," Mona said. Then she asked, "You like that boy?" Without waiting for a response she said, "You know the way to a man's heart is through his stomach or so they say! Although I found other routes work pretty well too. . . ." She laughed again and shooed Justina off.

Justina easily found the car, which smelled of mildewed carpet and old fast-food wrappers. She had to take a circuitous route since many roads were still not clear of debris. Stoplights were still out, as well, so driving felt like an adventure—no rules. You just got around however you could. Daniel's truck wasn't at his house, so she decided to start with Willie. She figured he was loading stuff in or out of the truck in the back of the house. She knocked on Willie's back door and was called to come in.

Willie was sitting in her same spot at the kitchen table, wrapped in heavy blankets with her legs propped up. Justina could see that her legs were much less swollen and discolored. The house still smelled unpleasant, although the kitchen wasn't as filthy as the living room. "Hi, Willie, how are you doing?" Justina asked, looking around for any evidence that Willie had food in the house. There were a couple of boxes of crackers and several bottles of water on the counter. Justina knew that Daniel had been taking food over to her and it looked like she still had something in the house, thank God.

"I'm doing as well as I can, honey. You see I'm stuck in this smelly ole house with no heat, but it'll all be fixed up sooner or later, I 'spect. Could be worse. How you doing, you still working over at the hospital?"

"Yes, I just came from there. And they were handing out some nice lunches, so I brought one for you and for Daniel. Here you go, bon appetite!"

"Well, aren't you just the sweetest thing. Thank you for thinking of me! I don't know what would have happened to me if not for Daniel, and you too. Not everyone remembers an ole woman when stuff like this happens. I bet for sure there's plenty o' folks who are not so lucky. I guess the good Lord is still looking out for me after all. He must not be quite ready for me yet!" She chuckled, her gold tooth flashing, as she tore into her packet and pulled out the sandwich.

Justina stayed for a couple minutes, then bid her goodbye, as Willie happily focused on her lunch. She grabbed the other package out of the car and walked across the street to find Daniel, eager to surprise him.

As it turned out, the surprise was on Justina. As she rounded the side of Daniel's house, instead of Daniel, she saw a cute little blond with a perky ponytail and tight, faded Levis. The girl was hauling pieces of broken sheetrock out to the alley. Justina stopped short—a little ripple of alarm and surprise running through her. Daniel hadn't mentioned having anyone with him. . . . She almost turned around and left, but she reminded herself that they were only friends and she just came to bring lunch. *I don't have a reason to be running away*, she told herself. Still, the urge to take off was strong—to leave and never mention stopping by.

She walked into the yard and the blonde girl spotted her, "Hi, can I help you?" She asked, clearly unsure why Justina was there. Justina sized her up quickly. She appeared to be about her age, early twenties, with curly blonde hair stuffed into a scrunchy ponytail holder. The girl had on a well-worn navy blue New York Yankees sweatshirt, too big, and Levis that appeared to have faded by wear, not because an extra chunk of money was paid so they looked like that. She had on contractor's gloves—thick and bulky—and work-boots. Justina thought she looked like someone who would be on a girls' softball team and knew how to change her own tire. She was clearly helping Daniel by hauling out pieces of wreckage from the house.

"Hello, um, I'm looking for Daniel. Is he around?"

"Oh, yeah, he's inside, with a sledgehammer! Are you Justina?" She acted friendly enough, although she was giving Justina the once-over, her voice was as light and perky as her little ponytail.

"Yes, I'm Justina. I was working at the hospital and I brought him a sandwich. They were passing out lunches." She felt kind of awkward, but the girl seemed to know something about her.

"Great. I'm Beth, I'm a friend of Daniel's here in the neighborhood. We made a deal, I help him with his house and he helps us with ours! Go on in, but be careful, he's a crazy man ripping out all that stuff!"

Justina went up to the house and found him working inside, his face covered with a dust mask and protective goggles. She watched for a moment while he ripped out the sheetrock in the living room. She couldn't help but admire him working—he was down to a t-shirt and jeans with dark sweat rings around the neck and armpits of his shirt. He was obviously in great physical shape she noted, not for the first time. There was nothing soft on that body. As he turned to bring a load over to the doorway, he spotted her and stopped short. "Justina! What are you doing here?" He asked. He sounded pleased to see her.

"Lunch. They were handing these out at the hospital. I took one to Willie already. I didn't know you had a helper." She trailed off, to give him a chance to explain the perky blonde.

"Wow, thanks, I am starving. No surprise there, right? And thanks for remembering Willie. She's been living on crackers and protein shakes in a can, except for when I can bring her something. I'm sure she was ecstatic to have actual meat and cheese!" He smiled at the thought. "Beth is the friend I mentioned before. Her house is trashed too, of course, so I said I would help her get it emptied out if she helps me first. I will have to wait for the insurance money, but I want to get the mold out before it gets worse, so it's important to move fast." He wasted no time getting his lunch opened up—first taking a big gulp of water. "Oh, that hits the spot. Funny how much I appreciate good clean water these days! Thank you!"

Beth came up to the doorway. "Hey, looks like you're having a lunch break. I'm gonna take a break and run home for a few, too. I'll be back in a bit, okay?" She peeled off her gloves and tossed them down on the steps, smiling and waving as she turned to go.

Well, she doesn't act like a girlfriend, Justina thought. But she still wondered. They seemed so familiar, taking care of each other as if it was the usual thing. She realized she was jealous and tried to stomp it out before it showed on her face or in her voice.

She hung out for a while as Daniel ate and told her about his progress. It looked like he had gotten a lot of the destroyed and moldy materials out of the house, at least in the living room, although he worried about the electrical and heating systems. "I will have to get someone come check all that stuff out," he said, "but it has to wait until we have electricity. And some money." He had already taken pictures and sent in paperwork to the insurance company, but he had told her this could be a long process, especially since he didn't yet know how much other damage he might discover. Plus, the neighborhood was still an overwhelming sea of destruction—piles of debris and sand everywhere. Not much would happen with the roads blocked in places and no power.

Warm food was now a luxury. Things were a long way from being anywhere near normal. And winter had apparently decided to come early this year. As Justina drove back to the hospital she wondered how long all of this could take and how long Daniel would want to stay at her house. She planned to be home for the rest of the quarter and then go back to the city for school. She wondered if Daniel would stay in his empty house or, worse yet, at Beth's. The more she pondered that, the more she got herself upset.

By the time she got back to the hospital and parked the car, she had convinced herself that Daniel would shack up with Beth. His relationship with Beth was the reason he didn't want to get close to her that night, but he didn't want to say that, she reasoned. He was trying to spare her feelings, especially because she had practically climbed into his lap. As she revisited that evening her stomach curled in agitation and embarrassment. How could she have been so pathetic? At the time it had felt so natural and comfortable, but now she wished she could go back in time and be less needy and forward. The more she obsessed over it, the more mortified she became.

When she found Mona to return the keys, Mona looked at her and asked, "Girl, what's up with you? You look like you are going to be sick. Did you find your man?"

"Yeah, I did. I kinda wish I hadn't." She considered leaving it there, but needed to talk to someone and was desperate to stop the squirming in her stomach. "His old *girlfriend*, who is now a *friend* and lives in his neighborhood, was there helping him out. He's then going to help her with her house. He never mentioned that before and they acted very cozy. I'm afraid I made a fool of myself, and now I wish I hadn't. I'm such an idiot. I thought that he and I were kind of starting to have something, but I think I made a big mistake. Ugh."

Mona wanted to hear what had happened to make her feel like a fool, so she gave a short version of the storm situation, what had happened since then, up to last night when she felt like they were so close but he didn't let it go anywhere.

When she was done Mona said, "Honey, I don't think you should be so worried. First of all, you don't really know this neighborhood. Let me tell you how it rolls here. Your man has probably known that girl his whole life. Their mamas probably were friends, borrowed each other's handbags for job interviews, and loaned each other a few dollars to keep the power from getting shut off when money was tight. That's how it is here, folks take care of each other, and lots of these families been around here for a while. Many of these people got a world of problems. It's a community, like a family, and when times are rough folks gather together to survive. So I wouldn't read too much into him having the girl there helping. I would be surprised if nobody was helping him." She continued, "Second, if he didn't like you, if he was a jerk, he would've taken what you was offering and then cleared out. He knows you are from a good family—he obviously respects you and doesn't want to abuse that. That boy knows you got a rich papa, he probably figures you are a precious little baby to your daddy. No way he's going to mess with that. You need to understand, he maybe feels like he is a second-class citizen compared to you. He figures there's no way someone like you is gonna really be with someone like him, so he's not gonna get himself in a heap a trouble by going there. That's what I figure." She took a deep breath and looked at Justina expectantly. Then she continued, "You know what I think this is all about? You're a college girl—you remember that stuff about Maslow? That famous psychiatrist or psychologist, something like that? So Maslow says that folks who can't take care of basic needs aren't worrying about the meaning of life—they's just trying to survive. Folks with a good house and a fat paycheck are more worried about world hunger and finding God or whatever, 'cause their bellies are full. So look at you all. You and that boy are in a different place, so it's hard to relate. He's trying to survive—he lives in the 'hood, his house is goin' in a dumpster. You are looking for love and personal satisfaction. You see what I mean? Does that make some kind of sense to you?"

Justina bunched up her lips and frowned as she considered this. "Yeah, okay, maybe. I just don't know if he even really likes me, you know? How did you get so wise, anyhow?"

Mona laughed richly. "Honey, if I knew the minds of men, I wouldn't be sitting here having this conversation. Trust and believe, Mona woulda found herself a rich sugar daddy and would be living the good life somewhere! You just gotta trust in yourself and in the good Lord to look after you and know that things happen how they's supposed to."

A voice from behind them said, "Hey, Mona, I'll be your sugar daddy. You just say the word, I'm there!" They turned around to see one of the security guys, a thick balding black man, perusing a box filled with bags of chips and water that was left over from lunch. He was obviously listening to their conversation with shameless interest. He gave Mona an exaggerated leer and chuckled evilly at her.

"Henry, you better be saving your pennies if you want any of this! You don't got enough sugar for this Mama!" Mona threw back at him, and they both had a laugh.

Mona turned her attention back to the subject at hand. She shook her head at Justina, sending the gold hoops dancing, "Girlfriend, you just need to relax and let nature take its course, if that's what is meant to be. You won't change it by giving your sweet self a headache. You just remember what I said. You might think he's the best thing you ever laid eyes on, but he don't see himself that way, and he got bigger troubles. I wouldn't expect him to be messing with you when his life is such a hot mess. Besides, we got folks out there needing us, we should get to it."

Justina nodded and said, "Yeah. You make me feel silly for fussing. I will try to let it go. Let's go get busy." She actually did feel better and admired Mona for her wisdom. She wished she were more like Mona who wasn't all that much older than her.

She decided she was going to make a real effort to put it all out of her head, like nothing had happened. Because, she had to remind herself, that really nothing had happened. All the drama was in her head. Nobody but Mona knew she was having herself a moment of angst. With that resolution, she got back to her day.

CHAPTER ELEVEN

Meanwhile, at Daniel's house, a similar conversation was happening. Beth returned from her trip home and immediately wanted to get the scoop. "So, Daniel. . .Justina's a hot little tamale, isn't she? So what's going on there? She's all bringing you lunch and stuff, hmmm?"

Daniel was blushing and feeling horrified, "I told you, Beth. I ended up at her house because of the storm. She was all alone, totally unprepared, and pretty freaked out. She's a sweet girl, and yes, she's very cute, but her daddy is some hotshot political guy and she's in law school. They are a different breed of cat, you know? I know she likes me, but it's mostly because she's grateful." He paused for a minute and then added, "I have to be fair, though. She has been a trooper since all this has happened—helping at the hospital and with Willie. I didn't expect her to be okay with hanging out in this hood, especially now. This is no country club!"

Beth cocked her head and looked at him speculatively. "Daniel, I think you do like this girl and you don't give yourself enough credit, you're an educated guy, good looking. . .but I don't know, her daddy could be an issue. She probably hangs out at those thousand-dollar-a-plate fundraising dinners you see on the news. Can't picture you doing that."

Daniel really didn't want to be having this conversation, especially with Beth. He shrugged, hoping a non-response might deter her from further commentary. He should have known better—she was nowhere near finished. "I have to say," Beth said, "She looked all funny when she saw me today. I pretended I didn't notice, but I think she likes you more than you realize. She acted all wierded-out that I was here. I'm just saying. As a female, let me tell you, we get jealous real quick and she did not expect you to be having any girls here with you. She didn't like it, okay? Just don't get sucked into something that's going to cause you grief. It's hard to find someone good, I know that much," she appeared rueful. "But you gotta be careful messing with those types of folks. They don't live in our world. She might entertain herself for a while until Daddy gets wind of it. And besides, don't you think people like us should stick together?" Without waiting for a reply she shoved her hands into her gloves and started loading up more sheetrock to take outside.

Daniel pondered this conversation for the rest of the day. On the one hand, it pleased him to think of Justina liking him; he had to admit that to himself. But on the other hand, Beth's comments about them living on different planets were true enough. He imagined what Victor's reaction would be if his little girl got involved with the guy he knew only as the handy man. He decided that his instincts not to get too close must be the right ones, although he had gotten used to enjoying her company. Certainly they could still be friends, no harm in that, but he shouldn't have done anything to let her think it might be more. He needed to control himself, regardless of his feelings for her.

It wasn't long before Daniel finished emptying all the wreckage out of his house. He left the upstairs alone because it wasn't damaged, but he had mostly gutted the downstairs—except for part of the kitchen and he left a few floorboards so he could walk around. He wasn't sure what he should do because he didn't feel right staying at Justina and Victor's place much longer, he had already been there a couple of weeks. Justina was now only going to the hospital half time, so she could study for the finals that had been delayed. He wondered if Victor was waiting for him to leave, although he was very polite and made no comments about it. If the weather hadn't gotten so cold, Daniel would not have stayed this long.

The power in Long Beach finally came back on, much to everyone's relief. Justina celebrated by filling up the freezer and refrigerator with food. She got all the basics that had not survived the prolonged outage. Life in their community was still far from normal, but at least they had heat. Many homes in the area had suffered extensive damage and dumpsters lined the streets in front of those homes. Many businesses had not yet reopened and remained boarded up.

One night at dinner Victor announced he had to go out of town for a few days—just to D.C. for some meetings—but they would be long days so he would not commute. When Victor made the announcement, Daniel watched his face carefully and waited for any comments related to him. He was getting uncomfortable about still being there, but Victor didn't say a word—at least not to him. Daniel wondered if there would be a discussion between Victor and Justina about it. He was kind of glad to have Victor leaving for a while; he always sensed he was being scrutinized for any inappropriate behavior.

The next morning, on the way over to Far Rockaway, Justina brought it up. "Papa asked me how your house is doing," she said. "He isn't comfortable with you staying here while he is gone." She made a face, rolling her eyes. "I told him I would tell you," she paused, "But don't worry about it. He won't know the difference. He is just very protective, that's all."

"No, Justina. I don't want to go against your father. If he found out, he would never trust me with anything and I wouldn't want to face him or lie to him. I can stay at my house—it will be like camping! Don't worry about me. Okay? I will be fine, really." He reached over and patted her hand, and she turned her hand around to give him a little squeeze.

She gave an exaggerated pout and then said, "Okay, how about this? You come over for dinner tomorrow. I will fix you something good so you at least have a warm meal before your camp-out at your house. Is that a deal?" Her smile was mischievous, like a high-school girl planning to sneak out of the house for a party.

He couldn't think of a good reason to tell her no, so he agreed. He did enjoy sharing a meal with her and it was much nicer than having yet another cold deli sandwich.

The next day, Justina stayed home to study and when Daniel arrived at the house she met him at the door with a bottle of champagne. He could smell something savory cooking and his stomach reminded him that he hadn't really eaten that day. He couldn't help but notice that she had put on a soft, fuzzy pink sweater and very form-fitting jeans. She looked so warm and soft— he tried to not get distracted by it. He wondered what she was up to—she was being very sweet and dinner smelled fantastic. The house was nice and warm, a pleasant change from his cold house. He could definitely get used to this and had to remind himself not to get too comfortable with this lifestyle.

They had a wonderful dinner. Justina had cooked a very tasty dish of paella and she kept the champagne, then the wine, flowing freely. Daniel realized she was trying to get him drunk so he wouldn't leave and she was doing a good job of making him comfortable. She was clearly in the mood to relax and enjoy herself— and to make sure he did the same. After dinner she asked him to build a fire in the fireplace, which of course he did willingly. He could see she was pulling out all the stops now, trying to set up a romantic atmosphere. On one level he thought he should steer clear, and he remembered the conversation with Beth, but then he decided maybe he should just go with it. After a few glasses of wine, the more pleasing path seemed the right one and he couldn't think of any valid reason to resist her—especially when she looked so tempting.

They settled in on the couch in front of the fire, Hercules joining in as he now had free rein of the house once again. It was like before Victor came home, except now there was good food, heat, and Justina's music (in this case she had some classic jazz and blues playing softly in the background). Daniel knew he was in trouble when she lit a couple of candles. They hadn't done that since the power was out.

Justina delayed conversation by playing with the cat, who was more than happy to cooperate. Finally she said, "Daniel, what is your plan? When do you think your house will be done? I mean, I don't think Papa minds you being here when he's home. And I love to have you here, you know that," she added with a flirtatious smile.

It was the same question he had been asking himself. He decided to be direct about it. "I've been thinking the same thing. I'm not sure how long it might take to get the insurance money and it seems that the insurance companies are jerking people around. I don't feel right about staying here much longer. Especially after you go back to the city—I'm sure your dad is not looking for a roommate." They both smiled at that. He continued, "I had hoped to get my house finished, but I need to get back to school. I don't like leaving the house half-done, but it will take time and money. I just don't know. He was really struggling with it right at that moment, his head was a little fuzzy from the wine, and she kept his glass full. On one level he understood what her goal was, but he had quit caring.

"I will be so sad to go back to school," She said, looking at him with luminous eyes. "And I'm going to hate it even more when you go away to school because I will never get to see you then." Daniel felt his insides writhe as she spoke—he felt the same way at that moment, but he couldn't tell her that. And the way she was looking at him. . .damn, he was in trouble.

He thought a rational approach might be a good idea, which wasn't easy for him at the moment. "Justina, you know we both have to finish our education. Mine in particular has been on hold too long. We don't really have any choice. I have to get my house taken care of too, there are so many things hanging over me. Staying here has been wonderful, I don't know what I would have done otherwise, and I love your company. But we can't shack up here forever. If you don't agree, check with your dad on that!" He tried to add in a light note but, judging by her face, it fell flat.

"Daniel, I am just going to miss you too much!" She said, her voice was threatening tears. Daniel realized the wine was making her emotional as she leaned into him and wrapped her arms around him, burying her face in his shoulder. She didn't seem to be crying, thank God, but she definitely was having an intense moment. He put his arms around her and held her.

"I know," he said softly, and left it at that. He was so uncomfortable in these types of situations and he knew he was way out of his element. She felt good in his arms, though, so sweet smelling and soft, even more so with that fuzzy sweater—cashmere or angora or something like that. He didn't want to let her go—he had to admit that to himself.

This time, when she sat up, it was Daniel that kissed her. Maybe it was the wine or maybe it was just that he wanted to do it. He didn't stop to analyze it. She tasted and felt so good to him. He didn't want it to end, although he didn't intend for things to go too far—at least not yet. She seemed to know that, because she didn't try to take it any further either. They enjoyed kissing and snuggling on the couch while the music played softly in the background. Finally she sighed, wrapping herself all around him.

"I wish we could stay like this forever," she said. He stroked her hair, "Me too."

"Daniel," she asked, "Do you like me?"

He laughed gently, thinking how funny the question was. "I'm not sure why you would ask that!" He said, wondering at her concern.

She clarified, "I mean, do you really like *me*. You don't think I'm a spoiled daddy's girl? Or a piece of fluff? I know that might sound silly, but it's important." She looked up and waited for his answer with huge, worried eyes.

He gave her a squeeze. "Justina, I like you a whole lot, but you scare me. I don't live in your world and I'm not going to. You are all about Gucci and charity events—I am beer and darts. You're a beautiful girl, you have a great future, and I'm pretty much a boy from the 'hood. That's the issue. You are going to end up dating a lawyer or someone like your dad who is super successful, not some-one like me." It made him sad to say it, but he knew in his heart it was true.

She shook her head. "I'm not like that. I don't decide whom I like because they are rich or have an important job. And I won't be with someone I don't care about in order to have those things. I've been around all of that and it doesn't impress me. I want to be happy. There are so many people in my father's world who are wealthy and powerful—the women have fabulous jewelry and the men are manicured with shiny shoes, but if you watch them to-gether most of them don't seem to care for each other very much. I am not going to sell myself out for that life, I don't get it and I don't want it." Her tone of voice was intense and Daniel found her very convincing, despite the fact that she was full of wine.

She went on, "You know I went to law school because of my dad, pretty much. Not so I can get lots of money or power or a hotshot lawyer husband. And whatever I end up doing with that degree will be something that matters to me, regardless of the money. I just want you to understand that." He could tell how important this was to her as a little worried frown creased her forehead.

"I hear you." He said. "I know you're not snobby and I see how you are with Willie and certainly with me, you are very sweet. I just don't need to be jumping into anything right now in my life, it's important for me to get my ducks in a row. I need to fix my house and I need to get my butt back to school. Those things need to be done. I don't feel like I should be with anyone until I get all that straightened out." He saw her face fall, so he continued, "I want us to be friends. I can't do more than that while my situation is so out of control, okay?"

She reached up and ran her hand through his curly hair. "Just so long as you're not telling me no, I'm okay." She said as she looked up at him smiling. "And you need a haircut!" He could tell she was making an effort not to be too intense, thank God. He had hit his drama limit for one night. Smiling, he said, "I need to go." He knew how easy it would be to stay, but he wasn't about to start down that slippery slope. He had to respect Justina's father—it was his house. And Daniel would never be comfortable coming back being there with Victor was if he had snuck around while the man was out of town. He peeled Justina off of him. He felt terrible for the disappointment in her face. His instincts had been right—she was trying to keep him there by filling him with wine and good food. She complained about him leaving, but didn't make it as difficult as she could have.

She followed him to the door, "Will I see you tomorrow?" She asked, eyes wide and concerned.

"Sure, probably. I'll text you, okay?" He made his escape while he still could, before he lost his resolve.

CHAPTER TWELVE

Justina did not feel entirely satisfied with the state of affairs, but she did think that they had broken through whatever barriers had been in place. It was very frustrating for her to not know what the future would bring and she worried about them both returning to school. She knew she should just live in the present and be content with that, but it went against her nature. She liked to plan and control her life and this situation made that almost impossible. At least Daniel wouldn't be going back right away, given all the work he wanted to do on his house.

She was happy, however, that he seemed to feel the same way she did. For a long time she didn't believe that to be the case. Now he showed much more affection towards her. The only problem was what to say to her father, especially since he would be back in town soon. She figured that conversation might be challenging, but she wouldn't hide the relationship from him. Daniel could come over for dinner in the evenings and that would have to suffice. She could deal with Victor later.

The decision was soon taken out of her hands, however. One evening when Justina had stayed home to study Daniel came over after working at Beth's house. Daniel had just come into the kitchen and was giving Justina a hug when Victor got home. They instinctively separated, but Victor observed them with understanding in his eyes, which narrowed as he looked at them. He didn't say a word, except hello, and went upstairs to put his things away and change his clothes.

"Crap," Daniel said. "That's not how this should go. He's going to have a fit." He frowned, running his fingers through his hair.

"I'll talk to him. Maybe tonight is not the best time—let's see how he is. He usually comes home tired and distracted by work. I will get him when he's rested. Let's get through tonight and I will talk to him tomorrow. Okay?" She primarily wanted to discuss the issue with Victor when Daniel wasn't in the house. She wasn't sure what her father might say and if it was ugly she didn't want to expose Daniel to that. Victor could be extreme some times and reasonable other times, it was difficult to predict which way it might go.

Victor was formal and polite throughout the evening and said nothing about the hug in the kitchen that he had witnessed. Justina could see him watching them, though, and knew he would have something to say. She was grateful that he restrained himself during dinner. Although Daniel and Justina both knew that, in theory, Daniel could still stay there when Victor was home, he left right after they ate.

The next morning, she got up early and started preparing for her discussion with her father. She wanted him to know how much she cared for Daniel and that she wouldn't rush into anything or jeopardize school. That would be a big concern for him, she was certain. Although she was an adult, in his eyes she was a little girl, and he believed he had a right and a duty to dictate most aspects of her life. Up to this point they hadn't fought about it much because she was away at school and mostly did what he expected her to do. It also helped that he wasn't around her too much, so he didn't have an opportunity to provide input. She suspected they would have had many more disagreements if they lived together on a full-time basis, instead of a few days here and there. The problem was that she didn't want to argue about every decision she made. This time it was different though. He knew something was going on and she was prepared to go to the mat over it.

When she got downstairs in the morning, Victor had already left for the day and had written her a brief note: "Had to go into the City. I will see you this afternoon, we will talk."

An immediate lump of dread jumped into her stomach as she read the note. She was ready for the discussion now, but she had to wait all day. And "we will talk" did not sound like he was in an open-minded mood. She hated confrontations and it sure sounded as though one was coming. In the past she would have just given in, rather than go up against her father, but this time she wasn't willing to do that.

The day crawled along ponderously slow. She couldn't study and couldn't focus on anything that required concentration. She went to the store and did the laundry—trying to kill time by keeping busy. The day would have been less painful if she had gone to the hospital—at least there she would be distracted. The good news was that he said he would be back in the afternoon, so hopefully he would be home sooner rather than later.

She decided she better send Daniel a text: *Hey, wait to hear from me before u come, still need to talk to dad.*

No answer.

She figured he was busy, and would check his phone later. Daniel would be back well after The Talk, she was certain, and she wouldn't allow her father to be nasty to him—not for one minute. Any confrontation must be resolved before Daniel arrived at the house. Time continued to inch along until finally, well after 5, Justina heard Victor pull into the driveway. She took a deep breath and greeted him at the door.

"Hi, Papa, how was your day? Was traffic awful?" She said, hoping to start on a good note and set the right tone.

He didn't answer right away, and instead hung up his coat and placed his briefcase in the hallway. "The meetings went long and traffic was a nightmare," he said. Oops, she thought. That can't bode well.

"Can I get you a glass of wine? I picked up steaks for dinner. . .I can fix them whenever you want."

"Yes, wine would be good. Red, please. Might as well pour yourself a glass too, we need to talk." He deliberately folded his jacket over the back of the couch and loosened his tie. She felt a flash of panic, realizing he had deviated from his usual routine of going right upstairs to change clothes.

It was obvious that he wanted this conversation to happen without delay.

She scurried into the kitchen and poured the wine, taking a minute to look at the clock and check her phone. Nothing from Daniel and it was getting late. He must be still tied up working, she thought.

She handed her father his glass and sat across from him, waiting expectantly. He didn't waste any time.

"Justina, we need to discuss the situation between you and Daniel. I could tell last night when I got home, something is definitely going on there. Don't play any games with me, I want to know."

She gulped. "Papa, I really like Daniel. We haven't done anything wrong, he always respects me and he respects you, but we do like each other. There is nothing inappropriate about that." She would not apologize for the relationship and figured she would start right out of the gate making that clear without getting hostile.

"Justina, you are my daughter. You know I want what is best for you. You need to be with the right type of boy for a girl like you. And now is not the time for you to get distracted with this, you need to focus on school. I understand how girls are—they get their heads full of romance and they forget everything else. I want a better life for you than that." He was beginning to raise his voice and the intensity in his tone was escalating. Justina decided it would be best to focus on the school angle.

"Papa, I am going back to school next quarter. I only have a year left and then I will focus on a career. You don't have to worry. Daniel and I talked about this, he knows that's what I need to do and he agrees."

"You and *Daniel* discussed this?" he demanded loudly, anger consuming his voice. "This is not his decision to weigh in on. How can he recommend what you should do? What kind of man drops out of school and just hangs around the neighborhood like he has? What is he able to do for you? He cannot take care of you. You will want to have children, be a mother. You need a man who can support you and care for you. He is not focused on building a future—he is drifting. But he is more than happy for you to finish school and be a lawyer with a good future? No! This is not going to happen. That's the final word!"

CHAPTER THIRTEEN

Meanwhile, Daniel pulled up after a grueling day of removing mildewed sub-flooring from Beth's house. As he came up the steps, Victor's voice came through the door loud and clear. Daniel stopped in his tracks as if hit by a sci-fi movie stun gun. There was no way he would go into the house after hearing that. Bile rose up in his throat and the blood drained from his face. He had suspected that Victor would react this way—it had been his constant fear. Justina never admitted this possibility, at least not to him, or perhaps she was just overly optimistic. After a moment of paralyzed immobility, he retraced his steps back around the house to get his motorcycle.

As he drove back toward his neighborhood, he replayed the scene at the Gonzalez house. He was mortified, and sick to his stomach, but not surprised. The part about him wanting her to have a good career for selfish reasons was inaccurate, but he recognized certain elements of truth in the rant. He had been aimless since his mother died and enough time had passed. He needed to be productive and get back to his life. Although horrified at what

Victor had said, Daniel understood that it might have been what he needed to hear. He knew that he had nothing to offer a girl like Justina, or anyone else, for that matter. Beth said the same thing, more or less, which confirmed what he believed from the beginning. His heart ached for having left Justina to fight this battle with her father, but he just couldn't face either of them, not now.

He drove, without any purpose, along Seagirt Boulevard for a while, skirting the beach. As he proceeded up along the water, he saw more broken homes and torn-up lives, the Rockaway stretch as bleak and dreary as his mental meanderings. The ripped-up boardwalk, like the one in Long Beach, and houses that once held families and memories, lay in disjointed piles, abandoned but surely not forgotten. There were no lights or other evidence of electricity and it looked as though many residents had moved on or were perhaps living elsewhere, waiting for help that might never come. The clumps of shell-shocked storm victims sitting on porches or in yards appeared to have given up and left. Here and there he saw someone hauling materials out of a house and a few children played in the wreckage, jumping from one pile of debris to another, but for the most part it seemed deserted. The grey desolation suited his mood.

Viewing the ongoing devastation helped Daniel to put his own miserable thoughts into better context. He saw what was happening in his own neighborhood and it sparked a desire in him to help people in these situations. It came to him with sudden clarity that he had found his motivation for getting back to school as fast as possible. He thought about organizations that help disaster victims, those unfortunate souls with no resources, and realized that was what he really wanted to do. It broke his heart to imagine so many lives turned upside down with little hope for prompt relief. He wondered how people kept their jobs when they had to leave the area to stay in safer housing or if they ended up unemployed. How could they afford to survive? Children would have to go to different schools. Small businesses had been destroyed beyond any hopes of recovery. It filled him with sorrow, but also strengthened his determination making him feel much better about his life. *First thing, though, I need to stop this business with Justina,* he thought. That situation was a recipe for disaster of another sort and he knew he would just end up getting hurt—it was inevitable. He needed to focus on something positive.

He turned around and went back to his own bleak and empty house. The downstairs remained gutted, but the upstairs was just frigid and dark. Camping, he reminded himself. He drove inland to find a store with anything he could heat up on his little charcoal grill and treated himself to a six-pack of beer. It would be a chilly night, but he had his resolve and, in a strange way, he felt happier than he had in a long time.

CHAPTER FOURTEEN

The scene at the Gonzalez house, however, was one of bitter dispute. As Daniel drove off, they heard the motorcycle engine rumbling on the way out. Justina realized what had happened. The rage rose up in her throat and adrenalin pounded through her veins. She jumped up and stood rigid before her father, her small hands clenched into balls of tight fury.

"How dare you say those things?" She demanded, her eyes wide and dilated, pink splotches mottling her cheekbones. "Did you just hear Daniel leave? He must have heard every one of your rotten words. I can't believe you could be so horrible! I am done with this. You can't decide who my friends are. You don't think he's had enough awful things in his life, losing his mother and now his house is ruined? Are you kidding me? He never did anything to you or me; he has been wonderful. And you talk about him like he is garbage!" She struggled to find the right words. Her heart pounded and she wanted to strangle her father. He was so bossy and always had to be in charge, judging everyone.

Victor appeared stunned by her fury, but not at all swayed by it. "Justina, what I said is the truth. You are too good for a boy who won't even finish school. He's a nice kid, but not for you to date! You do not show intelligent judgment here. You will realize this at some point. Now, we are done discussing this issue." He finished dismissively. He was not accustomed to being argued with and wasn't prepared to take it from his own child, a daughter no less.

"You're right, we are done. I am going to find Daniel!" Justina said, right up in his face.

"You most certainly are not going anywhere! And that is final." He grabbed her arm and held it tight. "You will calm down. He is an adult. He will be fine. You are not going to go chasing him around in that neighborhood, especially like this. No. You stay here." His voice was unrelenting with no room for argument.

"I am so sick of your bossy, macho, crap!" she said, the hysteria rising in her throat. "Do you even realize that I am an adult? You are never here, then you show up and you tell me how to live? That is so wrong. It is not up to you what I do! Why don't you just go back to wherever you've been and hang out with all those politicians you enjoy so much and leave me alone! That's what I want!" Justina screeched the last part at him, yanking her arm away and racing up the stairs. She would not cry in front of him, but she was so furious and frantic with worry for Daniel.

She tried calling him, but there was no answer. "Shit!" she cursed, throwing her phone across the room. Her tears and rage combined, creating the beginnings of a terrible headache. She was torn between running out of the house in search of Daniel or curling up in her bed and crying her eyes out. At that moment she hated her father, but also understood that leaving the house at that point might be a bad idea for many reasons. She couldn't imagine what Daniel must be thinking and feeling after Victor basically

Susan Lee Walberg

said that Daniel wanted her for her earning potential. *Oh my God, she said to herself, *what do I do?*

She finally decided, after calming herself somewhat, that she would go to the hospital the next morning and stop by Daniel's house on the way. Once she made the decision about the immediate course of action she began focusing on the big picture. Soon she would be back at school and she needed to get through that before moving forward with her future. She would have no freedom from her father so long as she was in school, she realized. Although one of her biggest concerns at the moment was Daniel, she recognized the truth of what he had said—they both needed to focus on getting their education first. She soothed herself by planning her last year of law school with an eye toward graduation. That was the only way to gain control over her life.

The next morning, after taking time in the bathroom trying to erase the evidence of last night's drama, she told her father she was heading to the hospital to work. As he looked at her over his reading glasses, his expression showed that he knew full well it was more than that, but he said, "Okay, have a good day. See you tonight." He was accustomed to having his directives followed, so after the blow-up the night before she hoped he would believe the matter to be settled.

She drove along the waterfront to Daniel's house. As she got close, she saw a fire truck and an ambulance on his street and black smoke billowed out of one of the houses. *Oh my God,* Justina said to herself, and pulled up as close as she could. The house was across the street and two doors down from Daniel's home. Flames flashed through the front door and windows and a gaggle of people stood watching the firefighters work.

Justina didn't see Daniel in the crowd. She went up to a young black woman who had a little boy of about five years old who hung onto her coat, crying. "What happened?" Justina asked her.

The woman just looked at her for a moment, her eyes vacant. Finally she responded, "Don't know for sure, but those folks just had some contractors in, you know we all been trying to get our houses fixed. I heard one of them firemen say that it was probably electric. Maybe those contractors didn't know what they were doing. That's my guess." The woman picked her son up, holding him against her side with one arm, and turned away, shuffling down the street with the crying child.

Justina looked around again for Daniel, or even Beth, but didn't spot either of them in the crowd. She wondered if there were any injuries in the fire, but didn't see anyone being brought out of the house. The neighboring homes may be at risk, she realized. They stood so close together that with one strong breeze and the whole row could go up in flames. She watched as the firemen got the blaze under control, although it was obvious that the building was destroyed. Justina decided she should leave and get to the hospital— there was nothing she could do for the victims of the burned house, except say a prayer.

At the hospital, things were backed up with no time to talk to anyone other than the patients. She checked in with Mona who immediately waved her toward a very pregnant Latina. The morning flew by and Justina became wrapped up in the people she helped. The situation at the hospital had not improved in terms of the volume of patients and the amount of sickness and injuries coming in the door. In addition, there were staff members who had been rendered homeless and slept at the hospital. It just didn't appear that things were getting any better and seemed to have gotten worse.

Justina checked her phone and tried again to call Daniel, but no answer. Like before, it wasn't long before the patients and their problems became foremost in her mind and attention. Some of the people she helped remained implanted in her brain long past the time she spent with them. There was the Peruvian woman whose meager box of salvaged belongings had been stolen from her smashed-up car, leaving her with no identification of any sort; the young Jamaican couple who were expecting a baby in the near term, but had nowhere to live; the multiple elderly persons, coughing and sick with no food, heat, or money, and no family to help. As she observed how the staff at the hospital just rolled up their sleeves and took care of business and patients as best they could, Justina realized that she had never truly experienced the real world. She thought about the people in the burned-down house and wondered where they were. She assumed Daniel knew them and figured she could ask him, if she ever saw him again.

Justina wondered how so much tragedy could keep on coming in an endless flow with no reprieve. Most every case was distressing on its own, but in the aggregate it was inconceivable. Although she realized that she was helping, in her own small way, she wished she could find a way to do more, to do something to create real change. She pondered the rhetoric she heard both through her father and his political allies and through reports on television—how they spoke so often about the poor and the vulnerable and the desire to help them change their circumstances. She wondered if any of them had seen the type of suffering she had witnessed and whether it truly affected them or if it was just talk. It didn't seem that anyone was rushing to help the patients at her hospital or the freezing, hungry people in Far Rockaway. There was one overarching theme among the storm survivors in Far Rockaway—they were devastated and had not received any credible assurance of relief from this disaster that had befallen them. The community was banding together to take care of its own and if it weren't for that, things would be far worse.

She decided again to approach her father and talk to him to find out what kind of help was planned. He was working for the Senator of New York who was early in a bid for a Presidential run. Surely they had discussed this issue. She felt obsessive in her need to know—the images of these people she had met were taking over her thoughts and fighting with Daniel for the space in her head.

One evening, after trying again to find Daniel and again failing (and again obsessing over it during the trip home), Justina approached her father to see what she could learn about the storm relief efforts. He seemed surprised that she had come to him with the question, particularly since she had little to say to him since the whole fight about Daniel. It was also unusual for them to discuss politics—their views on many issues were not compatible. He looked up at her over his reading glasses for a moment, eyebrows raised, before taking the glasses off, and giving her his full attention.

"Yes, there is work going on to manage the relief efforts from the storm. The Senator is working on pulling together a committee from both sides of the aisle, including various relief organizations, to look at what is being done and what needs to be done. One priority, of course, is to get the power going. Without power, homes cannot be completely repaired and made habitable, food cannot be easily prepared, and sickness will continue." He paused and she remained quiet, waiting for him to continue.

"As you can imagine, this is an enormous undertaking. It is not just our city—it affects tens of thousands of people, roads, power, and infrastructure, up and down the coast. Plus it is no easy matter to find the money or the labor for such a task. And every story, every family, has its own horrible losses. That is the challenge, but to your question, yes, there are many people devoting efforts to this cause." He smiled at her fondly, "You are getting to see how a disaster affects people, especially the poor, aren't you? It is heartbreaking—I know that. Maybe you can understand why I care so much for my work; I like to think that sometimes it can make a difference in the lives of people. You maybe don't realize that I've seen a lot in my life, things you will never probably have to experience. Those things impact you—they change you. Now you are learning that, huh?"

He reached out and took her hands in his. "You and I may fight on many issues, but in this I think we are the same. I am glad to see that you care about these things. You make me very happy. Your mama would be proud."

Justina squeezed his hands, smiling back through teary eyes. "Thank you, Papa." She said, then leaned over, and gave him a hug.

She got them each a glass of wine and settled down to talk with him about her experiences at the hospital. They were not too far into that conversation when her cell phone rang—it was Daniel.

CHAPTER FIFTEEN

J ustina could not ignore the phone—she had been so desperate to reach Daniel—but she did have a moment of angst over interrupting her conversation with her father. Nonetheless, she answered at once and got up and went into the kitchen to talk, giving Victor a *just a minute* gesture.

"Daniel, how are you? I have been so worried about you. Are you okay?"

"Yeah, I'm fine. I left my phone charger at your house and didn't think it was a good time to come get it, so I bought another one. I thought it might be a good idea to leave you and your father alone for a day or two. Your Dad doesn't want me there and I respect that." His voice sounded calm, not upset or depressed, from what she could tell.

"You heard me and my father fighting. I am so sorry for all those things he said. He has no right. I hope you know he was so wrong." She wanted him to understand that she did not in any way agree with her father or believe any of the things Victor had said. The very thought of it was abhorrent.

"No, he was right about some things," Daniel admitted. "He was right that I have been drifting for too long and that this is not what I should be doing with my life. Hearing him say that was actually not bad for me, maybe I needed that motivation. I am going back to school in a few weeks for the next quarter. I called them and they helped get me back in sooner rather than later. It's time for me to go back."

Justina considered this for a moment. She didn't like it, but realized that it was best for Daniel—he couldn't continue living as he had been. "I understand," she said simply. There was a long pause and then Justina broke the silence, "When can I see you?"

"Anytime," he responded quickly. "When are you going to be at the hospital? I'm not in a hurry to run into your dad just yet," he added with a slight laugh in his voice. "Also, I need you to bring me my stuff from your house."

She wanted to spend time with him, but didn't want to push. She was unsure of how he was feeling and didn't want a rejection. "Do you want to have lunch?"

"Why don't you come over after work instead? Meet me at my house, okay?"

"Okay. I'll see you then," she said, adding, "Thanks for calling, Daniel. I've been worried."

She returned to her father who had immersed himself in a thick document. As he heard her approaching, he looked up over his reading glasses. "Was that Daniel?" He asked.

"Yes," she responded. "And he's going back to school next quarter, so you don't need to act like he's a loser," she tacked on with a touch of defiance in her voice, but not enough to provoke an argument.

Her father smiled wryly, also wanting to avoid another fight. "I know he's not a loser, mija. I just want what's best for you. Okay?"

They left it at that, both satisfied with the semblance of a truce.

The next morning, Justina went to get Daniel's things out of the spare bedroom. His clothes were neatly tucked into his bag, which made her sad. He must not have been too comfortable—his packed bag was ready to go. She realized that they had been playing house and she liked it more than she should.

At the hospital, she tried to focus on her work. The day was a difficult one. She dealt with many people suffering because they failed to take their psychiatric medications, missed their methadone treatment, or had self-medicated far too much and were angry and abusive in both cases. The volume of patients in the hospital continued to exceed capacity; the ongoing health issues and problems of the population still persisting. The effects of living in unrelenting cold and mildew were apparent in the barking cough as well as skin and respiratory afflictions. The work that Justina had enjoyed in the beginning was wearing on her. Seeing the never-ending procession of resigned and desperate people was disheartening and she questioned whether her meager contribution really made any difference. She wondered how the regular employees could keep their spirits up, day after day.

And yet the patients responded with so much gratitude for every kindness and every bit of help and respect they received. So many of the people in the hospital were slumped, dejected, in their chairs and appeared to have given up hope. She loved how it felt to help these people and see their faces brighten when they realized that someone truly cared what happened to them. This was the part of her work that Justina most enjoyed.

Toward the end of day, Justina headed to the lobby to get a cup of coffee when she spotted the familiar curly blonde head of someone taller than anyone else in the hospital's lobby. No sooner had she recognized Daniel than she saw another blonde head beside his— Beth. They didn't notice her as they hurried into the Emergency Room entrance with strained focus showing on both their faces.

Her stomach lurched when she saw Daniel with Beth, but her immediate next thought was about what brought them to the hospital. The idea of coffee instantly forgotten, Justina scurried across the lobby to the Emergency Department. They were not difficult to locate, two blondes in a sea of every other human color. Daniel was leaning against the wall, near the triage desk, and Beth was close beside him, patting his arm and craning her neck to talk to him. Daniel's face appeared grey, despite his perpetual tan, his mouth pulled into a grim line. He slouched, hands in the pocket of his hoodie, looking at the yellowed linoleum and not responding to Beth in any discernible way.

Justina maneuvered through the crowded hallway, stepping over children playing on the floor and dodging wheelchairs. "Daniel!" she said, anxiety in her voice. "What's going on?" He looked up at her, his eyes red and his lashes wet and clumpy. He held his arm out to her, and pulled her close to his chest, without answering. Beth responded, "It's Willie. She's had a stroke or something, Daniel found her a little while ago. She's in with a doctor now. She's in pretty rough shape, but they will take care of her." The last part was clearly said for Daniel's benefit.

Daniel finally spoke. "It's my fault," he mumbled, his voice ragged. "She wasn't right yesterday. I should have gone back last night. She said she was fine, but I knew she wasn't. It's my fault," he said again.

Beth spoke up, "Daniel, you know that's not true. She's had heart problems for years. You got her to the doctor when she needed to go, you made sure she had her meds, and food. You did everything you possibly could for her. Don't do this to yourself, okay? You treat her better than her own kids. You know that."

He shook his head. "No, it's just like *her*. I was too busy taking care of myself, again, when I should have been there. It's the same thing." Even though Daniel was holding her tight, as if she was a life preserver, Justina had no part in this discussion and she realized it was a conversation that had happened before between the two of them. She didn't know the whole story, so she didn't say anything. She had no idea what she even could say, but Beth did.

"Daniel, your mother couldn't have been saved. It's not your fault. She had cancer, for Christ's sake. Don't do this. You got Willie here and she's getting care. We just need to pray for her now, that's all we can do, okay?" she implored, looking up at him to try to make eye contact.

He shook Beth's hand off his arm and muttered, "I'm sorry, I need to get some air." He pulled away from both of them, heading out the door.

Justina looked at Beth, not sure what to say. Daniel's grief was so heart-wrenching, and she realized how little she understood about his life. Beth broke the silence.

"He went through a lot when he lost his mom. She was very sick when he came home from college to help her. She didn't tell him for a long time, while he was at school, because she didn't want him to wreck his education. When she finally told him and he came home, he was broken-hearted. She was so thin, in so much pain. When she went into hospice, Daniel spent all his time with her. The night she died, Daniel was out with one of his friends who had come home from college. He hasn't forgiven himself, as you can see. Now as for Willie, it's the same thing. He's been doing everything to help her, but she's sick and now he thinks somehow it's his fault—like he could have changed the outcome. And it was just when he seemed to be getting past his guilt over his mom. I pray Willie pulls through, for Daniel's sake as much as hers."

Justina nodded and thought she was starting to understand him better—why he hadn't gone back to school yet—and why he was so hard on himself all the time.

"I don't know what to do to help him," she said. "I hate seeing him like this. What can we do?" It was clear that Beth had been through tough times with Daniel and, although Justina was jealous of their history, she sensed that Beth could give her a better understanding of how to handle the situation.

"Just be there for him and if he wants to talk, he will. But Daniel likes to deal with things on the inside first, so don't feel bad if he doesn't say much. Don't push him to talk about it or he will do like he just did, run away."

"Yeah, okay." Justina saw this in him—it made sense. It went against her natural instinct not to draw him out and talk about it, which was how she dealt with things. It made her feel powerless, like she wasn't doing anything to help him. She would have to trust what Beth was saying and focus on being there for him. She sighed and chewed on her lip, watching for Daniel's return.

As they waited, a heavy-set black nurse came out, calling for Daniel. Beth approached her and said, "We are with Daniel. He went outside for some air. Is there an update on Willie?" The nurse pursed her lips. "I can't share that with you, Daniel is the only person I have consent to speak with. When he comes back, send him to triage, and they will call me." With that she walked off, checking her pager as she went.

"I'll go find him," Justina said and she scurried out the door.

CHAPTER SIXTEEN

Daniel wandered around the block aimlessly, not seeing anything along his path. Walking in and finding Willie took him back to a time he had tried to forget. When he found out his mom had cancer he was blind-sided. She had been so strong, taking care of the kids and the house, never complaining and always making sure everything got done. He remembered when she told him that the doctors found a cancer in her, but she had been getting treatment and was feeling better. He had wanted to believe her so badly that he almost convinced himself it was true. He thought back to those final weeks.

Mom's clothes started hanging off her, and she made jokes about how hard she had tried for years to lose the baby weight. I knew she was sick, but kept thinking she would beat it. Then one day I accidentally walked into her room when she was only wearing a nightshirt. She sat on the edge of the bed, probably trying to get up enough energy to go to the bathroom. Her legs were just bones with dry skin stretched over them. I knew then how sick she really was and that she had been doing everything she could to protect me from it. "I'm okay, honey, really," she had said when she saw me start crying. "I want you to go on and have a good life, you understand? I don't want you to worry about me." I hung onto her and sobbed then, because I couldn't deny the truth any more—even she wasn't trying to deny it. I still see her, in my dreams, as skinny as a skeleton telling me it is okay.

He shook away the vision from that dream, which was still vivid and disturbing, but couldn't quit thinking about how his life had changed at that point.

I took the job at the bagel shop when I realized her illness had taken more than her health—it sucked up most of her money as well. So I started delivering bagels, which also provided free food. Although, Mom didn't eat much anymore, so nobody really benefitted but me. As she got thinner and weaker, I became more depressed and desperate each day. Every day when I came home from work I would call out to her as soon as I got in the door, terrified that she wouldn't answer. I checked her at night to make sure she was still breathing and brought her various tasty desserts from work to try to tempt her appetite. There were so many nights when she was having too much pain and I had to give her extra medicine. I would try to be strong for her, but I would go in my room and cry myself to sleep, hating myself for being so helpless, so unable to give her any relief. Then there came a day when she seemed brighter, more alert, and I felt a huge relief—a hope that she was finally beating this awful disease. At some level I must have known better, but I wanted to believe it so badly. She ate a slice of peanut butter cheesecake that I had brought from the bagel shop and encouraged me to go see my buddy Chris who had come home from school for Christmas break. She was insistent, at least as insistent as a virtually bedridden person can be, but she convinced me that she felt better and that she just wanted to rest. She said to me, "Don't worry, if I have any trouble I can call the nurse and she will be right here."

So I went and met up with Chris at a pizza and beer place. We laughed and joked and traded stories about girls, crappy professors, and life after high school. I never said anything to Chris about my mom, I just didn't want to talk or think about it for an hour or two. I just wanted to hang out and be a normal guy with no worries. As the evening ended, Chris was teasing me about hooking me up with his sister's roommate who was reported to be a very wild party girl. He promised to call me and hook me up, telling me that I needed to get a life and have some fun.

I kept thinking about that conversation on the way home that night, thinking maybe Chris was right and I should get a life. I thought that maybe one of these days I would go along with it, step out of my box for once. When I walked into the house, it immediately felt wrong, although everything looked the same—the scrawny Christmas tree with the gaudy blinking lights. . .I can still see that tree. I remember calling out to Mom, just like every other night, but I felt something was wrong and, sure enough, there was no response. I ran up the stairs and found her in bed with one arm hanging off the side, the phone lying on the floor. Her bottle of pain pills dumped out on her nightstand with only a couple left. Her arm was cold and felt like a dry bone. I couldn't find a pulse or hear her breathing. Finally I just lay across her, sobbing, unable to do anything else.

Eventually I called the hospice nurse, the number taped onto the phone. I didn't know what else to do or who to call. My mom had kept trying to tell me what hospice would do, but I couldn't listen. I didn't want to hear about this day. Everything after that was just a blur. Thank God for the hospice people, because I had no clue what was supposed to happen. All these people came tramping through our house—people to remove the medications, to take her body, and to talk to me about funereal arrangements, but I didn't understand anything. I just sat on the ratty old couch, staring at that Christmas tree and trying to process what had happened. Beth had come, she had seen the coroner's van, and she had tried to talk to me, to be supportive, to get me to eat some soup, but I told her to go away. All I could do was wrap myself up in a blanket and sit on the old plaid couch, staring into the blinking Christmas lights on our pathetic Christmas tree.

I still remember that night so well, like it was yesterday. I remember how guilty I felt, knowing that I had been stuffing myself with pizza and joking about getting laid while Mom was dying, alone and in pain. I can't get it out of my head—maybe if I had been there I could have gotten the nurse or given her the meds before her pain became too much. I still don't know if she took too many pills and if that was what actually killed her. If I had been there, I would have given her the right amount of pain medication as soon as she needed them. It's hard to say what the actual cause of death was— the cancer or the pills—although nobody was going to do an autopsy to see exactly why she died at that point and I don't think I really want to know. I don't really want to know if she did it on purpose or if it was an accident. I don't know how many pills she took, at that point there were so many different types of pills in the house—pills for nausea, pills for treating more pain, pills for treating less pain. At the end of the day, she was gone and I had been out having a good old time with my buddy.

I also remember that phone call to my brother, John. John had been distracted and said he was involved with some big work project. I remember that phone call, through the haze of that terrible night. John had basically said there was nothing he could do about it, "Sorry, man, but I am in deep shit with this project here. Can you take care of the stuff there? Let me know, I don't think I can make it, but let me know about the arrangements."

And that was it. I still can't forgive him for that, for not caring about Mom, and for not caring about me. It seems like I lost my brother that night, as well as my mom, although really he was already long gone—I just never wanted to totally admit it.

Daniel relived all this as he walked around outside and then thought of Willie. When he found Willie, she was laying on the couch virtually unconscious with her legs splayed out at odd angles, swollen and discolored, her mouth open. His sense of déjà vu had been immediate and soul piercing. Again, he could do nothing. Again he had been gone when he should have been there. Again he had to make a phone call for someone to come handle it because he could not. He thought about Willie dying and knew he couldn't even face that thought.

Willie was just like him in many ways. She had nothing, nobody, except herself. After Daniel's mother died they had formed a bond by taking care of each other. Willie's children were grown and gone and didn't come around to see their mother, so she took Daniel under her wing like another child. She would call him to come over and eat when she cooked something good, telling him it was too much for just her and she needed some help eating it all. Saying it was no fun for her eating all alone. Daniel would help her keep her house in order, fixing a leaky pipe or patching the roof. And when she was failing, where was he? He was out doing his own business. Not taking care of her when he should have known better. She hadn't been right earlier and on some level he knew it, but he was focused on his own problems and didn't let it register.

His mind kept going back and forth, Willie and Mom, over and over—limp and unconscious because of him. Rationally he knew that he hadn't caused their illnesses, but that feeling of responsibility was overwhelming and he couldn't get past it as he finally found a bench in the parking lot of the hospital and watched the black clouds, that so perfectly matched his feelings, racing across the sky.

CHAPTER SEVENTEEN

Justina found Daniel hunched over on a bench by the parking lot. He was huddled inside his sweatshirt, not seeming to notice the chilly wind or the dark layers above.

"Daniel!" she called to him as she approached. "Daniel, there's an update on Willie, the nurse wouldn't talk to us. Come in and she will talk to you." He looked up, his eyes still carrying a bleak and hopeless look. He got up without speaking and headed in. Justina almost had to run to keep up with his long strides.

The two girls waited as Daniel disappeared to talk with the nurse. Justina chewed on her lip and fidgeted, Beth played with her phone—checking e-mails and weather reports, whatever she could find to keep her fingers and mind occupied.

When he emerged, they could both tell that the news was not too awful—he actually made eye contact and held his head up, although the sadness was still in his eyes.

"She's not great, but she's going to make it—at least for now," he said. "She had a stroke. They are going to admit her. She's going to need some time to get rehabbed. Oh, and they said its good we got her here when we did," he added with relief in his voice.

"Oh, Daniel, that's such good news!" Justina said, hugging him.

"Thank God," Beth added, and then asked, "Did you see her?"

"Yeah, I saw her, but she was pretty out of it. She knew I was there, she squeezed my hand, but she looked really tired. The nurse said it could be quite a while before she's back to normal, if ever, and she may still have a hard time talking. But that's okay, it would have been worse if we hadn't found her. Maybe in a way it's a good thing," he added. "She shouldn't be alone in that house the way it is—at least here she's warm and getting looked after."

"That's right, she is very lucky," Beth said, nodding in agreement.

"Does she have insurance?" Justina asked, newly aware of those sorts of issues.

Daniel shrugged, "Don't know. Probably Medicare. Nobody asked me about anything, so I guess it's okay."

"I'll check about that tomorrow when I come in," Justina said. "If not, we can get her signed up for assistance." She wanted to be involved and hoped that she could somehow help Willie, in her own way. "I can keep an eye on her too and if anything is going on I can let you know. Once I get her permission, of course," she added with a smile, remembering the privacy issues that the nurse mentioned.

They decided to go and find something to eat, suddenly realizing how hungry they were. They piled into Daniel's truck and he drove up toward the airport until they found a diner where they stuffed themselves with burgers and beer.

They were all so relieved that Willie was okay and getting cared for that the mood of the group was almost festive. Daniel, in particular, looked more relaxed and the light was coming back in his eyes. He told the girls about his plans for going back to school and how getting compensated for the insurance for the house was progressing—or not, actually. Justina was so happy to see him looking forward rather than backward and showing some interest in his future. She realized that she hadn't seen that in him before and wondered if the fact that he'd saved Willie had helped him let go of some of his guilt over his mother. Whatever it was, she was glad to see it. She got out her phone and took some selfies with all of them while the mood was light. She wanted a picture of Daniel to have with her, although she would never admit that.

She regretted not spending some time alone with him, but it was late by the time they got back so Daniel dropped her at her car at the hospital. "I'll see you tomorrow?" she asked, and he confirmed it, giving her a quick hug and kiss.

The next day she went straight to Mona and asked about seeing Willie. Mona went and checked with Willie herself and came back smiling. "Yes, she would love to see you!" Mona said and she told her where to find Willie.

Justina hadn't been on the floors hardly at all since doing her volunteer work and was not too surprised to find the rooms upstairs nearly as full as the lobby and emergency room. At the nurses' station she found a nurse in a purple smock who directed her. She located Willie in a small room with another patient—a pasty white elderly woman who was asleep with her head back and mouth wide open, snoring.

When Willie saw Justina she gave her a weak but sincere smile, her gold tooth shining. She struggled to speak and held out her hand. Justina took her hand saying, "I'm so glad you're going to be okay, Willie. We were so worried about you. Daniel just about had a meltdown. Are you feeling okay?"

Willie nodded and a glint showed in her eyes as she motioned to the empty breakfast tray. "Good. Hot," she managed to say, although she was difficult to understand.

"How do you like your roommate?" Justina asked with a naughty smile. Willie rolled her eyes in response.

"Well, it looks like you are going to be here for Thanksgiving and Christmas so I will tell Santa to bring you something good, all right?" Without giving Willie a chance to try responding, she continued, "Okay, well I'm going to let Daniel know you are doing great and that you are getting some good food. I'm sure he will be by to see you today. I will stop in and check on you later, too. Okay?" Justina patted Willie's hand. Willie nodded, and tried to say something, but it wasn't clear. It was so hard to see her trying to speak—it broke Justina's heart. Particularly since Willie was such a character and always had something to say.

She sent Daniel a text on her way back downstairs.

"Just saw Willie, she is doing good and enjoying hot food!"

Daniel didn't reply, although that didn't surprise her. His responsiveness on texts was iffy at best. She knew he would appreciate hearing how Willie was doing, anyhow. Then she went back to check in with Mona and make sure Willie had her paperwork in order.

The doctors said that Willie was going to be in the hospital for quite a while and perhaps would be going to a nursing home because she had multiple health issues and the potential to become disabled. Although she had some ability to speak, she couldn't really walk and her coordination was almost nonexistent. She had a nurse's aid helping her eat and it took two people to get her out of bed and into a wheelchair. The good news was that the stroke hadn't caused her much damage mentally—she seemed to know what was going on—she just couldn't articulate her thoughts or move around. They were all hoping rehabilitation would help with those issues. In the meantime, however, the doctor advised them that they needed to get her blood sugar and blood pressure under better control. Overall, though, her chances for a decent recovery seemed pretty good, so long as her many health problems were managed.

Justina was relieved to know that Willie wouldn't be going back to that house any time soon. Ever since she saw it she knew that it was not a healthy place for anyone, much less an old woman with numerous health problems. Having Willie in the hospital was one less thing for all of them to worry about. It was nice to have some kind of good news these days.

CHAPTER EIGHTEEN

Time went by and the people in Far Rockaway were still without power. The November days were getting shorter and Thanksgiving was right around the corner. Ever since Justina's mother had died, Victor made plans for them to go into the city and have dinner. He always said it was because there was no point in doing all that work to cook Thanksgiving dinner for just the two of them, but Justina suspected that he didn't want to spend a holiday sitting in the house without any family except the two of them. At least by going out they could pretend it was a festive event, even if they both felt the emptiness.

This year, however, was different—at least from Justina's perspective. She knew from the people at the hospital that various locations would be set up to serve some form of Thanksgiving dinner to the residents still without power. Justina was beginning to feel like those were her people, her community, and she wanted to be part of helping them through the holiday. She couldn't imagine how awful it would be to spend the holidays in a shelter or in line at a relief station and she wanted to do something to help. However, she wasn't sure how her father would react. She didn't want to leave him alone and he was pretty set in his ways.

The week before Thanksgiving she met him at the door with a glass of wine. She realized that she did that whenever she expected a difficult conversation with him, but hoped he didn't make the connection.

"Hello, Papa, how was your day?" she asked and took his coat.

He took the wine she offered and said, "Thank you, sweetheart. It was a rough day, very long. There are many people complaining about the power company, the government, contractor scams, gas shortages...the problems with the storm just keep going. Homes have burned down because the electrical systems weren't fixed correctly by the contractors they brought in. It is a disaster, still." He sighed heavily and sank into his favorite easy chair.

"Yes, I saw one of those houses a while back, and the people said it was probably the contractor. It is still bad at the hospital too. So many people have been cold and hungry for too long, which is what I want to talk to you about, Papa. Thanksgiving is next week. I know you like to go into the city, but I would like to work at one of the relief stations. They are setting up stations all over Far Rockaway so people can have a Thanksgiving dinner. There is going to be one close to the hospital and some of the people from the hospital are volunteering. I would like very much to help, as well, but wanted to talk to you first."

Victor hesitated only a moment and then said, "Yes, I think that's a great idea. It's a much better way for us to spend our holiday this year. Find out what time they need us and let them know we will be there." He nodded decisively and took a sip of wine.

Justina's eyes widened and she said, "You want to go? Really? I didn't think. . .." her words trailed off. This was not the answer she expected.

"Yes, I would very much like to go. It would be good to see what is happening in the real world. All I hear is complaints on the phone all day. I would like to go meet some of these people and serve their dinner. We are among the fortunate ones."

"Wow, yes, I agree. Okay, I will set it up. Thanks, Papa. This means a lot to me. And you can meet some of my friends at the hospital!" She smiled widely, relieved that the conversation had gone better than she could have hoped.

Later that evening she called Daniel about Thanksgiving. "Hey," She said, "Papa and I are helping at the relief station on Thanksgiving. Can you come too?" She thought how nice it would be to see him on the holiday and maybe it would even help repair some of the damage between him and Victor.

"I can stop by, but I told Willie I would spend the afternoon with her," Daniel said, "Sorry about that. But I will stop by."

Justina swallowed her disappointment. "No, that's okay, you should be with Willie. Nobody should be alone on the holiday. If I don't see you before, I will see you then."

The sun came out on Thanksgiving morning and Justina and Victor were up early to get to the relief station by 10. They both wore jeans and thick sweaters. Justina always thought it was odd to see her father in jeans—he just wasn't a jeans kind of man—but she had to admit he looked good, as always. When they got to the relief station and she introduced him to Mona, she felt proud of him.

"It's good to meet you and thank you so much for coming over to our 'hood to help out! I have heard all sorts of good stuff about you from Justina!" Mona shook Victor's hand. "They are setting up over there," she motioned to some long buffet tables that were being assembled. "They have some apron-type things, too, so you don't mess your clothes. Now I gotta go, I am picking up some donated drinks. Okay?"

"Sure," Justina responded, and they went to help get things set up. The food was being served in the church parking lot and the doors to the church were open for people who wanted to go in.

There were at least a dozen volunteers, although it was hard to keep track, as people came and went with the various donations. Justina was impressed with all the food that was brought, especially knowing there were many such stations around the area. They had a full, traditional turkey dinner to provide and even desserts. It made her happy to be part of something so positive after all that had happened to the community.

It didn't take Victor long to get into a conversation with one of the organizers and Justina watched him with amusement. Even on a holiday, in jeans, he was working the crowd! Before much time passed, the Rockaway residents began showing up and formed a long, hungry line. Justina watched her father as he served up mashed potatoes to see his reaction to the unhealthy, dirty, coughing, population. She had gotten over the shock of it from working at the hospital, but she wasn't sure about Victor. She felt another wave of pride seeing how he chatted with the various people coming through the line, speaking Spanish to the Latinos and greeting all of them with holiday wishes.

Once the first batch of people had been served one of the organizers, a young black man in a Giants cap, stood up and made an informal speech. He gave thanks that the community was intact even if the homes were not and thanked the various donors. A young, olive-skinned woman also spoke, expressing gratitude for the community and her neighborhood church that hosted the meal. Another woman with frizzy orange hair gave her thanks and ended by reminding everyone, "We will overcome this. . .do not forget we are New Yorkers!" Everyone cheered at this and she stepped into the crowd amid high-fives.

When they seemed to be wrapping up the speeches, Mona went up to the head organizer and spoke in his ear. The man immediately looked over at Victor and Justina and announced, "I just found out that one of our gracious volunteers, Victor Gonzalez, is an adviser to Senator Goldberg. He has been here incognito! We would like to thank you for being here, Mr. Gonzalez. Would you like to say a few words?"

Victor glanced over at Justina and at Mona, who was grinning like a Cheshire cat, and walked over to the podium.

"Good afternoon, everyone. And Happy Thanksgiving! I know this may be the most difficult holiday many of you have seen. I am not here today as a politician, but as a neighbor and part of your community. I do want to let you all know, however, that everyone in Albany as well as the Senators and Representatives are very aware of how bad things are and are working on many fronts to get your power back, get the insurance companies to pay, and to get relief money from the Federal Government. I'm not here to make a speech. I came here to serve a meal. I just want all of you to know that we understand what is happening here. These are not easy things to fix—the problems are all over the region. I am proud to be part of a community that pulls together like this one—that is what I am thankful for today. God bless you all and Happy Thanksgiving!"

He stepped aside amid some clapping and a few shouts of "amen!" and went over to the organizer to talk with him. Mona sidled up beside Justina. "Girlfriend, that is one fine Papa you got. . .if that wasn't your daddy, I might be putting some moves on that one!" She winked as she said it, and then went on, "in all seriousness, you should be proud of him. He's a good man, despite all your troubles with him. I wish I had a daddy half that good. That's what you should be thankful for."

"Yes, I know. Thanks. Papa is good at stuff like this—he can't help himself. I think it comes naturally." She looked over at Victor just in time to see Daniel approaching. She was surprised to see him go directly up to Victor and shake his hand.

"Wow, there's a shock." She whispered to Mona. "That's Daniel talking to my dad! I wouldn't have thought he would want to talk to him." Mona raised her eyebrows and they both watched the brief conversation, which appeared amicable.

"Good for him," Mona murmured. "He's handling it like a man. And he's a good-looking guy, too! You are surrounded by them! I need to be hanging out with you a whole lot more!"

Justina laughed and then Daniel came over to where they were standing. She introduced him to Mona. Daniel didn't say anything about Victor—he just chatted for a minute and then said he was headed over to see Willie. He gave Justina a hug and left.

They served another round of meals to the Rockaway residents until it started getting late and it was time to pack up. Without power, Far Rockaway was not a place to wander around at night.

Justina and Victor were quiet on the way back home that night, but it was a contented silence and Justina thought it was maybe the best Thanksgiving they had enjoyed in many years.

CHAPTER NINETEEN

The Christmas holidays were coming and Justina knew that once Christmas passed she and Daniel would be back at school. Christmas had never been the same since her mother died. Just like Thanksgiving, they didn't do anything at home. They went into the city every year and stayed at the Four Seasons. Her father had actually gotten to know the staff and management there and they did have beautiful holiday decorations in the city and at the hotel. Justina still missed doing a traditional Christmas, but didn't feel like she could tell her father. Plus he loved going to church on Christmas Eve, which was one activity they did agree on. The churches in Long Beach could not compare with the beauty of the churches in the city. Justina loved the feel of the old church they attended with its vaulted ceilings and traditional ceremonies. She had mixed feelings about it this year though. She really wanted to spend time with Daniel before he left for school.

Victor was going to be in D.C. for a few days right before the Christmas holiday, so Justina thought she would have some sort of Christmas celebration with Daniel. She figured he probably wouldn't enjoy the holidays much this year. She could at least make a nice dinner for him and maybe put up some Christmas decorations to try and make the house more festive.

Justina remembered that they had a fake Christmas tree up in the attic. They hadn't put it up since she was younger and would still get excited about the whole Santa thing. She thought it would be fun to put a tree up now—it had been such a bleak time— maybe a few Christmas lights would cheer everyone up and make it feel like a holiday. She ventured up to the attic in search of the tree and found it easily enough—there weren't too many boxes in the dusty attic. She noticed the trunk and several boxes in the corner and she knew they held her mother's things. Her eyes rested on the boxes for a minute. She had not looked through them since she was a child. *Holiday,* she reminded herself. She didn't want to get maudlin—it was time to try to get festive.

The tree was smaller than she remembered and she was able to pull the box down the stairs without much difficulty. She found the box of lights and ornaments, which weren't as nice as she recalled but were sufficient for her purposes.

She pulled an old Ella Fitzgerald Christmas CD out of her father's collection. The CD had probably been her mother's. She put it on to get the right mood going while she set up the tree. It was a simple job and it took little time to put it together. She didn't care much for the bright colored lights—they were somewhat gaudy— but she knew that as a kid they had seemed like the coolest thing in the world. She was just grateful that enough of them still worked to decorate the tree, since she doubted she could go right out and buy Christmas lights this year. Things were nowhere near back to normal yet and there was a definite lack of festivity this year. Many of the businesses and homes in Long Beach were still boarded up and many residents did not view Christmas as a top priority this year.

She sent Daniel a text to let him know that Victor was gone and that she wanted to see him before Christmas. She invited him for dinner the next day. Not only did she want to see Daniel, she wanted to get him away from Beth. That girl was way too much in Daniel's face. Justina found it hard to believe that nobody else in the whole neighborhood could help Beth and her family—to lend them a truck or give them advice on contractors. She knew Beth was taking every opportunity to latch on to Daniel and it drove her crazy.

Especially during the holidays, they should be spending time together. It seemed that ever since he decided it was time to go back to school, he had been more distant and was busy all the time. She just needed to get back on track with Daniel before school started. Daniel appeared happy to accept her invitation, so she started planning a nice dinner for him.

She bought all the ingredients for homemade lasagna and got a loaf of French bread, salad fixings, and even a small tiramisu at the local bakery. Although a number of shops and restaurants were re-opened along east Park, many were still boarded up. It was sad to see the main street in Long Beach—usually so bustling with people shopping and going to eat—half deserted. *At least it isn't full of National Guard and police anymore,* she thought to herself. It was still sad, though, the number of people who hadn't returned yet and the number of homes and businesses boarded up.

She got a couple of bottles of wine out of the wine cellar and put them in the refrigerator. She cleaned the house, which it didn't need, since the cleaning lady had been back since Victor's return. She tried on several outfits, trying to decide on her best look for the night. Casual? A little dressy? A little sexy? She finally decided on a form fitting red sweater and black leggings.

She put the Ella disc on the CD player, lit a couple candles, and set the table with their good china and crystal. She turned on the

Christmas tree so that the tree and candles would be the only light in the living room when he entered. The room had a warm and inviting glow with a festive ambiance. She thought it looked just right. She brushed her hair until it was as glossy as a raven's wing and applied her makeup with great care. Then she sat and waited for Daniel's arrival.

CHAPTER TWENTY

He arrived late and before he was even off of his bike she had the door open, eager and welcoming. "Merry Early-Christmas!" she said, giving him a hug. "I did some decorating so we can have a little Christmas celebration before Papa gets back and we go to the city." She frowned as she saw his face as he looked at the tree with its bright blinking lights. "What is it, what's wrong?" she asked.

"It's nothing, it's just that your tree looks like the one we used to have. Same lights and all." He made an effort to smile. "It's fine, I just haven't been thinking about Christmas. It's very nice you did this, thank you."

He hugged her and gave her a quick kiss, commenting, "Wow, something smells fantastic! I hope that's our dinner!"

He disentangled himself from her, but gave her a warm smile. He could see she made an effort for everything to be perfect that evening and he felt bad for reacting to the tree. If she noticed he pulled away too quickly, it didn't show on her face. She took his jacket and invited him into the dining room where she had the wine out and ready. She poured them each a glass and held hers out toward his.

"A toast?" She asked, smiling. "To moving forward!"

They clicked glasses and Daniel tried to decide if moving forward meant the same thing to her as it did to him. Somehow he doubted it. Justina bid him to have a seat and started bringing the food out from the kitchen. She kept up a lively conversation, asking his thoughts on Willie's progress, his house, his classes in the next quarter. She told him she'd gotten her roommate's agreement to let her keep Hercules at the apartment and told him about the interesting people at the hospital. She kept his glass full as she got the dinner ready and Daniel felt himself starting to relax, although the whole Christmas tree thing had shaken him more than he wanted to admit. He realized he was drinking too much wine, but he didn't care.

The dinner was wonderful and Justina was being charming. The more wine he drank, the easier it got to relax and roll with it. In the soft lights, Justina's hair gleamed and her eyes looked huge and luminous, her lips full and soft. He knew he was at risk of weakening in his resolve. He struggled to remember why exactly he was trying to resist her.

When they finished eating, Justina brought out a bottle of dessert wine—he hadn't realized there was such a thing! She filled his glass, telling him to enjoy it while she cleaned up the kitchen a little. He did as he was asked, even though he knew he had already drank too much.

She emerged from the kitchen and came up behind him, wrapping her arms around him loosely.

"Let's go in the living room," she suggested. "Bring the wine!"

"Sure," he said and grabbed the bottle and his own glass. He realized he wasn't very steady on his feet, although Justina appeared unaffected.

As he sat down, she snuggled up close and peered up at him with those big gorgeous eyes.

"Are you going to miss me?"

"Of course I am," he answered and wrapped his arms around her.

She buried her head in his shoulder, curling up almost in his lap, and he held her close. He could tell how contented she was to be held, like a happy kitten, snuggling into him. He stroked her silky hair and sat back against the couch. When he looked up, there it was again, the Christmas tree with its bright cheery lights. He didn't want to think about it, but his mind flashed back to putting up the tree the year before. He did it more to make his mom happy than for himself. He really hadn't cared much about the tree, but it had always mattered to his mom.

Christmas was her thing.

He recalled how she had tried to show interest in it. Even though she was so sick by that time, she was still trying to make him happy. And then she was gone and he had to take the damn thing down. Daniel had taken the tree and all the lights straight out to the curb for the garbage man to pick up so he wouldn't have to see it again. He tried to force those images out of his head and focus on where he was now, but it was getting more difficult. Justina sat up and looked at him, her hair gleaming in the lights from the tree. "Thank you for being here, Daniel. It means a lot. Christmas is hard for me, I know you understand."

He put his hand under her jaw, cupping her face and bringing her closer in, kissing her hard. At first she responded, but then pulled back, looking at him with alarm.

"What's wrong with you, Daniel? You're not acting right." She frowned, her face perplexed. He knew he had been rough with her and he was drunk, depressed, and bitter. The tree and the whole Christmas thing was the last straw, bringing back a fresh wave of painful memories.

"I'm sorry, Justina. I shouldn't be here. I'm not fit company for you tonight. Maybe any night."

Justina looked at him with pure shock on her face.

"I'm an asshole, okay? I'm a screwed up asshole and your dad was right. You need to find a decent guy who will treat you how you deserve. I need to leave."

He moved her off of him and stood up unsteadily, reaching for his jacket.

"Daniel, what is going on with you? I don't think you should be out on your bike, you had too much wine." She looked at him with hurt and confusion spread across her face and he hated himself even more.

"My life is too messed up, Justina. I can't drag you into it and I never should have let it go this far. I'm sorry. I never meant to hurt you. I never meant to hurt anyone," he trailed off. He opened the door, stumbling into the chilly December night.

"Daniel, wait!" She came out on the steps after him, but he waved her back.

"Go inside, Justina. It's cold out here and I need to go. Just forget about me, okay? I'm sorry."

Daniel wouldn't look at her as he started his bike and pulled away. He felt like a jerk, but he just couldn't deal with her or anyone.

He just wanted to curl up in a dark place and be alone.

CHAPTER TWENTY ONE

J ustina stood in the doorway and watched Daniel drive off in disbelief. She couldn't begin to understand what had just happened. She was completely unaware of the chilly night air as she watched as his taillights disappear down the road. What could have caused him to act that way? Everything was going so well—or so she thought.

She finally went back inside and worked on cleaning up the rest of the mess from dinner while the tears trickled down her cheeks. She couldn't believe he had just left like that, with no warning. All this time she had worried about Beth, about her father, but this wasn't about them—she was pretty certain. She replayed the evening in her head, over and over, trying to make sense of it. She was hurt, but also puzzled and wanted to talk to him. She wanted to understand. If she understood, maybe she could help fix whatever was wrong. She went and got the bottle of Muscato out of the living room. *Screw it,* she said to herself and refilled her glass. She felt a headache coming on and tension was building up the back of her neck. She got her bottle of Xanax out and took one, then headed to the living room, plopping down in front of the tree.

The Christmas lights blinked at her in the dark room and she sat staring at them, sipping her wine absently until her eyes started getting heavy. She finally wandered upstairs, falling asleep without even getting undressed.

The next day was Christmas Eve and Victor was coming home. Justina woke up late with a throbbing head and heavy body. She shuffled into the bathroom and stared at herself, trying to care about the mascara smeared all around her eyes and her scraggly hair. Looking at the clock, she sighed and turned on the shower. She stood under the hot water with her eyes closed, willing herself to get moving. She had finally gotten herself showered and dressed when she heard the front door. Her father called out to her. She sighed again, *here we go*, she said to herself, working up a happy face for him.

"Mija, are you here?" Victor called up the stairs.

She came down the stairs, smiling for him. "Hello, Papa!" she went to him and gave him a hug.

"Feliz Navidad," Victor said. "Are you ready to go pretty soon? I just need to get some clean clothes. . ." He trailed off as he noticed the Christmas tree and then said, "What is this? You wanted a tree this year?" He looked at her quizzically.

"I just thought it might be festive," she said, deliberately vague.

"Of course. Whatever you want. You still want to go to the city, right?"

"Yes, I am ready to go, just give me a few minutes. I think it will be wonderful and I look forward to going to church. It will be very nice." She gave him her brightest smile and went back upstairs to pack a small bag.

The drive to the hotel was quiet. Justina didn't have much to say and Victor seemed preoccupied as well. She had tried to ask him about his meetings, but for once he didn't seem inclined to talk about work. Once they were checked in to their adjoining rooms, Victor indicated that he had a couple calls to make so he would knock on her door when he was ready to go out. As soon as she was in her room, Justina pulled out her phone and dialed Daniel. She thought about the night before and how much he had drank. She hoped nothing had happened to him. She fretted to herself about him having an accident or getting in trouble.

No answer. She texted him a message that she wanted to talk to him and asked if he was okay, but again she received no answer.

"What are you doing, Daniel?" she fussed to herself.

She put on her dress and high heels for dinner, and freshened up her makeup, checking the phone every few minutes. When Victor knocked on her door, she still had not heard from Daniel. She tucked the phone and room key in her purse and prepared to go downstairs, as they did every year, to have a couple of drinks and dinner before going to church.

"Ah, you look lovely," Victor said when she came out into the hallway. "I am a lucky man to have such a stunning date!" She smiled at his gallantry and took his arm. After they were seated, Victor pulled a small package out of his jacket pocket. "I have something for you, Justina. I wanted to get a special gift for you this year." He watched in anticipation as she opened the pale blue velvet box, revealing a sparking diamond tennis bracelet.

"Papa, it is so beautiful! Why did you do this? It is so lovely." The diamonds glowed in the dimly lit room and Justina was dazzled by their shine.

Victor smiled, but sadness was also in his eyes. "You are my girl, Justina. It is always a pleasure to buy something beautiful for a lovely woman. I know we have had our disagreements lately and I have not been there for you like I should. I don't think it will get any better any time soon, but I want you to know that I love you and would always prefer to be with you. I hope you know that."

Justina stood up and went over to his side of the table to hug him. "I know Papa. And I love you too." She stepped back slightly, "Can you help me with this?"

She held her slender wrist out for him to fasten the bracelet.

They had a delicious dinner and Justina enjoyed the softly lit ambience and quiet Christmas music being played on a piano. She excused herself a couple of times to go to the ladies room, but there were no texts or calls from Daniel. She knew better than to check her phone in front of her father, especially considering how nice the evening was going. Still, she left the phone in her open bag where she could see if the notification light came on, just in case.

Church service was incredible and Justina lost herself in it. It seemed that the pews were fuller than usual with people packing every available space. *Maybe other people need to be here this year more than usual too*, she thought.

The church itself was so amazing. It was a very old building with vaulted ceilings and candles everywhere, casting a warm glow over all the church goers. She loved the traditions of the church and the Christmas service was particularly uplifting. It made her feel so good to be there and she wished Daniel could be with her. She wondered if he ever went to church, and realized there were many things about him that she didn't know. *And maybe never will*, she thought to herself. Fortunately her thoughts were interrupted by the next part of the program, which involved standing and singing several Christmas songs, so she pushed thoughts of Daniel out of her mind. She loved the spiritual Christmas songs, singing them was always uplifting and, at least temporarily, made her concerns seem insignificant. The sermon on hope and renewal also seemed to have special significance for her this year and she was grateful to be there and to be reminded of her many blessings.

It was very late when they got back to the hotel and Daniel had not called or texted. Justina resolved to try again the next day. She was still very worried about him and didn't intend to leave him alone, despite what he had said. She didn't sleep well that night— her sleep was filled with disturbing dreams that she couldn't remember the next day. She only knew that she felt more tired than she had when she went to bed and she woke up too early. There were still no messages from Daniel. She knew her father wouldn't be ready to go have brunch for at least a couple hours, so Justina got dressed and brushed her hair, heading out in search of a very strong cup of coffee.

She found a coffee shop and ordered a double latte. Finding a seat in the corner, she settled in to watch people and try to reach Daniel. She tried calling again and again, but there was no answer so she sent another text. She went through her e-mails and social media sites, flipping back and forth—checking for messages while she drank her coffee. She eventually went back to the hotel where she knew her father would be ready to have Christmas brunch.

Victor was in very good spirits and they had a leisurely meal before heading back to Long Beach. Christmas Day traffic was light and they were home in no time. Justina immediately went upstairs, telling her father she wanted to lie down for a while, since she hadn't slept well the night before. She immediately called Daniel and again there was no answer. She paced back and forth in her room, having an argument with herself about whether to continue trying to call him. One the one hand, she was thinking about his drinking that night and his odd behavior and she was concerned about him. On the other hand, perhaps he really was done with her and calling him was just a desperate act. She called again anyway.

This time the phone was answered immediately, but it wasn't Daniel. It was Beth. "Hi, Justina?" Beth asked.

Justina didn't answer for a moment, but finally said, "Yes, this is Justina. Is Daniel all right? Why isn't he answering his phone?"

"He's asleep right now," Beth answered. Then she added, "He has pretty much been sleeping since late yesterday. That's why I answered his phone, so you don't keep calling. He's not going to answer."

"Is he sick?" Justina asked. *Why would he be sleeping so long? And why is he with Beth?*

"No, not in the usual sense. Don't you know? His mom died at Christmas. It was a year ago yesterday. He's very depressed."

"Oh my God, he never told me that. No wonder he was so wierded-out the other night. He was acting very odd and I didn't know why…." she trailed off. It really wasn't Beth's business what had happened.

"Yeah, he is taking it very hard. He was just sitting in his kitchen drinking beer and it was freezing cold. I finally got him to come over here. Nobody should be alone at Christmas, especially Daniel, especially this year."

Justina winced. "He wouldn't talk to me," she said defensively.

"I know how he is, but he told me he isn't going to see you anymore. I think you should leave him alone for a while. He has enough on his mind—he doesn't need to worry about you too." Beth added, "I'm not trying to be mean, but he needs to move on. Being around you just makes him feel like a loser and he doesn't need that."

Justina frowned. "When he wakes up can you just let him know that I was worried about him? Please?" She hated begging Beth to give Daniel a message, especially with the way she was acting—so possessive—but apparently there was no other option.

"Yeah, I guess. I just don't want to upset him."

"Just please tell him. Okay? Thanks." Justina hung up before Beth could say anything else.

As soon as she hung up, Justina hurled her phone across the room. It landed unharmed on an overstuffed chair.

"Damn it!" she exploded and paced rapidly back and forth. So many things were going through her head. That stupid Christmas tree. Telling Daniel that Christmas was hard for *her*. That he had clearly been drinking too much and not acting normal. But she had been totally clueless, a spoiled brat.

She went in the bathroom and took a Xanax, trying to calm herself down. She wanted to go to Daniel to apologize, to do *something*. But he was at Beth's. And he didn't want to see her.

In desperation she went looking for Victor. She found him in the living room, reading a journal of some sort. He smiled at her when she came in. "Did you have a good rest?" he asked.

"No, Papa, I didn't. I need to talk to you. And I need you to listen to me without being mean. Okay?" She hated going to him with this. She was so upset, she needed to talk to someone. If her mother were still alive, she would have preferred to talk to her.

Victor took his glasses off and set the magazine aside. "What is it, mija?"

"Please don't yell at me, but it's about Daniel," she said and when she saw his face tighten, she held her hand up. "Please, Papa, I need you to talk to me. I just found out that his mother died on Christmas Eve. I didn't know that and I made it worse. I made a big deal about Christmas and I think I upset him. Now he has been sleeping since yesterday at a neighbor's house and I don't know what to do. I think this is my fault." She looked at him with sad eyes, wanting him to say something to make it right. She felt like she was going to start crying again and concentrated on not doing so.

"Justina, I am sorry. This is not your fault, you know that. When your mother died, it was very hard and holidays were the worst. You understand that. As a child it was different for you, but I can tell you, it is always very difficult. There is nothing for you to do—you need to let him deal with it on his own. There is no cure for grief," Victor said, sadness heavy in his voice.

"Papa, I know you don't like Daniel, but he is a very good person. I can't stand for him to feel worse because of me, don't you understand?"

He sighed and rubbed his temples as though he had a headache. "Justina, it is not that I don't like Daniel. We have been through this. He is just not the right type of person for you. I am sorry for what he is going through, that is a terrible thing for anyone, but there is nothing for you to do about it. And you need to understand that he has to get through this himself. It sounds like he knows that and I expect he knows he isn't in the market for a girlfriend anyhow. You need to leave him alone, he needs to figure out his own life and it is not for you to do." She started to interject, but he stopped her with a shake of the head. "No," he said. "You focus on your future right now and let him alone to figure out his life. It is not the time for either of you. Some day you will see that I am right. I am not trying to be cruel, mija. I am telling you the truth."

She looked at her father in silence, contemplating what he had said. She realized there was some truth in it, but leaving Daniel alone was almost more than she could do. She wanted to help him, Especially now that she knew the whole story about his mother. She wanted to make it better. "Papa, how do you let a person go?" she asked, her voice sad.

"Sometimes you never really can," he answered.

CHAPTER TWENTY TWO

Shortly after Christmas, Justina returned to the city, cat carrier in hand, to go to school. When she got to the apartment, she found out that her roommate had virtually moved out and was staying at her boyfriends' house most of the time. She realized, with some surprise, that she didn't mind being alone, which was new. Besides, she had her cat, who was a constant companion. She found the routine of being back in the city comforting, almost calming, after all the drama and distress she had been exposed to. It was like another planet—one she was used to. Despite her angst about Daniel, she was happy to be back in her own place.

Even though being back in her routine had seemed great at first, she never quit wondering about Daniel. She had hoped that he would call. She knew he was back at school and she should be happy for him because it was important to him, but she still wished he hadn't pushed her out of his life. Even if he was busy he could certainly find time for a quick text if he wanted to, so she knew he meant what he said. She had to let it go and focus on the other part of her life, but at times it was all she could to keep from calling him to tell him how much she missed him and to find out how he was doing.

It wasn't long before she got a welcome distraction from a surprising source—her father. Victor was continuing his work with the Senator who was making inroads with his party and trying hard to address many of the hot-button issues in the country. One of those issues was the relief effort after the storm, which Victor had discussed with Justina in the past. As it turned out, their newly formed committee was going to be doing a lot of work in New York City. Victor immediately thought of his daughter's passion for alleviating the hardships caused by the storm and he asked her if she wanted to be involved. Perhaps she could even get some credit at school as this committee included lawyers, engineers, business people, government agencies, and other community leadership. Justina jumped at the opportunity before even talking to the school. This was exactly what she needed, to do something worthwhile! She knew her father was trying to keep her busy, but she didn't care.

Victor put her in charge of organizing and tracking the meeting discussions and outcomes, and she was quickly swept up in the planning and organizing. It was exciting to be part of something so important and she was completely engrossed in the process. She was starting to understand how her father could be so absorbed in his work— so much was at stake.

When the day of the first formal meeting arrived, Justina was nervous and excited. She had organized the meeting herself and she hoped she hadn't bungled any details. She hadn't done anything like this before so she relied heavily on her father for general direction, but at the same time wanted to show him she could do it so she didn't defer to him as much as she maybe should have.

There were about 20 people in the committee and Justina had their nametags ready along with packets of materials. She greeted them as they came in and everyone was very pleasant, until the last of the check-ins arrived. A woman approached the table and gave her name. Justina didn't recall having her on the list or getting a confirmation that she was attending. Her name was Naomi Johanssen and she was the president of a consumer group on Long Island. She towered over Justina in her stilettos and asked in icy tones why her name wasn't on the list. Naomi's red lips were drawn into a tight, thin line and she tapped her long crimson nails as Justina frantically pulled a new packet of materials together.

How in the world did I screw this up? Justina asked herself, her mind racing to figure it out as she tried to appear in control. Once she had given Naomi everything she needed, she breathed a sigh of relief, but was still anxious and wondering how she had made such a mistake. *I know I never heard from her,* she obsessed silently.

Fortunately she didn't think there were any other opportunities for error, the packets and presentations were ready to go, the food was confirmed, and all she really had to do was listen and take notes. *Okay, I can do this part without screwing up,* she thought. *I am, after all, a law student!* Taking notes was all she did most days.

The morning went by quickly and Justina became focused on the discussion and presentations of the group.

This is so cool, she thought to herself. *I almost understand Papa now!* It was fascinating to see and hear a group of people so focused on something she cared about. The food showed up on time and was enjoyed by everyone, so she figured her worries were over. Then disaster struck.

During lunch, Justina took a peek at the agenda to refresh her memory of the afternoon's topics. To her horror, she saw that Naomi was scheduled to give a presentation right after lunch. Justina knew she had never received anything from the woman and couldn't recall any discussion about it with Victor. *Oh my God, not again!* She felt the panic rising in stomach and spreading throughout her body, making it difficult to breathe. There was only one thing to do—go to Naomi and ask if there was a presentation.

Justina looked forward to that conversation about as much as a public execution.

She looked around, but the woman was nowhere to be seen. Everyone had finished eating and had taken their last few minutes to go out and make phone calls or check e-mails, so the only people in the room were the catering staff who were cleaning up. Justina went back through her e-mails and lists and, sure enough, Naomi was on her original list. But she couldn't find anything she ever received from her. *Crap.* She should have followed up on non-responders. Her father was going to be mortified. She already felt miserable.

As the lunch period drew to a close, everyone gradually came in and took their seats. Just like in the morning, Naomi was the last to show up. *Probably sharpening her fangs to take a bite out of me,* Justina thought. Naomi waited until everyone was seated to make her entrance. Justina followed her up to the podium and asked her if she had sent in a presentation, because it had not been received. Justina could feel her hand shaking. She gripped the podium so it wouldn't show.

"You don't have my presentation?" Naomi demanded—loud enough that nobody would miss hearing it.

"I'm sorry, I have double checked everything and it was never received. I don't know what to tell you."

"Don't you think that, perhaps, if someone is on the agenda you should make sure you have their presentation?" Naomi snapped loudly, "What do you propose we do about this?"

"Excuse me, Ms. Johanssen, I have it on a flash drive," a young man who had been sitting along the side of the room in the back approached them. He fished around in the breast pocket of his jacket and produced the flash drive. He quickly got it loaded, giving Justina a quick smile as he deftly brought it up on the screen.

"Well, I'm glad to see that someone was paying attention," Naomi stated. "Thank you, Eric."

"Yes, thank you," Justina repeated. "And again, I apologize," she said, retreating as fast as she could.

She saw that her father, who was at the back of the room conferring with the Senator, appeared to have partially caught the exchange and she shot him an apologetic grimace as she took her seat.

Her heart was racing and her hand shaking as she struggled to focus. Regardless of any other screw-ups, she absolutely had to get the notes of this presentation correct and she felt too rattled to think straight. She got through it though, and fortunately the rest of the afternoon was uneventful.

Justina felt humiliated, though, and horrified for her father who had brought her in for her own benefit. Now she had publicly muffed it. When the meeting was over for the day, the group adjourned into the next room for appetizers and drinks. Justina did not really feel like mingling after her screw-ups and anyway, she was just a student, not one of these people. She got a glass of wine and found a corner where she could observe and wait for her father. She wished she had brought her Xanax with her! She knew he would talk to her when he could and she wasn't sure how he would react. She was mulling over the possible scenarios when her rescuer from earlier approached.

"Hey, have you recovered yet?" he asked, smiling.

"Oh, hi. No, I'm not recovered. My Dad hasn't had a go at me yet! But thanks for the help earlier. I can't imagine how that would have gone if you hadn't had that flash drive. I just can't figure out why I never got her stuff. What a nightmare!" She rolled her eyes, still feeling tense and not quite ready to laugh about it yet.

He laughed, a deep, warm laugh. "She's a crazy bitch, trust me, I work for her. And you know the worst part? I would bet she has her own flash drive in her briefcase, but she wanted to nail you. That's how she is." He paused for a moment, thinking, then asked, "Did you check your spam filter? I bet your computer blocked her for some reason. Check that and see." A waiter came by with a tray of mini crab cakes and Eric took a cocktail napkin and several of the appetizers. He held the napkin out to Justina, "Crab ball?" he asked with a wicked grin.

The way he said it made her laugh. "Yeah, sure."

"Anyhow," he said, "I haven't introduced myself. I'm Eric. I work for the evil queen. And you are?"

She swallowed her mouthful of crab and said, "Justina. My Dad is Victor Gonzalez—he works for Senator Goldberg. That's how I ended up here."

"I wondered how they found such a beautiful coordinator," he said, again with that charming, wicked grin.

"Yeah, and such an incompetent one. My father must be so proud. Fortunately he's been too busy to rip me up yet." She felt another flash of panic as she thought about it and took a big gulp of wine.

"Don't worry about it. Those things happen to all of us now and then, it's part of life. You just should have picked someone other than Naomi!" He noticed her glass was nearly empty and said, "Let's wander over to the bar. I'm feeling quite thirsty!"

Justina couldn't say no. Eric was gorgeous—he was tanned with black hair, perfectly cut, and he had stunning blue eyes that sparkled. He was not very tall, but powerfully built...and his smile. He had perfect teeth inside that wicked grin. He was young and she wondered what kind of work he did, so she asked.

"I'm just an intern," he said. "I'm nearly done with my Masters in Public Administration. I love politics, that's where I want to be, so I'm working with the consumer advocacy group for this quarter. It's been an interesting experience, I can say that!" Again—that smile.

She smiled too and said, "Despite my father, or maybe because of him, I'm not so into politics. In fact, my father and I often disagree. I'm in law school and I'm very interested in this particular issue that was discussed today. I did some work in a local hospital right after the storm, so my father knows the recovery efforts matter to me a whole lot."

"Wow, law school. Good for you! You will make a gorgeous lawyer. I'll call you when I get sued!" He laughed easily and Justina found herself relaxing and enjoying the conversation— that is until she saw her father approaching. "Oh boy, here we go." She said.

Victor, however, was at his most charming, apparently not wanting to berate his daughter until they were alone. "Hello, you two. Enjoying the wine?" he asked smoothly, looking at Eric with a question on his face.

"Papa, this is Eric, he works for Naomi Johanssen—my new best friend." She said, trying to keep reference to the afternoon debacle light.

Eric extended his hand and greeted Victor warmly. "Sir, very nice to meet you. You and the Senator are doing a great thing here. I've been honored to participate." Justina marveled at how quickly Eric transformed from flirt to schmoozer and thought he probably was cut out for politics. She had seen her father turn it on and off the same way. She knew she had a long way to go before she was that polished.

After the pleasantries were exchanged, Victor told Justina he would catch up with her later; he had some things to go over with the Senator. She assured him that was fine and was marginally relieved that the discussion would be postponed. Perhaps by the time they caught up it would seem less awful.

As soon as Victor left the room, Eric resumed his previous persona. "So, I can send you the presentation from today if you'd like. It would probably help with the notes. But. . ." he paused for effect. "It comes at a price. I'd like you to have dinner with me sometime soon." He smiled his charming smile, eyebrows cocked, waiting for her response.

Justina couldn't help feeling flattered. . .and she did want that presentation. She agreed before even stopping to think about it. She had no sooner given him her phone number and e-mail address before Naomi beckoned Eric.

"Oops," he said. "Gotta go. I'll call you soon to collect that dinner!"

CHAPTER TWENTY THREE

As soon as Eric walked away, Justina wondered how wise it would be to see him for dinner. He seemed pretty smooth. Then she reminded herself that it was just dinner and she didn't have any commitment—certainly Daniel had made that clear. So why not have dinner with an attractive guy and get help with her notes in the process? She shrugged it off and thought to herself that it would be nice to go out, she hadn't done much of anything in a while. Her father called later on, wanting to meet for coffee the next morning before his meetings started. Justina grimaced to herself, but agreed. She knew she didn't really have a choice.

The conversation with her father the next morning was not at all what she was expecting. First of all, Victor barely mentioned the incident.

"Nice work yesterday," he said. "I know you haven't done anything like that before, good job. And don't worry too much about Naomi. Everyone knows she is difficult and she loves nothing more than to put a pretty girl in her place! She's a nasty piece of work, but she's important to our fundraising, her connections are very necessary." Justina nodded, nibbling on a bagel and letting him talk. He continued, on a different note entirely. "Her intern, Eric, seems like a very bright young man and he likes you. I will bet he is going to be successful—he clearly knows what he wants. Did he ask you out?" Not one to dance around a topic, Victor had clearly picked up on Eric's flirtatious attitude, even if only from across the room.

Justina felt herself squirming and her face was warming up uncomfortably. She so wished her father would leave things like this alone, but he never would. "He asked me to dinner," she admitted. "He is also giving me Naomi's presentation to help with my meeting minutes." She waited for his commentary, which was sure to follow.

Right on cue, Victor gave his opinion. "I think that's wonderful. You should be going out with young men like that, enjoy yourself. You have the whole world to pick from. I am very glad to hear that." He didn't mention Daniel at all, but he didn't need to—his meaning was clear.

"Papa, it's just dinner. Someone like him probably has a different date every night. It's no big deal, okay? I am not looking to get on the party train. Okay?" she attempted to get him to drop it, which he did, having made his point.

By lunchtime Justina received an e-mail from Eric with Naomi's presentation attached. "I'll call you later today," his note said, "I look forward to seeing you again." She was pleased that he followed up so quickly and was being so charming. *Not like some people,* she thought with sadness and a little bitterness.

True to his word, Eric called in the early evening to set up a date. "Can you do dinner Friday?" he asked. "I want to see you as soon as possible!" She was surprised—Friday was prime time and only two days away. How could a guy like that be open on a Friday night in New York? It didn't seem plausible, but she had to admit she was kind of excited.

"Yeah, I think I can do Friday," she said, not wanting to appear too eager. "Should I meet you somewhere?"

"No, no," he said instantly. "I will pick you up, no point in making you drive around the city when I invited you out! That would be bad form! Tell me where you live and I will be there at 6:00."

She gave him her address and general directions and then asked, "Where are we going, so I know what to wear?"

He chuckled. "Of course, the most important question, what to wear! Just wear something nice, but not formal, don't go to a lot of trouble. You will look amazing whatever you wear! I will surprise you with where we go, I haven't decided yet."

Wow, she thought. *He never lets up with the charm.* She laughed and agreed. Once they hung up, Justina was already considering her closet and finding it sadly lacking in attractive options. After spending the rest of the evening going through her wardrobe, when she should have been studying, Justina decided on a simple black dress and gold accessories. She hadn't had a real date in a very long time and had kind of forgotten how much fun it was.

She tried not to think about Daniel, except to tell herself that he told her to be on her own. This was only dinner anyway.

Friday night arrived and Justina was ready and waiting at six. Actually, she was ready and waiting shortly after 5, just in case he was early. She wouldn't want to get caught in a bathrobe.

Eric was precisely on time, looking sophisticated in a navy blazer, neatly pressed khaki pants, and beautiful Italian leather shoes. Justina always noticed a man's shoes. Eric immediately told her how stunning she looked, making her blush a little, and escorted her to his sleek black sports car.

The restaurant he took her to was a very small, intimate Italian restaurant. She didn't know the city all that well, and wasn't even sure where they were, but it was a wonderful place with softly lit tables and Frank Sinatra playing in the background. Eric was a charming dinner companion and he ordered a bottle of wine almost immediately. The waiter seemed to know Eric—they were friendly, chatting back and forth. Justina thought how at home he seemed. Confidence just oozed out of him and he was constantly engaging, asking her about her father, school, and other basic getting-to-know-you type of questions.

Finally she asked, "What about you? You are having me do all the talking!" she was curious where he came from and what his story was.

"You are doing all the talking because I love to hear you and I want to know all about you! My story is not interesting. My family lives in Cape May, New Jersey. You know Cape May?" She nodded and he continued. "I grew up there and my parents and sister are still there, but I wanted a faster pace. I love the city and politics in particular. So here I am, going to school and hoping to work my way into a cool job. I'm done with school at the end of this quarter. That's it—that's my story. Not too exciting." He smiled wickedly—completely contradicting his self-assessment.

"Where were you when the storm hit?" Justina asked. To her the storm was still hugely important as she assumed it must be to everyone living in the region.

"I was in the city when it hit," he answered. "Cape May, along with other areas in Jersey, was evacuated. By some miracle, though, the homes are mostly unharmed. My family is fine. They had a tree down on the corner of the garage and they were lucky." He didn't seem overly concerned about the storm. Justina figured he probably hadn't seen what she had seen. She wondered a bit about the way he had poured it on to her father about the importance of the relief work they were organizing, but she knew he was ambitious and would of course say that.

When he dropped her off, he walked her to the door and took her hand, kissing it in an old fashioned gesture. "I would love to see you again," he said. "I enjoyed your company tonight so much. Can we go out again?" Again, Justina agreed without even thinking about it. She had thoroughly enjoyed her evening too and felt like she could get used to this sort of treatment.

He called several days later to set up another date for the coming weekend. This time he took her to dinner and then a small jazz club. They did a little dancing, but mostly talked and relaxed, which was easy to do in the club's relaxed atmosphere. When he took her home she thought she might at least get a kiss, but he just kissed her hand and touched her cheek softly, telling her he had a wonderful time and would call soon.

Justina had never been treated this way and was a bit overwhelmed. *This is what it's supposed to be like,* she thought to herself. *I've heard of this dating thing. I didn't think it really existed anymore!* She thought about her limited range of previous experiences and realized they were sadly lacking in many respects. Daniel didn't really fit in that category though—that situation was so different. They were never really dating. She didn't know how to classify it.

She didn't want to think about Daniel anyhow—it was upsetting to her. On the one hand she felt rejected because he had ended whatever it was that they had, but on the other hand she felt guilty for dating Eric. She tried to push it out of her head, she would deal with that tomorrow.

One problem with having a social life was that her schoolwork was starting to slide. She decided to go home for the weekend, see her father, and catch up on her studying. She knew her grades were going to drop if she didn't get back on track quickly. When she got the inevitable call from Eric, she declined and explained her reasons for going home. He made all the appropriate groans and sighs of disappointment, but said he certainly understood. She wondered how he managed to keep his grades up with all the schmoozing he did.

She didn't want to admit to herself that she was hoping maybe Daniel would be home. She told herself she needed a break and to see Victor and maybe Mona and Willie. But the hope of "running into" Daniel was lurking in the back of her brain, where she forced it to remain.

Her first agenda when she got into town was to see how things looked—how the cleanup was going. Long Beach looked pretty good except, of course, the boardwalk was totally gone and not yet replaced. All that remained were the concrete underpinnings stretched along the beach like a giant skeleton. The beach just didn't look right without it, she thought sadly, and wondered how long it would take to put a new one in. The other thing that made Justina sad was that, judging by all the boarded up homes and businesses, many people had not returned home yet. There were many homes with large dumpsters in front, out of which boards and sheetrock were protruding. *How many years will it take to get back to normal?* She wondered.

She then drove over to Far Rockaway. Things there did not look noticeably better although, admittedly, she hadn't been gone that long. So many homes still looked uninhabitable and there was still more trash piled up in yards than one would expect to see. The neighborhood was clearly still in a state of distress. She took a few pictures with her phone camera, thinking she would show her father what things were like as of now. He and other Committee members had toured various areas affected by the storm, but she didn't know if they realized how little had been achieved at this point—a couple months later.

Her next stop was to see Mona. She missed her friend's wisdom and humor. As they talked, she deliberately didn't tell Mona anything about Daniel. That was still a painful subject and she didn't want to talk about it. Besides, she was hoping it would straighten itself out. It felt really nice to be back at the hospital and to realize how many friends she had there.

Willie was delighted to see her, as well, and was looking really well—the best she looked since Justina had known her. It was obvious that getting the right care and food was helping her a great deal. She still complained about the "healthy" diet, but she was obviously happy. Justina was glad to see her in such good spirits, although she felt a pang when Willie told her that Daniel and Beth had been by to see her the week before. Justina wondered if they had gotten back together. It seemed like Daniel was with Beth all the time.

She decided to drive past Daniel's house, just in case he was home. She knew she shouldn't and that he probably wouldn't be there, but she couldn't help herself. Her heart about stopped when she came around the corner and saw Daniel's truck out front instead of in the back, where he usually left it when he was gone. *Oh my god*, she said to herself, suddenly terrified of what she would say to him.

She didn't need to worry, however. As she got closer to the house, it wasn't Daniel who came out—it was Beth. She emerged with a toolbox, carefully locked the door behind her, and hopped into the truck.

CHAPTER TWENTY FOUR

W hen she got back to her apartment in the city, there was a card waiting under her door. She immediately knew it was from Eric. The note card had a floral design on the front. Inside it said, *Welcome back! I missed you over the weekend!* Justina smiled to herself and tucked the card into her purse. That guy was relentless!

She thought about how lucky she was that Eric had shown up in her life when he did. It was pretty clear that Beth and Daniel were closer than ever—she was apparently driving his truck and going in and out of his house like she owned it. Thank God Beth hadn't seen Justina that day! It was very painful to think about, so she pushed the image out of her head. She couldn't take any more agonizing over it. She had already screwed up her planned studying by fretting over Beth and Daniel most of the weekend. She turned her phone off that night, took a long hot bath, and did some much-needed reading. Hercules made it known all evening that he did not appreciate so much time alone.

Eric called the next day and invited her out for the following Saturday. He was charming as ever, which reminded Justina that she did enjoy being treated like she was special and appreciated. Several weeks went by and she continued to see Eric on the weekends. He continued to be charming, but nothing more than that.

She was kept quite busy, trying to keep up with classes and work with her father and the Relief Committee. Her minutes from that first meeting had apparently met everyone's approval because she didn't hear anything back to the contrary, even from Naomi. She did have her father review the notes before passing them along and she knew that if there was a problem, Naomi would be the first to complain. She became more comfortable in her role and enjoyed all she was learning and all the people she was getting to know.

One of the things she was working on was organizing a big fundraiser. She was getting guidance on it from a few different committee members, since she had never done anything like this before. It was exciting to be involved. The fundraiser was to be a big formal dinner and auction at one of the better hotels in the city. The committee members all gave her names of various donors to invite and she kept very busy putting those lists together and issuing invitations.

Eric was involved in the fundraiser too and the two of them spoke regularly about it, in addition to going on their regular dates. Justina continued to be impressed with Eric's ability to strategize—he seemed to have an innate ability to figure out an angle for anything. She had to admit, it was a form of brilliance. It was no wonder that her father liked him so much—he definitely had the skillset to be a great politician.

She still wasn't sure why Eric was pursuing her, although he hadn't really made any significant moves on her. He kept things warm, gave her a goodnight kiss after their date, but seemed determined to not try for more. She wondered if it was because of her father and figured it probably was. If he crossed the line with her and she told her father, it could work against him. He was shrewd enough to be careful that way—she could see that.

As the fundraiser drew near, Justina started working out the seating. She was a little surprised when her father invited her and Eric to sit with him, Senator Goldberg, and the Senator's wife. When she expressed her surprise, Victor indicated it was the Senator's idea. "Justina, right now the optics are very important for the Senator and it helps him to have the Latino demographic at his table. You know that these races are very tight and, if Senator Goldberg is going to get the nomination, he needs to have every demographic supporting him." Her father didn't seem perturbed by this and Justina wondered if this was the reason he was in the role of advisor to the senator from the start. She realized again that she had a lot to learn about how the world worked.

Eric was beside himself when he learned of the arrangement—he could barely contain himself. "Naomi is going to be pissed!" He chuckled evilly, "You know what she would do to be sitting at that table? And what an honor to be sharing dinner with, perhaps, the next Presidential candidate and his wife! I have barely met him and now I have a chance to get to know him a bit. Wow!" Justina could see that he wouldn't be thinking of anything else until after the event, he was already plotting his strategies for making an impression.

When the day of the event arrived, Justina was terrified that she would make a mistake on an even bigger and more public scale than before. She went over everything with her various resources on the committee, as well as her father and Eric, and it seemed all was in order.

She spent the afternoon at the salon, getting her nails done and her hair piled up atop her head and fastened with little rhinestone clips. She was excited, but terrified as she put on her pale blue beaded dress. The thin straps and up-do showed off her smooth shoulders and graceful neck to great advantage. She thought with satisfaction that at least if she screwed up, she looked good. Hopefully that would help, although she suspected it would be a disadvantage with Naomi!

Her father arrived at her apartment early to take her to the event. As they were getting ready to leave, her father surprised her with a velvet box. "I want you to wear this, mija," he said, and opened it to reveal a stunning diamond choker. "It was your mother's. I think you should have it and it would be gorgeous with your dress. You look beautiful, I am so proud of you," he said, his voice thick with emotion. He fastened the necklace on her and she looked in the mirror, admiring it.

"It's gorgeous, Papa!" she said, getting a little choked up as well. "Thank you so much!"

"Sometimes you look so much like her," he said, his eyes resting on her face in a combination of pride and sadness.

"Papa, don't do this, okay?" she asked, not wanting to get teary-eyed. It always affected her when her father was like this—it was so rare—he was normally so strong and in control. "I don't want to ruin my makeup, so don't make me cry!" She gave a little faltering laugh, but it served to break the moment.

Her father had hired a car and driver and he ceremoniously held out his arm to her to escort her to the car. She noted with pride how handsome her father was in his tuxedo, his black hair greying just a bit the temples, his skin smooth and freshly shaved. She wondered why he hadn't found a girlfriend; he was certainly a distinguished gentleman and had plenty of choices.

They arrived early at the event, since they were responsible for making sure everything was running smoothly. Her father helped her sort out what she needed to do to greet people and get them oriented and then he went off to handle the media who were already there, hoping to get an early peek at the various VIPs arriving.

Eric and Naomi showed up shortly thereafter. Eric looked gorgeous in his tuxedo and Naomi looked as dangerous as ever in her form-fitting red dress, slit almost all the way up to her hip. She gave Justina a chilly greeting and quickly moved away, clearly signaling that Justina was not worth even a minute of pleasantries. Eric looked at Justina and shrugged with his characteristic evil grin. "Wow!" he said, giving her an up and down perusal. "You look so hot! How come your Dad's not here watching over you to make sure all these corrupt political types don't eat you up?"

She giggled. "You got him figured out, all right. He's dealing with the media vultures, I guess they are a bigger danger!" She motioned across the foyer where her father was engaged with several reporters, presumably advising them of the protocols for the evening.

"You have done great with this guest list," Eric commented. "Everyone who is anyone is here!" His eyes were shining with excitement.

"Thanks. You know, your Governor from New Jersey is here too, since New York and New Jersey are collaborating on these events. You should probably go meet him! You never know, he could be a Presidential candidate as well," she pointed out, knowing that Eric would be making an immediate beeline to the Governor. She thought how funny he was, so predictable!

Eric winked at her, "Yes, you are right! I also need to go keep tabs on Naomi. She's trying hard not to show how annoyed she is that I am at the "important" table and she's not! So I'm sucking up. I think I am going to be helping people check in, so I better go do my job. If I don't see you again, I'll see you at the table!" He gave her a wink and a leer, quickly heading off to do his duty.

Victor came over moments later. "I want to you help steer people into the banquet room," he instructed. "There are several bars set up in there so we can keep people contained and that way it will be easier to get them seated in a timely fashion. We want everyone seated in advance of the opening speeches so that the reporters can get photos of the guests before the events begin. I've told the reporters that they cannot circulate during the speeches and auctions—they are only allowed to circulate before and after and can only take pictures from the back of the room. We don't need this to be a media circus. Okay?" Justina loved seeing her father like this—organized and all business. It was very impressive. "Yes, Sir!" She said.

"Just be wary of the dirty old men and wolves," he admonished, his tone not entirely joking, and she thought of Eric's comment moments before. Her father was nothing if not consistent.

"I know, I know," she said, having heard similar warnings before.

He raised an eyebrow at her. "I'll be watching. It's an open bar and not everyone behaves, so be aware. Some of these men think they can do whatever they want—they have money and power and you are a beautiful young woman. If you have a problem, come to me or go to the security staff and we'll handle it discreetly. Understand?"

She could see he was not joking. She realized he'd been at many of these events and had probably seen plenty of bad behavior. "Yes, Papa. I understand," she said.

Nobody gave her any trouble other than some harmless flirting and compliments, which she didn't find at all offensive. At the designated time she began circulating and encouraging stragglers to go to the banquet room. She found that once they knew there was a bar in there, they went willingly.

Once that was accomplished, she got herself a glass of wine and headed to the table. Eric was already there and soon the Senator's wife approached. Eric immediately jumped up and went around the table, pulling out her chair and introducing himself. *He's shameless,* Justina thought with amusement. Eric was on—the charm, politically correct comments, and amusing observations were flowing from him and the Senator's wife was clearly entertained by him.

Soon the Senator, Victor, and the Senator's public relations advisor—a beautiful blonde named Marci—joined them. Despite being seated between two very attractive young women, Eric was so laser-focused on the Senator and his wife that Justina had to suppress a smile. He was amusing, though, and everyone enjoyed his running commentary and witticisms.

Once the tables convened, the reporters started circulating. This was a big deal at her table and their group was posed in various standing and sitting arrangements for photographs, some were taken of the whole table and some were only of the Senator and his wife. Justina thought it amusing that Eric put his arm around her possessively for the shots including them. She was surprised he didn't try to get in between the Senator and his wife!

The evening was a huge success, with over a million dollars raised for the storm relief effort. Everyone ended the night with a stomach full of surf and turf and too many drinks. Guests were glowing and laughing as they gathered their coats and handed their tickets to the valets.

As Justina waited her turn in the ladies room before leaving, she pondered how many dye jobs and diamonds were in the room. It was pretty impressive, but her mind flashed to the waiting room at the hospital and the people there who couldn't get medicine or food. The contrast made her sad, although she knew that this group had just laid out a lot of money that would hopefully help the other group.

She was reflecting on this when she came out and looked for her father. As she rounded a corner toward the lobby, she spotted her father and Eric. She would have broken right into their conversation, except she heard her name.

"Well, that's Justina," her father was saying. "She's very smart, but she does have a very soft heart."

Justina stopped and stepped back, trying to listen. She'd never actually seen her father and Eric having any sort of discussion before, and didn't know they were on such close terms. Eric made some response she couldn't hear, but her father said, "No, I am fine with you seeing her. I want you to see her. She needs someone like you who knows what they want and is working toward it. So yes, by all means." Justina's jaw dropped. Her father was telling Eric to see her! But it got worse.

Eric's laugh was soft. "Thank you, sir. I just didn't want to make any mistakes that could cost me an opportunity to work with you and the Senator. I would be honored to help his campaign any way I could. If you are happy with me seeing your daughter, it is no hardship for me—she is a lovely girl and I like her very much. You must be very proud of her."

Her father nodded, pleased. "Yes, of course. She is my pride and joy and I only want the best for her, so you treat her right. I'm glad we understand each other."

"Yes, Sir," Eric said, then quickly added, "Oh, there's my car. Thank you for the discussion, I will see you next week?"

"Yes, I will see you then," Victor affirmed and Eric hurried outside to collect his car.

CHAPTER TWENTY FIVE

Justina couldn't move—she just stood there, cheeks hot and eyes burning. She turned and went back to the ladies' room, unwilling to face her father. Fortunately the crowd in there had dissipated. Justina leaned against the sink, looking at herself in the mirror. Her eyes were glittering, but otherwise she looked the same—lovely dress, jewelry, and hair, nothing out of place—which was unbelievable considering how she felt. She took several deep breaths and tried to calm herself at least enough to make it to the car before she came unglued. She put a little powder on her hot cheeks, took one last deep breath, and headed out to join her father for the long ride home.

Victor was by the door, chatting with the driver as they waited for her. "Well, there you are," he said affably. "You know you didn't have to get all prettied up for the ride home!" he joked. He moved to take her arm but she pulled away, giving him a tight, cold smile. She quickly stepped outside and went around to the other side of the car, which had been pulled up right outside the door. She waited for the driver to let her in.

As soon as they were settled in the car, Victor asked, "Honey, what's wrong?"

She looked at his handsome, smooth face, which seemed softer in the soft glow of streetlights coming through the windows. He looked so concerned, which somehow made her even angrier. "I really don't feel like talking right now," she said curtly. She knew once she started she would lose it completely and she was so angry she didn't even have the words to describe how she was feeling, anyhow.

He frowned, looking puzzled. "Everything went beautifully tonight. You should be very proud of the job you did in helping put that together. We raised much money for the relief efforts and I received many compliments for my beautiful and talented daughter! You have nothing to be upset about."

"No?" she asked, unable to contain it anymore. "Not even my father bargaining over me like a piece of meat? You don't think I should be upset about that? What, are you giving Eric a job in return for him taking me out and being an 'appropriate' boyfriend, so I don't do something stupid and date the wrong person? God forbid I should make my own decisions and date someone who isn't a social climber!"

"Justina, what are you saying? What did I do? I never told Eric to date you. What is this about?"

She could hear in his voice that he knew what she was upset about, but was going to downplay it—like she misunderstood. She was so tired of being treated like a stupid little girl. "You know what? It doesn't matter. You can have Eric and your committee and all of that. I'm done. You and Eric can weave your little plots and strategies, but leave me out of it. I will make my own decisions about my life, so don't worry about it. I'm done," she said again.

"Justina. Honey, Eric is trying to make his way in this world—there is nothing wrong with that. He likes you and that's a separate issue. I really don't understand what you are upset about. I like him, he's smart and ambitious."

"Oh, he's smart and ambitious all right. So much so that as soon as he found out who my father was he wanted to date me. And he was very careful to be Mr. Appropriate so that my father would never disapprove, God forbid. Then he could suck up to you for a job. And you want him to date me so I forget about Daniel! You think I don't know what you're trying to do? Please!" She finished in disgust and turned away from him, pointedly staring out the window.

"That's not how it is, honey. We should talk about this more when you are calm. You are upset and now is not the time to talk." His voice remained calm and soothing, but his words got another response from her.

"Yes, I'm upset, but don't you dare act like I am over-reacting or hysterical! I am not going to be a pawn in you or Eric's power games. That's it. There's nothing else to say." She didn't want to hear anything else from him. All he would do is try to placate her by minimizing what had happened and she was far too humiliated to hear it. Victor remained quiet after that, knowing any further discussion would be useless, and he dropped her off at her apartment.

Justina couldn't believe she had been so stupid. She knew Eric was totally focused on getting ahead and she had even suspected he was treating her carefully because of her father. Why didn't she realize he had used her to get close to Victor? *How stupid could I be? How could I not have seen that? Because I didn't want to,* she answered herself. She had felt abandoned by Daniel, so she allowed herself to be taken around and treated like a princess. She allowed herself to buy into it because she needed to believe it. *Idiot,* she told herself. She resolved to call Daniel the next day and not to let her own insecurities get in the way of anything with him.

She slept very poorly that night, drifting in and out of restless and agitated dreams. Half awake, she felt like she was spinning, alone, unconnected to anyone or anything. She couldn't forgive

Eric, who clearly used her; She couldn't forgive her father, who was meddling and trying to control her; and she couldn't go to Daniel with any of it because she had been so stupid and immature in the first place—she could never admit to him what had happened. Daniel would never be able to understand any of it. She especially missed her mother at times like this, when she knew she had screwed up and needed some advice or at least someone to listen to her and not judge her.

Once she had given up on sleep and had gotten up, she decided that her next best option would be to call Mona. She felt like she had made so many mistakes, she needed her friend's wise perspective because clearly hers wasn't all that useful.

Mona was practical as usual. "You know that's your daddy. He don't mean no harm, he's taking care of his princess. He's not coming from an evil place—he thinks he's taking care of you. He's the man and you're the little girl. And it don't matter no how, you're all he has, and vice versa. You can't trade in your daddy and that's who he is, you must find a way to deal with him without losing your sweet self. That's all."

"I know what you're saying, but it's like I can't make any decision unless he approves—otherwise, see what he does? He will try to sabotage me. I feel like if I am close to him, he won't let me breathe. How can I ever grow up and have a life with that? It's crazy." Justina was so frustrated that she couldn't really explain how her father was. Anyone who had not experienced it couldn't understand how he just took over and controlled everything. She didn't see how she could be close to him and still move on in her life and make her own decisions.

"Honey. You are so open and trusting, your heart is all on your face. You should try to have a life of your own without lying to him, but without letting him in the middle of it. You can't get rid of him, that's your daddy and you know you love him. No matter what other people say or do, family is family and blood is blood. That's the way it is. Your daddy understands that—he understands the family ties—but he doesn't think you are an adult yet and he has nobody else. And he's the macho guy. No little girl could ever know more than him about what is best. You just need to remember that and adjust yourself."

Justina thought about it for a minute. "You are right about family and the whole macho thing. And I do love him and I know he adores me but I have a right to a life, too. I just need to think about this and not bring him into it. You're right. I do let him know everything, like a little girl with no secrets. I guess it's time to be more discreet, at least until I figure out what I am doing!"

"That's right, girl. Now, with respect to this Eric guy. Cut his ass loose. He is no good for you—he is all about himself. You know that and your gut is right. He just played you like a pro. It's not your fault, you were all hurt because you wanted Daniel to drop everything and be your love slave." She tut-tutted as Justina started to protest. "No, it's true. You were hurt and looking to feel better. Daniel is his own man and he won't be with you unless he thinks he is worthy of it and taking care of himself. Daniel needs to have self-respect and he's been in a bad place. You probably never knew a man like that and you took it all personal. You should appreciate that kinda man. He will never be with you because of who your daddy is. And he won't ever live off of you. Maybe you think that doesn't matter because you would do anything for him. Trust Mona on this one, you won't love him long if you have to take care of him and he's not doing anything. He knows that. I know that. You just haven't learned it yet. Trust me and trust him. If you can't respect each other and be equals, there will never be a future. But don't waste no more time with Eric. He is not worthy of you. You are hot stuff and he knows it, but he wants to use that for his own gain. No good."

Justina thought for a moment, chewing her lip. Finally, she said, "you know, you are right. I've never wanted something or someone that I couldn't have, which makes me a spoiled brat, I know. I've had a few reminders of that lately. I'm done with Eric, no doubt. He's a jerk. Did he think I would be too stupid or weak to figure him out or that with all his charm he could work around it? Or maybe he thought we would be a good pair of schmoozers. Really, it's so insulting. I would have figured him out. I already knew he would do whatever it took to get ahead. But what to do about Daniel?"

"You don't do anything. He told you what he needs to do and you need to respect that. He's a man; he needs to know that he can take care of himself and anything or anyone else. You should appreciate that. He's a real man, not someone who will use you to get by or to get ahead. Just be there if he wants you, for now, and let him do what he needs to do. Quit worrying about the men and figure out your own life. Those men ain't goin' nowhere, trust me. You're such a little hottie, gonna be a lawyer. Are you kidding? Relax and let it go. Whatever should be will be, just go with it. That's the best advice I can give you. Okay?"

It was hard for Justina to agree to Mona's advice. She wanted to *do* something. She was so upset about the whole situation, but she knew Mona was right and that was the reason she had called her in the first place. Mona was very wise about these sorts of things, something that Justina apparently was not. She missed her friend a great deal, especially during chats like this, when she realized she wasn't close to anyone else who she could confide in. At least not anybody who she felt gave wise advice.

As they got off the phone, Justina agreed to stay in touch and to come to the hospital again next time she was home. She thought maybe she would go home sooner rather than later and get a little more time with Mona, smooth over things with her father, and go see Willie again. At least Mona helped her to refocus her energies. She set to work on something she could control—her homework—with a promise to herself she would get her act together and then call Daniel.

CHAPTER TWENTY SIX

Daniel had thought a lot during his trip back to Maryland for college. He thought about Justina and the disastrous evening they had shared. He had plenty of guilt about what had happened, but also sadness at leaving her. He hoped that when he got to Maryland he would be able to refocus his thoughts and move toward his goals. He did not intend to muddy his time at school with relationship issues and was planning to take a really heavy load of courses to finish sooner.

Daniel found an internship project that focused on building housing for the poor and he immediately volunteered. He could get the experience he was looking for and it would give him the satisfaction of doing something meaningful as well. His schedule was quickly filled with classes, work on actual housing development projects, and homework. He reconnected with a couple of classmates he had been friends with before, and soon he was completely embroiled in his new/old life.

He moved back in with his friend Marcos, who always kept him entertained. Marcos was in perpetual motion. He did great at school, but never seemed to do any homework. It would cut into his time playing soccer and going to parties with hot dates! He got Marcos up to speed about the whole Justina drama, leaving out some of the embarrassing moments. Marcos said he was happy to hear it because he was always trying to get Daniel to lighten up and be more sociable. Daniel realized how much he had missed his guy friends, especially Marcos, and was feeling really good about focusing on his new/old life. That is until he got a call from Beth.

"Daniel, your little friend made the local news. She was at some fancy fundraiser and it looks like she had a pretty hot date. I don't suppose you've seen the paper down there in Maryland? It has gotten all sorts of coverage here in Rockaway, since the event benefitted storm victims..." She trailed off, waiting to hear Daniel's response.

"No, I haven't seen anything. Is it online? I can go look. I know she's been working with her Dad on a relief committee." He didn't recall her mentioning any fancy event, but he hadn't talked to her in quite a while. Certainly she had never told him about having a date, but he would check out the article and see for himself. Sometimes Beth had a way of misinterpreting things anyhow. Still, he wondered if his expectations for her had already come true and her father had hooked her up with some up-and-comer.

He chatted with Beth for a minute and then went straight to his laptop to check the news. It didn't take long to find the article— the local news had done a big spread—including several photos of various important people.

And there she was, in a group with the Senator, her father, and, yes, a smooth-looking guy with his arm around her like it belonged there. Justina looked gorgeous—hair up, sparkling diamonds, and a glittering gown. She seemed to be just glowing, radiating right off his screen. Her date was great looking too and they looked good together with their dark hair and brilliant white smiles.

Daniel felt his heart sink. He had known this could happen, which was why he tried to keep some distance from her, but this had taken no time at all. She had only been back at school less than a quarter! It reaffirmed for him that she had never been serious about him in the first place. She got caught up in playing house and was maybe lonely and that was it.

Leaving the picture up on the screen, he went and got himself a beer. *Lucky I have a 12-pack*, he thought to himself, as he sat down to read the article. Justina was barely mentioned, except for an aside acknowledging her help in organizing the event. Her date wasn't mentioned at all, except as identified in the photo. Daniel wondered what that guy had done to get a seat at her table, since he didn't appear to be anyone important. Not that it mattered, he told himself. He was her date, which was probably all it took.

Daniel felt kind of sick, thinking about how Justina had been so persistent in her attempts to reel him in and how he had bought it. The only thing that saved him was his own lack of confidence and fear and now he knew he had been spot-on correct. It didn't make him feel any better, though. He really hadn't thought she was shallow like that. He had thought that maybe, just maybe, there could be something between them once they were done with school. Although he knew that Victor would never totally approve, once he had his degree and a career it wouldn't matter—he would be able to hold his head up. Now he figured Victor had some role in the scenario he saw in the paper, but Justina was clearly a willing participant. The whole thing sent a strong message to Daniel, loud and clear. *Stay away from her—she will only be trouble.*

He closed his laptop and got another beer. He tried to find something on television to distract himself, but that image of her was burned into his head and every time it resurfaced he felt his stomach turn and clench. No way he was going to get anything productive done, so he finally settled on watching a basketball game and working his way through much of his 12-pack before passing out in a restless sleep.

The next morning, he awoke feeling like he had been run over by a large truck. He made a whole pot of coffee and drank most of it before heading to class. He was within walking distance of school, which was helpful on a day when he needed to clear his head.

He mulled over the whole Justina situation. His initial reaction was to follow up on one of the girls who had been flirting with him since he got back. It would be very easy to bury himself that way, he was pretty certain he wouldn't have any problems getting a date. But then he would have to face the same set of challenges—getting close to someone and dealing with all the emotional drama—and he wasn't really ready to face all that, especially with a new person.

He figured he would need to focus more energy on school and his internship. He was really getting a lot out of the internship. If he spent more time on it he would learn that much more and probably get even better references out of the project. He decided that would be the most useful way to quit thinking about Justina. He for sure wouldn't be calling her. He always wanted to talk to her, but wouldn't do it. He was trying to stick to his word about keeping some distance and focusing on school. Now it would be easy—all he had to do was think about her with her new boyfriend or whatever he was. No way would he be desperate enough to embarrass himself by reaching out to her.

He knew that Beth had called and told him on purpose as well. Although he considered her a good friend, he also knew that she would get back together with him in a heartbeat if she had the chance. *And if I didn't know it before, I know it now,* he thought. He admired Beth's energy and strong will, she never let anything get her down, but she didn't interest him romantically. They dated when they were very young and was more a product of proximity than anything else, at least so far as Daniel was concerned. Beth had just never left the neighborhood and hadn't gone out into the world at all. Daniel felt bad for her; she had been caught up with her family and never got a chance to have her own life. He hoped someday she would.

He thought back to their high school days. Daniel had always felt responsible for his family even though he was still a kid. He was working after school and weekends to help his mom with money. He had always been quiet and serious. The other kids gave him a hard time, trying to get him to go out and party, play sports, and do all the things that the other kids did. They would ridicule him, saying that he thought he was better than everyone, that he was a nobody, and he needed to get over himself. The girls were a different story, always trying to flirt with him and get some reaction.

Beth was his champion, during those times, and her spunky personality served well in that respect. She knew that Daniel was never the same after his dad left and that he felt responsible for everything. Beth's mother and his mom were friends, neighbors, and helped each other out, so it was natural that the two kids were friends as well. Daniel felt like Beth was a sister to him, but at some point they had drifted into more of a boyfriend-girlfriend relationship, which both the mothers encouraged. Beth's mother, in particular, was always calling and asking if Daniel could come over and help with some minor thing, then she would invite him to dinner, then to hang out and watch TV, then she would disappear and leave him and Beth alone. Daniel's mother encouraged him by saying, "You don't need to hang around here and keep me company, go have fun!" Daniel had been a rather passive participant in the relationship. Even though Beth was very cute and sweet to him, he was not interested in her the way he should have been. In retrospect, he knew he shouldn't have let it go on but, in truth, it made his life at school easier. Having a cute girlfriend helped get the other kids off his back, he was no longer the weird guy who wouldn't join in on anything. He was a guy with a girlfriend, so spending his time with her was understandable.

And Beth was not very high maintenance. She came from a family that also had no money and she didn't expect fancy dates or expensive gifts, which was a good thing because there were none. It was a treat to go to a movie or out for pizza. He thought back to when he was accepted at the University and had to tell her where things stood. He didn't intend to try to have a girlfriend long distance and go to school. He told her that there wasn't a romantic future for them, it wasn't what he wanted, and she deserved someone who would be better for her.

Going to school was his chance to make something out of his life and he didn't have to apologize for that. He felt that he needed to focus. That was when he found out that Beth really had expected them to spend their lives together and, in retrospect, he should've known that. He wasn't a very good boyfriend to her—he was just drifting along with her because it was easier.

The day he told her she sobbed and begged him to rethink what he wanted. She said she understood his need to go to college and told him that she would wait for him—she wanted him to be happy. He was forced to tell her that he didn't want her for a girlfriend; he wanted to be friends, which was the worst possible thing to say. She was broken-hearted. Daniel had never actually seen Beth cry, she wasn't the type to cry, and he felt like a complete asshole as she cried until her whole face was one big blotch. He still remembered that as one of his worst days—he felt like a total creep.

He had avoided her for a long time after that because he was not sure how to handle things with her anymore. Whenever he was home from school he would avoid going past her house. All of that changed, however, when his mom got sick. Beth and her mother were the ones who helped Daniel get through it—he could never have done it alone.

He had been so devastated and had no idea how to care for his mother. Plus, he didn't really want to accept how sick his mother was, but Beth and her mother knew. They helped his mother with trips to the doctor and picking up prescriptions so Daniel wasn't really forced to face the details. Everyone in the neighborhood saw how hard he was trying and it broke all their hearts to see him going to his job at the bagel shop, trying to keep the house in good repair, trying to be the man of the house, and take care of his mother. Beth had become a part of his life again during that time, although she wasn't overtly trying to get back together with him—especially given all that was going on at the time.

After his mother died, Beth was there for him and at some point he realized they were drifting back into the same old patterns. It was then that he pulled away from her a bit. He still felt close to her as a friend, and would spend some time with her, but he kept a distance between them. He didn't want to have another bad conversation like when they broke up. He was so devastated by losing his mom that he just couldn't deal with any girl drama. Beth seemed to get it and never forced the issue.

Thinking about it now, he was glad they remained friends but he knew that Beth could cause him trouble in the most seemingly innocent way possible and, perhaps, without even conscious intent. In this case he was glad she had called and told him what was in the paper, but he knew that call had some degree of self-interest. For that reason, he didn't want to confide in her about anything in his personal life—it just wasn't a good idea. Whenever he forgot that, he ended up getting a reminder. He also knew that Justina was jealous of Beth and Beth had done her best to show how close she was to him at every opportunity. *What a mess*, he thought, *and so ridiculous. Here I am all alone in Maryland, working my butt off. What are they all worked up about, anyhow?*

For Daniel, other than worrying about Justina, things were going quite well. He was involved in his internship, so he was learning how to build a structurally sound home from the ground up. He was also getting a chance to work with architects and experienced engineers and contractors, so he felt like he would be ready to tackle some real-world projects when he was done at the end of the year. He took an overload of credits too, so he would get done sooner. Overall it was a good time for him. His confidence was growing and he felt like he was going to be able to do something that mattered. He got a lot of praise from the various professionals he was working with, both for his knowledge and his eagerness to jump in and do whatever was needed. They all liked that he wasn't just a books and paper guy, he liked to do real work. Daniel felt like he had found his calling, which was a great feeling after feeling lost for so long. Being back with Marcos kept him from getting too serious—it was very hard to be serious for long with Marcos around.

He thought about going home—he knew he should do some work on his own house—but decided it could wait. He wasn't planning to see Justina and was a bit annoyed with Beth, so the only one to see was Willie. He worried about her, but at least he knew she was being taken care of. Last time he visited she was doing well. He figured he would put in as much time and energy as possible at school and then he would go home for a longer period during the break. Maybe the better plan was to cut loose and join Marcos for an off-campus party...*time for life to move on*.

CHAPTER TWENTY SEVEN

Justina, meanwhile, had made a few decisions of her own. She stuck to her resolution to quit her father's committee. She couldn't stomach the idea of seeing Eric. When he had called her after the charity dinner, wanting to set up a date, she told him flatly she wasn't interested in seeing him anymore. He, of course, was shocked and wanted to know what was wrong, but Justina refused to get into it with him. She just told him that she felt he wasn't the type of person she wanted to be involved with and hung up. He tried calling a couple more times, but she wouldn't answer.

She was surprised at herself, she had never done anything like that before. She had always been so passive and tried to please everyone. She was proud of herself for taking a stand.

With respect to her father, things were strained, mostly on her end, and she told him she no longer wished to work on his committee. He tried very hard to change her mind, because he knew she cared so much about the relief efforts, but she told him she thought it would be better for her to find her own direction. Victor was a little surprised, but acknowledged that he respected her decision and her independence. She could tell he was trying and maybe her father was having his own little learning moment. She hoped so.

She wanted to forgive him and thought a lot about what Mona had said about his actions not coming from a bad place—that he meant well for her. She knew that was true. And it was also true that all they really had was each other—their little family was so small. She finally decided to reach out to him and see when he would be in Long Beach. She would go home again and see him as well as Mona and Willie. And she would not worry about trying to see Daniel this time.

She finally did connect with her father and found a weekend to come home toward the end of the quarter. She would also be there a few weeks later, during the break, but that was okay. It was only a short train ride and she was ready to come home. She certainly enjoyed Long Beach more in the spring than in the winter.

As soon as she got off the train she relished the smell of the ocean air. She never got tired of that—it was something you didn't get much of in the city. Her father wasn't home yet when she got there, so she opened up a couple windows to air out the house and put a bottle of her father's favorite chardonnay on ice. She still felt that she was fully justified for being upset with him, but she was ready to let it go and move on.

She spent a nice evening with Victor. They stayed away from sensitive subjects—he seemed to know better than to push her about the committee or Eric and didn't mention Daniel either. Maybe he had learned a little about interfering in her life! Probably not, but one could always hope. Victor did give her updates on the committee's progress. She wondered briefly if Eric had made inroads with her father or the Senator, but wasn't going to ask. It wasn't important enough to disrupt the harmony she and Victor were carefully creating and, really, she found she didn't care. Eric had been a diversion, she realized, and a mistake that she wouldn't make again.

The next morning Justina went to the hospital. She wanted to see Mona and Willie. It felt so good to be back there—it was a place where she had felt useful, like she made a difference. And, of course, Mona was always great to see. It turned out, however, that Willie was no longer there. She was in a nursing home across the street. Mona called to make sure a visitor would be welcome and then Justina headed off to see her.

When she got there, she was pleased to see that the nursing home was nice—it was clean and the staff was very friendly. Justina had never been in a nursing home before, so she wasn't sure what to expect. She was less pleased, however, when she found Willie's room and discovered Beth already there visiting. She put a smile on her face, though, and greeted them both. Willie looked good and her speech and coordination seemed to have continually improved.

Beth got up as soon as she saw Justina. "Hey, how are you? I was thinking of getting a soda, do you want anything?"

Justina declined and Beth stepped out, giving Justina a little time with Willie. Willie gave her that distinct gold-tooth grin and held out her heavy arms for a hug.

"How you doing, girl?" she asked, her speech only partially slurred. "It's good to see you! Been wonderin' how you been doin'!"

Justina couldn't help smiling back. Willie always made her smile—she was such a character. "I'm good, just home for the weekend. I had to come see how you are doing! How are you feeling? Are they treating you right here? You look good and it sounds like you are recovering."

"Yeah, they treating me all right 'cept they still keep trying to give me all this healthy food. I sure would love a big old plate of ribs." She sighed. "And they work me all the time. Got this therapist for my speech another one for walking and stuff... they done wear me out!" She was smiling as she said it and Justina could see that the care she was getting was good for her. She had been trying to get along by herself for far too long and it was wonderful to see a sparkle in her eyes.

Pretty soon Beth came back with her soda and they chatted for a while about how things were going in the neighborhood. Beth gave Willie all the local gossip about who was pregnant, who was getting a divorce, and who was moving away because they couldn't keep their house. Willie just clucked and shook her head, her eyes and gold tooth shining the whole time. Eventually, one of the nursing aids came in to get Willie ready for lunch, so it seemed to be time to leave. The each gave Willie a hug and promised to come again soon. As they walked out, Beth asked Justina casually, "Have you talked to Daniel lately?"

Justina immediately felt on her guard, but wasn't sure why. "Not recently. I know he's real busy with everything he's doing at school. I'm sure I'll see him at spring break."

Beth was quiet for a moment, then said, "You know they did a big article on that fundraiser you helped your dad with. We saw it in the local paper. You looked fantastic. Who was your date?" she asked in an innocent tone.

Justina's heart just about stopped and before she could think, she blurted, "Daniel saw that?" She immediately wanted to bite her own tongue off for saying it, but it was too late.

Beth was all wide-eyed innocence. "Oh, yes, he saw it. Didn't he mention it?"

Justina regained her composure a little. "No, he didn't mention it," she said smoothly. Of course, that was because she hadn't heard from him, but she wasn't going to tell Beth that! She figured she could do some damage control. "That guy is an intern for one of the VIPs at the event. I'm not dating him. He was just sucking up for the camera. He's a schmoozer." At least Beth would know she wasn't playing Daniel, even though she knew for sure Beth would never whitewash the incident. She was probably the one who told Daniel about the paper!

Beth shrugged. "Hmmm. He sure was cute and he seemed to like you!" she added. Then she motioned to a side street. "I gotta go. See you later!" She headed off down the road at a jaunty pace, her ponytail bouncing back and forth.

Justina stood there for a moment, collecting her thoughts. She had a pretty good idea of why she hadn't heard from Daniel now. Despite what he had said that night before Christmas, she didn't believe he had truly meant it. She wondered if Beth would call him and tell him about the conversation that day, but decided probably not. There was nothing to say that could cause trouble unless she lied. Justina wasn't sure if she would do that or not. Despite what Daniel had said about his relationship with Beth, Justina had a pretty strong sense that Beth felt possessive of Daniel and would make trouble if she could do it without looking like she was trying.

Justina was certain about one thing, she needed to call Daniel and downplay the whole thing as best she could, without lying about it. She knew that this was exactly what he expected would happen, he had said as much. Now he would think she had just been playing with him all along and that he was right to not see her anymore. She sighed to herself, trying to figure out the best way to approach it. She wasn't sure if he would even answer his phone. She was nervous about calling him. She didn't want to lie to him and reminded herself that she didn't actually owe him an explanation. But she knew that if she didn't say something she'd probably never hear from him again, and she couldn't blame him.

She didn't need to worry because when she called he didn't answer. With Daniel she never knew if it was because he didn't have his phone with him, if it was turned off, or if he was avoiding her. She left a message, saying hello without mentioning the other issue. If he didn't call back, she would try leaving another message with more detail, but she didn't want to start out with that.

She watched her phone all evening. Her father came home with some take-out and they ate and watched the news. Justina's phone never rang. She was edgy—that kind of nervous guilty feeling that is hard to relieve. She wanted Daniel to call, but was anxious about talking to him.

The next morning, before heading back to school, she called him again and again. He didn't answer, so she left a different message. "Hey, Daniel. I'd really like to talk to you. I saw Beth the other day. I want to make sure we don't have any misunderstandings. I want to tell you what's going on. Call me, okay?" She wasn't sure what else to say without going into a long story. Daniel responded with a text: *Can't talk, very busy. No misunderstanding, u have ur own life. C U later.*

CHAPTER TWENTY EIGHT

Daniel laced up his shoes and headed out to go for a run. This thing with Justina was making him crazy. He didn't want to think about her, but was unable to let go of her. He kept envisioning that picture of her with that snotty-looking rich guy. What was he expecting, anyhow? He was a poor guy from the hood. He could never compete for a girl like that, could never offer her the kind of life she obviously enjoyed. He circled the campus, not even seeing the beautiful brick buildings and well-designed landscaping.

He knew he needed to let it go. He was doing well in school. He was back in the top 5% of his class. Since doing his internship and a volunteer project, a couple of professors made it clear to him that his skills and talents were being noticed. He was especially interested in structural engineering, given the rebuilding efforts he had seen and been a small part of in New York after all the devastation that happened there. Seeing all those homes and lives destroyed had made a huge impact on him and had given him the direction and motivation he needed. When he was being honest with himself, he knew that Justina had been part of the reason he had finally pulled his head out of the sand and returned to school. She made him want to be the kind of person who could hold his head up without apologies. As much as that whole situation had been hurtful, he knew at least one good thing had come of it—he was going to make something of himself and do something to help people.

As he neared the end of his route, he had managed to refocus his thoughts and put Justina in the back of his head. He stretched at the bottom of the stairs to his apartment and headed up with fresh resolution. He decided to go to the library and do some studying. His bedroom was dim as he entered and he realized that he hadn't even bothered to open the blinds in a couple of days— he had been in such a funk. As he got undressed to take a shower, he saw the light on his phone blinking with a new message.

No way, he mumbled to himself. *I am not going to get sucked into any more drama! I'm done with that, time to move on.*

He definitely did not need to hear from Justina again, he needed to focus and get her out of his head. He kicked his sweaty clothes aside and hit the shower, deliberately putting the blinking phone out of his mind.

After showering and eating a quick sandwich, Daniel walked to the Engineering Library and headed upstairs to the computer center. He hadn't even gotten to his preferred corner when he heard his name. He turned and saw his buddy Marcos coming after him almost at a run.

"Man, where you been?" was Marcos' greeting. "I left you like three messages, man, I thought maybe you ran away with your *novia*. Did you hear about Mexico City?" Daniel had a flash of guilt about the phone, but his curiosity took over—especially given the manic way Marcos had approached him, something was clearly going on.

"What? No, I haven't heard anything. I was running before I came here. What's up?"

"Man, there has been a massive earthquake down there. Professor Alvarez is putting together a team to go and help out. It's a total disaster. It was like an 8.2 magnitude. The city is trashed. We gotta go down there. The school will cover the costs, they need everyone they can get to help dig out and get things put back together. Are you in?" Marcos spoke rapid-fire, his eyes glittering and his usually well-styled black hair disheveled. His adrenaline was clearly pumping overtime. He looked like he was on the verge of jumping out of his skin.

"Whoa..." Daniel said, letting it sink it in. "Give me a minute, when did this happen and who is going and when?"

"We are going as soon as we can. Don't know yet about getting in and out, it's hard getting information when stuff like this goes down. Is your passport current?" A chirping noise sounded and Marcos fished around in his baggy khakis to pull out his phone. He looked at it, shook his head, and put it back in his pocket.

"What's up?" Daniel asked, noting the worried look on the face of his usually playful friend as he pocketed the phone.

"I'm waiting to hear from my mom. We have family down there. My mom said she would let me know as soon as she gets through. No phones are working though. It's impossible to know how bad it is or how widespread the damage is at this point. My aunt and cousins' *barrio* is outside the city, but not too far away, and the size of that earthquake. . .it's not good, man."

Daniel was at a loss for words, "That sucks," he said, and then added, "I don't have a passport. How long does it take to get one?"

"You can put a rush on it, but you better get on it quick if you want to go. If we can even get in, that is. Still waiting to hear if planes are flying in or out of the city. So you're in? Want me to let Dr. A. know to put you on the list." Daniel made a snap decision and nodded as Marcos' phone chirped again. "I better go, man," he said. "I gotta call some other family here in the States. I'll talk to you later." Marcos was already turning to leave while pulling out the phone again.

Daniel went online and quickly found out that he would need his birth certificate which, of course, wasn't with him in Maryland. He hoped it was still intact in the box of papers in his bedroom. Those documents were upstairs and hadn't been destroyed by water. He headed back to his apartment and sent a few texts to his professors and to Marcos, letting them know what he was doing. Then he gathered up a few things to take with him. He briefly thought of calling Justina to see if she was, by chance, in Long Beach—but he quickly talked himself out of it, remembering his earlier resolution. No point in stirring that whole thing up again and causing himself unnecessary distraction. *Need to let that go,* he reminded himself. He wanted to tell her about this, but resolved that he would not backslide from his earlier commitment. Besides, he had a lot to do to get ready for the trip. He looked up the news on the earthquake as well to learn more about it. Although communication coming from Mexico had been sketchy, as Marcos had said, it was clear that it was a major disaster—the biggest earthquake ever to hit that area.

Once he got home, he decided to go to the passport office in New York. While he waited for the documents to be ready for pickup, he would use the time to go see Willie and Beth. He didn't know how long he would be in Mexico. He ducked into his house quickly to gather up his papers, fortunately finding a copy of this birth certificate that wasn't in such bad condition. He immediately filled out the passport application, then headed over to Beth's house, and then to see Willie.

The visit with Beth was uneventful, mostly because he refused to get drawn into any discussion about Justina. He focused on the upcoming trip and didn't give her a chance to get in his personal business. He hadn't seen Willie in a little while, so he was pleasantly surprised to see how well she was doing. He had brought her a little bag of chocolates and was rewarded with her gold toothy smile and a big hug. Willie fussed at him about going into such a dangerous situation, but she seemed to understand why he needed to do it.

He stopped at a deli to pick up a sandwich, knowing his house had no food in it whatsoever, and then headed home. Things were as he had left them—in disarray, chilly, and not smelling very good even though he had hauled out so many loads of damaged materials. Now that he had filed for the passport, all he had to do was wait. He looked around and wondered if he would ever finish the house. He just didn't really care about it after all this. It was discouraging and without his mom, there didn't seem to be much reason. He found a couple beers left in the lifeless fridge to wash down his sandwich. *How ironic,* he thought. *I must have put these beers in the fridge when the power was out…and I went there to look for some beer now…old habits die hard.*

He thought about all the people who had just given up on their homes and businesses when they couldn't afford to fix them or just didn't want to go through the trouble of getting help and money to do it. He had seen a number of small businesses still boarded up—apparently for good—and he wondered what happened to those people who had lost not only their livelihood but also, perhaps, their hopes and dreams? He knew the insurance companies were dragging their heels and he didn't know if he would ever get any help making the repairs anyhow. He certainly understood why people had just walked away. It was so depressing.

He thought of his mom as he worked on his second beer in the cold, gutted kitchen. She had been so proud of maintaining that little house, proud of being a single mom who had a good kid. She always let him bring his friends there and would offer them a treat or a snack, even when money was tight.

He never appreciated it then but, once she was gone and he had to figure out how to manage, he realized all that she had done. He knew she would want the house restored, he just didn't know if he had the heart to do it. He remembered how much pride she had taken in their home and how she tried to make it all that she could.

"Daniel, we're going to remodel the kitchen," she told me one day when I came home from school. I was confused, not sure what she intended. "See, I got these curtains and we are going to fix the décor in this room!" She held up a set of bright yellow and white gingham curtains and valance. She handed them to me, giving me step-by-step instructions on how to "install" them, since she wasn't tall enough.

The second part of the "remodel" involved painting the kitchen cabinets and putting several chicken decals on the doors. I remember her standing on a step-stool, her grey-blonde hair up in a scrunchy, and her baggy blue denim shirt streaked with the white paint she had used on the cabinets, asking me whether the chickens should be higher or lower, centered or to the side. She had made it seem like a party, that kitchen renovation.

She called Beth's mom and invited them over to see the "new" kitchen and everyone pretended that the dingy room really was bright and attractive. We all celebrated those little things, he thought, because there wasn't much else and despite everything we didn't yet know what a true tragedy was....

He looked at the stained and torn yellow-gingham valance over the kitchen window and the faded chicken decals on the remaining cupboard doors, remembering that as a happy time—before she got sick, before she spent most of her time in bed in a darkened room. He had barely been in her room since she died. He left the door shut so he wouldn't have to deal with it. His last and most vivid memories of that room included hospice workers and, ultimately, a coroner. He didn't want those memories kept alive by seeing all that again.

He wondered to himself if maybe she would not have wanted the house fixed, if it meant he wouldn't be able to move on. She had always wanted him to have a good life, so maybe giving up on the house and moving on wouldn't be disloyal to her memory. He vacillated over it and wished he had more beer in the house.

Maybe it was going back to school, maybe it was getting called to the disaster in Mexico, but he felt he was at a crossroads. He didn't feel like he was part of this neighborhood any more, he didn't really feel he was part of any world, he thought he must be ready for a new life. He chose not to decide about the house yet, which felt like a decision in and of itself.

CHAPTER TWENTY NINE

Justina pushed through the last of her finals, feeling pretty confident that she had done well. Her volunteer work was really satisfying and she felt like she was starting to carve out a life for herself. She found that the idea of being alone didn't bother her like it used to, which was a good thing, since she seemed to be alone most of the time these days.

Hercules greeted her at the door, mewing for a treat and some attention. "Hey, buddy," she greeted him, scratching him behind the ears. She was opening him a can of cat food when her phone buzzed. It was her father.

"Hi, Papa," she said as she answered it.

"Hello, Sweetheart, how are you?" he asked, but it didn't sound like he was really listening for the answer.

"I'm good, just finished finals, I think they went well," she said, figuring she would head that off at the pass.

"Good, good," he said, still sounding distracted. "Justina, I have to go out of the country for bit, and I'm not sure how long. I just wanted to let you know. Have you been watching the news? Have you seen the earthquake in Mexico City?"

Justina felt a flash of alarm. "No, I don't watch television during finals, you know that. It's too easy to get distracted. How bad is it? Why are you going?" She hated when he went far away, she was always afraid he wouldn't come back. Ever since her mother had gone and not returned, it was a fear. She had adjusted to her father's travel, since it was so constant, but still liked to know he wasn't too far away or would not be gone long. And going far away to a place where there were dangers, well, she felt anxious anytime he did that.

"I am going as part of the international relief effort. The Senator is heading down to see the damage and offer assistance. I am going to help him. Being bi-lingual is an advantage in this instance, so I will be helping coordinate things. You know we try to help our neighbors and this is a bad one." He continued, "I told Celeste not to worry about cleaning the house until further notice, but if you are going to be there, give her a call, she can get some groceries for you." His tone was all business now, clearly he was going down his list of things to do before leaving and calling her was one of those things.

"Papa, I want to go with you. I can help too. I speak Spanish, remember?" She flashed back to the hospital and all the hurt and sick people lining the hallways, suddenly homeless and desperate. "I could help at the hospital, like I did here. They will need help. Please, Papa. . . ."

"Absolutely not. I don't know how bad things are down there—it is a disaster zone—the worst earthquake ever. Even buildings that are still standing could come down. There could be aftershocks. I am not allowing you to be in danger. And I don't want to have to worry about you. How could I do my job when I would be wondering all the time if you were safe? No." he finished definitively.

Justina felt her frustration mounting, compounded by all the other things her father had done in the recent past. "Papa, when will you let me be an adult? I am sure there are places outside of the dangerous area where they still need people at hospitals to co-ordinate and help all the hurt people. I can't just stay in my gilded cage forever! I want to go with you!"

"No," he said with finality. "You are not going and that is all." His tone was clear—he was not going to budge. But Victor was not the only one who could be stubborn. Justina was his daughter and equally determined.

"Okay," she said with defiance in her voice. "I can go on my own. Then you don't have to bother with me. I can take care of myself." She paused and then continued, "You know, you have been controlling me long enough, Papa. I am done being your little princess. I want to do work that matters—it's what I want to do with my life. Nothing is more important than that. I would love to go with you and work with you on this, but I am not letting you tell me no. And that is all," she added, throwing his own words back at him.

"Justine, you can't—" he began, but she interrupted him.

"Yes, I can. And I will. I have decided. So am I going with you or should I call the volunteer groups I know and ask for a ticket with them? I mean it, Papa."

Victor sighed an impatient sigh. He was not used to his daughter going against him, especially when it wasn't safe for her, and he really hadn't expected to have to deal with this right now. He was quiet for a moment, considering, and she let the silence stand. She knew she had him in a corner. His desire to protect and control her was overwhelming, but he could better protect her if she was with him rather than with some group he didn't know and couldn't keep tabs on.

Finally he spoke. "All right, Justina. I see you are becoming as stubborn as your father. Here's the deal, you can go and help but only at a hospital that is outside of the danger zone. One that is structurally sound. And I am coordinating it. You will stay with me. You are not going around on your own and you will work with an American team. There will be plenty to do, in many places, I am sure. Are we agreed? You know I am not happy with this, not at all."

Justina felt the thrill of victory—she had never won a battle of the wills with her father! "Yes, Papa, I can agree. I can be ready right away, I just need to get someone to watch the cat! And Papa," she added, "Thank you. I want you to learn that I am not a child. I want you to see that I can be useful, too. It is important to me." She felt she needed to tell him that so he would understand that she wasn't just being impulsive.

"Yes, mija, I see that. I would like to have you with me so long as you are safe." He paused and then resumed his all-business tone. "You will need to meet me in Los Angeles, we are flying from there. The Senator has meetings with the California Governor before we go to Mexico City. Have my assistant get you a ticket for tomorrow; she will set up all the details. Okay? You are sure you want to do this?"

"Yes, Papa, I do. And thanks, I will call her now. You won't regret it," she added.

"Okay, I will see you there. I have to go now. Have a safe flight, I love you!"

"Love you too, bye!"

Justina flew into action as soon as she ended the call. Her first call was to set up the travel arrangements. Her father's assistant was extremely helpful and promised to locate tickets and e-mail them promptly. Her finals were done, so that wasn't a problem, but she had to find someone to feed the cat.

Fortunately, one of her neighbors—another law student—was going to be staying in town and working, so that was arranged with relative ease. Her roommate was totally unreliable, so that wasn't even an option unless she wanted a starved cat with an overflowing litter box. She thought of Daniel and wanted desperately to talk to him. She decided that leaving the country for a disaster warranted a call, even if he was mad at her, so she called. No answer. She debated leaving a message, but decided not to. He didn't want to know her anymore—or so it seemed. She decided to put it on hold until she got back, by then she would have plenty to tell him and surely he would be interested and cooled off by that time.

What clothes do you take to an earthquake in Mexico? She tore apart her closet and drawers to find things that would be appropriate, although she didn't really know what that might be. She settled on khakis and t-shirts. She dug out her passport, noting that it was nowhere near expiring. Thank God for that—an expired passport would give her father an excuse to keep her home. She spent the rest of the day doing odds and ends to get ready, texted some friends to let them know what she was doing, and picked up a supply of cat food and litter for Hercules.

She spent the evening eating take-out and watching the CNN coverage of the earthquake. She watched in horror as the various rescue teams pulled apart piles of debris, pulling out mangled bodies, and badly injured people of all ages. Men and boys were scaling mountains of fallen buildings, like so many ants on an anthill, forming chains to work up and down the piles. City officials and people looking for loved ones were being interviewed. The footage revealed a vast array of human tragedy and grief—all coated in dust and tear stains—with the connection cutting out on a frequent basis. The reality of what had happened became very real to Justina and she finally understood what her father was worried about. The entire city looked like a war zone and the reporters estimated that thousands of people had died, although the rescue efforts would be going on for days.

The city scene reminded her of September 11th, the horrific attack and aftermath, the closest thing she'd seen to this type of devastation. September 11th had become her generation's version of the Kennedy assassination. "Where were you when. . .?" Like most Americans, she would never forget that day.

I was home from school with a cold, and the housekeeper, Celeste, had come to stay with me. Papa was working in D.C. for the day. I woke up late in the morning, suddenly hungry after not eating since dinner. As I came down the stairs, I could hear the television on and Celeste crying. I was quiet as I entered the room, wanting to know why she was crying. Over her shoulder I could see the television, which showed a plane flying straight into one of the Twin Towers. The next clip showed the collapse of the building and terrified people running in all directions with plumes of grey dust engulfing everything. I must have made some noise because Celeste heard me and jumped up. "No, no, honey, you should not see this," she said, her voice thick from crying and her eyes puffy.

"What happened?" I asked. Like most Americans, including children, I couldn't imagine what happened that day or why.

"We don't know for sure," Celeste answered, "But I think bad people did this. You should not watch. Let me get you something to eat." She started to reach for the remote control, but I grabbed her hand.

"Celeste, please. . .is Papa okay?" I had forgotten where he was that day, as my brain flashed to Mama and the plane crash. I started crying and Celeste took me into her plump lap, stroking my hair.

"Your Papa is fine, he is in D.C. today, remember?" I remembered then, but was still terrified.

"I want to call him, can you call him, please?" I begged. I had to know he was not hurt and the television kept showing the plan crashing into the building, over and over. It was like all my nightmares from Mama dying, playing out right there on the television. Celeste saw how upset I was and tried calling Papa, but there was no answer.

"Honey, you know he is probably very busy working because of this, okay? He is not in New York, he is in D.C. I will keep trying to call, but he is okay, I promise." Her words soothed me and she turned the television off so I wouldn't keep watching it.

Papa finally called and told me he was fine, but he was going to be delayed coming back. "No planes are flying now, mija, and everything is crazy trying to travel. Celeste will watch you and I will be home late. I have to get a car, it's the best I can do. Be a big girl for me, okay?" I agreed, but was crying again.

I had finally cried myself to sleep, but I had nightmares that woke me up. I must have been crying or screaming, because Celeste came into my room to calm me. "Where is Papa?" I asked, and she told me, "he is on his way, just get some rest."

After the initial shock, we found out, bit by bit, of all the people we knew who had lost someone. Celeste had lost a nephew; Papa had known people who died that day; and so did other friends and neighbors—people working in the buildings and those who were rescue workers of some sort. My nightmares didn't go away, and if a plane flew over while I was sleeping I would wake up, terrified. Planes, in my mind, had become something to be feared.

There was a memorial held at the local church, which Papa and I attended. He didn't want to take me, he said I would be upset, but I insisted. I loved going to church, I always felt so good there, but this wasn't like a regular day at church. People brought pictures of missing loved ones and everyone was sobbing and clinging to each other. All those crying people made me cry too and I cried even harder when they started playing "Amazing Grace." All that pain and sobbing left me devastated. Papa took me out of there and cursed himself for letting me talk him into going. I don't think he realized, either, how upsetting it would be. After that I started seeing a therapist. It was a very long time before I got over the nightmares or the fear of planes.

The scene of Mexico on the news was too much like the one she remembered from September 11th—grey piles of debris and dust everywhere, people climbing up the piles of devastation in the hopes of finding someone alive, people wearing protective masks because the air was too thick and toxic to breathe. And the throngs of sobbing, desperate people searching for loved ones, showing photos, and posting notices on any available wall. It was an image that would never leave her.

The magnitude of the destruction in Mexico City made her realize that whatever puny help she could give would not make much difference to people who had lived through this awful experience. She felt inadequate and overwhelmed just thinking of it, but then reminded herself that she had made a difference for people at the hospital after the storm. She realized that there was only so much that any person could do to relieve suffering this great, but that doing something was better than doing nothing. She had to remember that when it became overwhelming. *Helping even one person is better than doing nothing, she reminded herself.*

Feeling sobered and insignificant, she flipped off the television. With her head full of images of grief and pain, she went to bed.

CHAPTER THIRTY

Daniel watched intently from his window seat as the plane began the descent into Mexico City. The flight had been a long one and the atmosphere on the plane was somber. The passengers were all headed to Mexico City as a result of the earthquake, some to find and help family, others to be part of the rescue effort. The conversations swirled around Daniel—various stories of missing family, comparisons of news reports on the damage, and discussions of the work that needed to be done. There were several doctors on board to help with the injured and a group of firemen and EMTs from Los Angeles going to help with the rescue efforts. Daniel discovered that the two women sitting in front of him were nuns, which he would never have guessed. They were wearing fleece jackets and Birkenstock sandals, nothing like his traditional view of how nuns should look. He only realized it when they were addressed as "sisters" and he was a little surprised, but then realized that they would probably have a very meaningful role for the people in Mexico City. He was impressed with the array of people making the trip and it gave him a feeling of pride to be involved in it, although the stories he heard were overwhelming.

The group of firemen behind him had helped out after the 9-11 attack and they were discussing the challenges of finding survivors. Daniel listened intently, hoping to learn all that he could about what he had just volunteered for. The *Spanish for Dummies* book that Beth had dropped off for him sat unopened as he listened to the pieces of conversations, both about what was coming and what had come before.

There were discussions about contaminated or inadequate water supplies, how to manage large numbers of dead bodies, and the logistical challenges of trying to feed and house thousands of displaced people. The physicians talked about amputations they had performed both in the field and in various settings after a disaster, waterborne diseases and dust inhalation, and how best to manage those issues. Daniel felt like he was getting a crash course in disaster recovery, and he realized he was just beginning to understand what true devastation was, although he had certainly been through a different sort of disaster, which had caused serious damage and trauma.

The airport in Mexico City was largely undamaged and planes were coming and going. Daniel was set up to ride with a Red Cross group that was going to the city, since his group from the university had flown in the day before. It took forever to get off the plane and the airport was chaotic with people coming and going in every direction. Rapid-fire directions being given in Spanish by the various airport staff and security personnel who were tasked with organizing the chaos. Outside the airport, buses and taxis that were beat-up Volkswagen bugs and vans clogged the pick-up area and Daniel doggedly followed the Red Cross workers who were clearly accustomed to navigating the confusion and crowd of similar airports.

The apparent leader of the group, a tall, thin woman with auburn hair and pale skin, spoke in perfect Spanish to one of the airport workers who directed her to a rickety bus that appeared to have once been white but was now a dusty grey with patches of rust. As soon as they were all onboard, the driver lurched away from the curb, carrying on a loud conversation in Spanish with the Red Cross woman while rapidly weaving in and out of traffic and honking at anyone who dared to slow his progress.

As they got closer to the city, the after-effects of the earthquake became more apparent. Bricks and stone that had broken off houses and apartment buildings were laying in mounds where they had fallen. Eventually they got to the outskirts of Mexico City and the bus pulled to a stop outside a single-level motel that was shabby, but appeared relatively undamaged.

Daniel wasn't sure what to do once he got there, but he did not need to worry since Marcos was waiting for him. He was leaning against the building and eating a taco from a street vendor who had conveniently set up shop in the parking lot.

"Hola," Marcos said and gave Daniel a half-hug. "How was the trip? I got a car. We aren't staying here. Let me grab your bag," he said as he grabbed Daniel's oversized backpack. "Hey man, you hungry?"

Daniel shook his head no and waited while Marcos paused to chat with the bus driver, who had stepped out of the bus and was lighting a cigarette. Daniel realized he was a fish out of water and was grateful he had Marcos who could help him get acclimated. He also wished he had paid better attention when he took Spanish in high school, but that had been a long time ago. He couldn't make out a word that was being said except for *cerveza*, which came from the driver and made the driver and Marcos laugh.

They eventually made their way to a pale blue, dented-up Volkswagen bug and Marcos showed his Mexican roots by careening through traffic, much like the bus driver, while chattering to Daniel.

"I'm glad you're here, man. This place is a disaster—I mean total frigging disaster. They are still digging people out. It will probably be days or even weeks before they can even think about putting anything back together. We are staying with the cousin of Professor Alvarez. Her name is Maria. It's not fancy, but she is very nice and makes great tamales."

Marcos grinned at that and before he could continue, Daniel asked, "What about your family, are they okay?"

Marcos nodded yes while simultaneously honking at a taxi driver who cut him off. "Yes, they are fine, they are far enough outside the city. They totally felt the shaking and I think their house is cracked up a bit, but no real issue—thank God."

"Anyhow," Marcos continued, "we are helping with the search and rescue, but I can tell you it is not pretty. You okay with that?"

Daniel nodded, he had suspected as much from what he had heard on the plane. "So we will stop at the house, drop your stuff, and head into the city. Time makes the difference right now. You are ready to go? It is really bad, I am warning you. They are finding a lot of bodies as well as survivors. It's not easy."

He could see that Marcos, despite his attempt at his usual lighthearted demeanor, was upset and anxious and in a hurry to get back to the city where the damage had been the worst. He imagined how it must be for Marcos who, although born American, had close ties with Mexico and was obviously very familiar with the city.

He mentioned this to Marcos, who nodded, "Yeah, these are *mi gente*, my people. It is awful to see such suffering. It will take a very long time for this city and these people to recover." Daniel thought about his own neighborhood and the disaster there and felt the same way. Many people there had never recovered and had never returned to their homes or businesses—at least not yet. It was awful to think about so many lives swept away with no warning and no way to recover.

They pulled up to the house, a small stucco adobe building with wrought iron railings and grates on the windows. There wasn't much of a yard—it was mostly ragged grass and dust with a couple of rusty cars parked out front that looked like they were most likely inoperable. Maria, who was 40-ish and slightly plump, met them at the door wearing a yellow cotton dress and flip-flops.

"Bien Venido, welcome," she said, a broad smile covering her face. "You are Daniel, yes?"

He nodded and said "Yes, thank you for letting us stay here. I'm so sorry about what has happened here." He wasn't sure what to say—what do you say to someone whose city has been destroyed?

She just nodded, "Si, si, thank you, come in," and she led them into the house. He could tell that her English was minimal, but certainly better than his Spanish. She spoke rapidly to Marcos who nodded and took Daniel back to a bedroom with two small beds.

"We are bunking here in her sons' room. They moved out. Like I said, it's not fancy, but wait till you taste her cooking! And she is good people. This is better than a hotel."

The room was plain—the only decoration was a collection of soccer trophies on the beat-up dresser in the corner. "One of her sons plays soccer," Marcos said, when he saw Daniel looking at them. "He is playing for Brazil. Maria is so proud of him, it was all I heard about last night." He motioned to one of the beds and said, "there you go, there is your new home," then he added, "You ready to roll? There is only so much time to find survivors, every minute can make a difference."

Daniel threw his pack on the bed. "Let's go. I'm ready."

They drove quickly into the city where the destruction was progressively worse as they got further in. The first thing Daniel noticed was the broken glass—windows were broken out everywhere. At first there was just the broken glass and some areas where the pavement had split and heaved, leaving one side at odds with the other. Then there were chunks of rubble that had broken off buildings and were lying in piles. As they got closer to the epicenter, the buildings were more and more broken with tops askew like crooked berets and huge crumbled sections obliterating the sidewalks and roads. Yellow *precaution* tape was drawn across doorways of apartment buildings where the facade had been ripped off, leaving the rooms inside naked and exposed. Marcos parked alongside a huge pile of concrete chunks, rebar, and broken glass.

"This is as far as we go with the car," he said. "We are going to the hospital first. It was demolished and there are still people inside." He reached back behind Daniel's seat, pulling out a couple of paper facemasks and thick gloves. "You will need these—the dust is awful and the concrete will cut you up fast."

Daniel followed Marcos through the piles of debris. Men of all ages were climbing up mountains of broken concrete, passing chunks of debris down the chain, working to unearth the inhabitants of the building. As they arrived at the remains of the hospital, Daniel watched as people were being pulled out of the wreckage.

"It looks like they got in, finally," Marcos commented. "Come on, let's go." They climbed up the pile of broken walls and windows until they got to the opening where people were being brought out. Marcos went up to an older Mexican man, who appeared to be in charge, and spoke with him in Spanish. The man glanced over and Daniel and nodded, pointing inside. Marcos motioned to Daniel and they climbed into the hole that was opened up.

Daniel could hear people calling out and crying. He didn't need to speak Spanish to understand their pain and anguish.

They passed a young man carrying out an elderly woman who appeared to be dead and another carrying a sobbing teenage girl whose arm was bloodied and bent at an unnatural angle. The air was hot and filled with dust. Debris continued to fall here and there as the building settled.

"They had an aftershock this morning," Marcos mentioned, as they worked their way toward the back of the opened area. "Be careful."

They stopped as they heard a man's voice calling out from behind a pile of rubble. Marcos and Daniel started moving the chunks of debris out of the way to find him. By the time they got through, their arms and faces were filthy with dust and scratched from the pieces of rebar and concrete. Sweat and filth was coating them from top to bottom. They finally found the man—his leg was pinned beneath a piece of steel beam. Marcos spoke to him in Spanish, apparently discussing what they needed to do to get him out.

"We can't move this beam, it is too heavy," Marcos told Daniel. "We need to try to dig out the area under him."

The man was gritting his teeth and tears had made tracks through the coating of dust on his face. He was obviously in horrible pain but trying to stay strong. Marcos kept a one-way conversation going with the man as he and Daniel tried to pry the pieces of concrete and metal out from under the man's lower body. When they got him loose enough, Daniel took hold of his shoulders while Marcos held onto his legs to pull him free. The man screamed in pain as they pulled him loose. Daniel looked down and saw that the man's leg had been totally crushed by the beam—his pants were in shreds and his leg was a pulpy, bloody mess.

"Mi Dios," Marcos muttered. "We need to get something to carry him on. Stay here with him, I will be right back," Marcos instructed.

He returned shortly with another man, carrying a makeshift canvas stretcher. The man who came with Marcos quickly looked at the leg and then they moved the injured man onto the stretcher. "He's a medic," Marcos explained. As soon as they loaded the injured man onto the stretcher the medic was called to help with another victim, leaving Daniel and Marcos to carry the man out.

Once outside, Marcos took the lead and they brought the injured man to an area where victims were gathered. Nurses and medics were moving through the crowd, giving the victims whatever help they could until they could be transported to another hospital. There were a couple dozen people being treated, all of them covered in dust and most of them crying from shock and pain. Daniel realized that while the injured were brought to one spot, the dead were being taken to another. He wondered what they did with so many bodies and how they could treat so many injuries.

Daniel and Marcos spent the rest of the day digging out survivors and those who had not been so fortunate. A tractor had arrived to load the chunks of debris onto a dump truck, making a clear path for ambulances and vans to come in and pick up the injured and transport them to a hospital. A cluster of people was gathered around, as close as they could get, hoping to find loved ones coming out of the wreckage. Police kept them back a distance, trying to preserve some sort of order, but every time a survivor or body was brought out, the crowd pushed inwards trying to identify them. The work was physically grueling, but emotionally it was far worse, especially when they found someone only to discover they had already died. By the end of the day they had gotten as many people as they could find out of the unit they had opened up and began work on the outside again, looking for another possible pocket of survivors. Every so often one of the rescue leaders would yell at everyone to be quiet so that they could listen for sounds of survivors. Now and then they were rewarded with a whimper or a cough and would start digging—just as often there was only silence.

As the sun went down they quit for the day, so they could get some rest and be up with the sun the next day. Daniel had never felt so exhausted in his life—his body was sore and scraped up all over and his head was full of images of human misery that he knew would be with him forever. He was coated in filth and sweat and, despite bottles of water being provided throughout the day, he didn't think he could ever get enough to drink. Marcos didn't seem quite as exhausted—he had enough energy to stop and pick up some beer at a market on the way back to the house.

When they got to Maria's, he could smell the savory scent of meat cooking and his stomach suddenly reminded him that he hadn't eaten in many hours. Marcos gave him a beer and directed him to the shower. If it weren't for being so hungry, Daniel thought he might pass out in the shower. He didn't think he would ever get the dust and smell off, it was in every pore, but the shower revived him enough to go eat some of Maria's delicious *tacos carnitas*.

Professor Alvarez showed up for dinner. He told Daniel and Marcos to call him Eduardo. Apparently the day spent in the wreckage had earned them first name status with their professor. He had been at the hospital wreckage too, but had only seen them in passing. Eduardo was a slender man with black hair that was thinning on the top. His face looked worn and old, much older than just a few days earlier. He had been at the other side of the hospital for much of the day—where the dead were being taken.

He explained that there were so many dead that they were being taken to a baseball field—there was nowhere else to put them. Families could go there to identify their loved ones. He rubbed his eyes wearily as he explained the logistics, hunched over in exhaustion. Daniel listened in horror—the reality of that many deaths was becoming clear. While he worked all day to find survivors, he was focused on that task, and hadn't thought about how those efforts were going on all over the city—and that so many bodies were being found in addition to the survivors.

The magnitude of it all hadn't struck him until that point, as he visualized a baseball field filled with corpses of men, women, children, and elderly. He didn't know whether to cry or throw up. The day was so intense and then the exhaustion, beer, food, and reality caught up with him. He finished his beer and went to bed. The minute his head hit the pillow, he was out.

CHAPTER THIRTY ONE

When Justina arrived at LAX airport, a driver holding a sign with her name on it greeted her. The driver took her to the nearby Hilton where her father was staying. After she was settled in, they met in the lounge. Victor looked as polished as ever and hugged his daughter tightly.

"It's so good to see you," he said and then added, "I still wish you were not determined to do this thing, it is not a place for you."

She shook her head at him and motioned to the waiter, asking for a glass of wine. "Papa, I watched the news last night. I see what a horrible disaster this is. I understand what I am doing, okay? This is what I want to do—I want to help people who are in a bad situation. Don't you understand that?" Her dark eyes were intense and serious, much like his when he was determined.

"I know, I know," he said. "I am very proud of you. I admire that you have such a good heart. I would just prefer for you to be getting your education, settling down with a nice husband, and having a normal life. It is what is right for a woman—to have a husband and children."

She rolled her eyes at him, "Papa, please. I am so *not* looking for a husband. Besides, you won't want me to be with anyone I like. We already saw that . . ." as soon as she said it, she regretted it—the topic of Daniel had been taboo between them.

His mouth tightened. "Justina, I will not have you getting involved with a delivery boy! That is absolutely not acceptable for someone like you. Can we just let this go?"

"Yes, Papa, of course we can. You already made me lose him anyway, so you can relax. We should just drop it." She really hadn't intended to fight with her father, especially given the situation they were heading into. There were more important things going on than her love life or lack thereof.

She excused herself to go to the ladies room. She came back acting as though the conversation had not happened and Victor did the same. He explained to her the situation in Mexico City and the various efforts being made there. "I spoke with the coordinator at an international aid group that is down there now. She gave me the name of the contact. They are taking care of victims being brought to a hospital outside of the inner city where there is minimal damage. Some of the hospitals in the city have been destroyed, so the patients who are rescued, as well as survivors found in the city, are being taken to these locations. You will go there and help with translations for the doctors who are English-speaking volunteers. Some speak Spanish, but some do not. It will be a great help to have you there and you will be safe."

Justina nodded, "Okay. Do we know how many people are injured? On the news it looks like so many."

Victor shook his head. "We don't know yet. And there are recovery efforts happening all over the area, so it's hard to get a sense of it. She did say that they are very busy, but they expect that over the next few days they will be doing less rescuing and more recovery. The more time the rescue goes on, you know, the less survivors. . . ." He trailed off with a frown. "I will be going with the

Senator and the U.S. Ambassador to Mexico to see the damage in the inner city—and don't even ask," he added as he saw her face. "You are not going. They are still having aftershocks and buildings that are weakened can still come down. It is a filthy, dangerous place to be right now. Not a place for a woman. Anyhow, we will be showing support and strengthening our relationship with the Mexican President. This trip is important not only because of the relief we hope to provide, but also politically. We need to have a strong relationship so we can deal with sensitive issues like immigration."

Justina could hear her father gearing up to talk shop, which wasn't her biggest concern at the moment but she listened and sipped her wine.

The next morning they left early. The flight into Mexico City was a smooth one, mostly spent in a conversation with their seatmate—a slender Indian man named Raj who was from an international relief group. He explained to them the geography of Mexico City, which had contributed to the severity of the earthquake.

Apparently Mexico City was built on an old lakebed. The soil and silt layered beneath the city was not very stable and that increased the impact of the quake. For this reason, he explained, the damage was most severe in the city center and historic area and mostly affected older buildings that were taller. There were stricter building codes now, he told them, so the newer buildings—even the tall ones—fared much better.

Justina asked him about casualties and injuries. He shook his head, "We do not know yet. It will be thousands dead, I am sure. But there are other issues—so many people have lost homes, children have lost parents, people are missing, power is still out in a large area, and the water supply will surely be contaminated. People have nowhere to go. We have to try to feed them and give them medical care and clean water. The military is patrolling to prevent looting and people are setting up tents in the streets. It is a very bad time in the city, but apparently the area outside the city is relatively unharmed."

"How many people are homeless now? Like thousands?" She tried to wrap her brain around that many people wandering the streets.

He shook his head. "More like tens of thousands. I think this is the worst quake to hit such a populated area. It is a national disaster and the Mexican government has been slow to launch an organized response. The Mexican people have taken control into their own hands, setting up groups to do search and rescue and provide whatever supplies they can. The Mexican Red Cross is working with the American Red Cross and other groups, but these efforts have been disjointed in terms of the Mexican government's involvement. Many who have arrived to help have personal ties to Mexico and they are not part of a formal, organized government response. The people there have stepped up and the community has done an impressive job of organizing some of the efforts needed. Still, it's such a big disaster—many types of expertise are needed. I can only hope for the best. It will take a very long time to recover from this."

Justina nodded, processing all this. "What about the hospitals?" she asked.

"Yes, there were a couple of very large hospitals that were badly damaged. One of the main hospitals is completely collapsed and they are still taking people out of it. It was an older building, very old, in fact. It totally collapsed and they couldn't even get the ambulances out to move survivors. I think they are just now clearing the streets to get vans and ambulances in to move people who are rescued. The community hospitals are trying to absorb the overflow from these hospitals and help all the people injured in the city. It is a huge job. Especially considering that they lost many doctors, nurses, and other healthcare workers in those two hospitals that collapsed. So there are fewer beds, less doctors, and so many injured. It is a nightmare."

Justina told him what she was going to do, and he nodded. "That will be a good way to help. There are many doctors going to help, but they need to be able to talk to the patients. They need to tell the patients what is going on and make sure they understand what their choices are and what they have to do. There are so many aspects to a disaster like this—you can't imagine. There are supplies and medicines being sent in, but getting those things sorted and distributed is a huge challenge. That is what I will be doing, trying to coordinate those efforts."

Justina was glad to have a chance to talk to Raj, she felt better prepared for the situation. Victor had his laptop open and was working on a speech and presentation that they were preparing. She was getting nervous and it was helpful to have someone to talk to, even though she was overwhelmed hearing about the magnitude of the work to be done.

There was a car and driver waiting for them when they arrived and they were quickly taken from the airport to a nearby Marriott. Justina was surprised that everything appeared to be intact. She had expected to see some damage. "How far away are we from the city center?" she asked her father, who had been to Mexico City on a number of occasions.

"Not too far, maybe a half hour, forty minutes, depending on who is driving," Victor said, with an attempt at a joke. "I have been told the worst damage is localized, but the damage is very severe. Getting in and out is not easy—the Metro is down in the affected boroughs and the roads are still blocked in many places."

"Okay. Where is my hospital?" He smiled at her possessive reference to the hospital.

"We will go in the morning. I am not exactly sure where it is. The driver can tell us tomorrow."

They had a quiet evening and an early dinner. Justina spent the evening in her room watching the depressing local news and the CNN coverage. She fell asleep with images of grief stricken women crying and clutching inert babies and children sobbing and hanging desperately onto filthy stuffed toys or blankets.

Her dreams were a jumble of plane crashes and crumbled buildings with her wandering through rubble, looking for someone—she didn't even know who. She felt desperately lost and terrified. In her dream she was sobbing uncontrollably and she woke with red eyes and saturated patches on her pillow.

At breakfast, her father appeared to not notice his daughter's subdued appearance or at least he didn't comment on it. Victor was in his typical work-mode, getting organized for his day of meetings and tours. There were times when Justina admired his highly organized and focused approach to life and other times she wished he would loosen up a bit. On this particular morning, she was grateful for it because it took his focus off of her.

She felt tired and off-balance from her disturbing night's sleep and didn't want to discuss it. Instead, Victor included her as he went over his list of things to do. "Our driver's name is Manuel. He is picking us up at 8:00 and he will take us to the hospital first. I will go in with you and make sure you are settled. You will be working primarily for a Dr. Chukwu. He is originally from Nigeria, but coincidentally lives in New York. He is here with several other physicians from New York who are part of a relief organization based there. He will be your primary person to go to with any problems or questions, okay? The coordinator told me he is wonderful and that he is very happy you are coming, so you should be fine. Then I will be going to meet with the U.S. ambassador and the Senator. I probably won't be back until late afternoon, and if I can't reach you on your phone I will have you paged, okay?"

Justina nodded, picking at her muffin—her long hair hanging down around her face, partially obscuring it from view.

"Better eat up," Victor advised. "It may be a long day once you get started. I doubt you will have regularly scheduled lunch breaks and not sure you will like your lunch choices anyhow."

"I'm fine," she assured him and looked at her phone. "Isn't it time to go?"

Victor checked his watch and nodded, pocketing the phone. "Let's go."

Their shiny black car and smartly dressed driver, Manuel, were waiting outside. Manuel immediately greeted them and opened the door for Justina, then Victor.

The hospital was about 15 minutes away and was already a swarm of activity. A variety of vans and ambulances were lined up at the hospital entrance, blocking the driveway as they helped people into the hospital.

Victor instructed Manuel to meet him out at the curb and they proceeded into the hospital.

They were immediately absorbed into a noisy swarm of patients, families, and healthcare workers—a cacophony of voices of all ages and in various levels of distress. Justina looked around to try to make sense of the process while Victor was scanning for someone in charge. He finally spotted a young man wearing scrubs, who didn't appear to be in the middle of a patient emergency, and asked him about Dr. Chukwu. They were pointed in a general direction as a nurse grabbed the young man and pulled him over to a little girl who was alternately coughing and wailing. She had a bloody leg wrapped in a makeshift bandage.

They proceeded through the hospital, occasionally asking for the doctor and being waved onward. Finally a nurse said she would bring him out and disappeared into the crowd. She returned several minutes later with a huge black man in tow, his physique more like that of a football player than a physician. Dr. Chukwu had a reassuring presence about him, perhaps due to his large size and placid face that was broken only by a very broad and very white smile. His voice, too, was soothing—it sounded smooth and melodious. His greeting was formal and welcoming at the same time.

"Miss Justina, welcome, we are very happy to have you here! The people here are mostly very hurt and need to have their conditions explained. I need you to help with that. We cannot treat patients without making them understand the treatment." His head bobbed as he spoke, the light glinting off his little wire-rimmed glasses. Justina nodded and looked to Victor who patted her arm and took his leave—his mind already focused on the next thing. Justina was immediately at ease with Dr. Chukwu, and eager to get started.

"Come," he said, beckoning her to follow through the solid mass of humanity that clogged every inch of visible hospital space. They wasted no time getting to the patients, Justina scrambling to keep up with his long strides.

"You need to talk to them in very simple language, okay?" He instructed. "Many of these people are in shock or so badly shaken up they can't process much of what you say. Try to make it as plain as possible, all right?"

"Yes, I understand. I can do that," she assured him, dodging an elderly couple in her attempts to keep up with him.

Their first patient was an elderly man who had been partially trapped in one of the apartment buildings that had collapsed. His shirt was in shreds, soaked with blood, and a rag had been wrapped around his arm at some point before he made it to the hospital. Like all the others Justina had seen in the lobby, gritty dust seemed to coat every pore and hair on his body. A persistent low moan of pain came from his dry lips, broken only by a frequent hacking cough. When he saw Dr. Chukwu, his eyes widened, and he looked to Justina. She realized that perhaps he had never seen a man that dark or that large before, so she started explaining to him in Spanish who the doctor was and reassured him that they would take care of him. Doctor Chukwu explained to Justina what he needed to do to treat the arm as well as the cough and dehydration, so she could make the patient understand.

The man seemed relieved to talk to her and she kept a quiet conversation going with him while the doctor cleaned and stitched up the ragged gash in the man's arm. He gritted his teeth in pain, still moaning off and on when it was particularly uncomfortable, but he was clearly trying to focus on Justina rather than what the doctor was doing. Overall, the first patient went well, Justina thought. She felt that she had made a big difference for the man. Dr. Chukwu complimented her, telling her that she had a calming way with the patient and that they were a good team.

The next patient was the worst one. It was a little girl who had been pinned under a steel beam that crushed her leg. She looked to be about six years old and had on a tattered pink dress with little ponytails atop her head, secured with Hello Kitty clips. Her mother was with her, sobbing and begging for help for her baby. After Dr. Chukwu's exam, Justina had to tell the mother that her daughter was going to lose her leg. The mother fell to her knees clutching Dr. Chukwu's coat, begging him to not do it, to save her leg, to make her little girl better. Justina had to translate back and forth and it was the hardest thing she ever had to do, the tears were coming freely down her own face without her even realizing it.

The pink tights she had been wearing were torn completely off at the top of her leg and the leg was completely twisted and crushed. She was still wearing one white patent leather shoe on the unharmed leg. She was screaming in loud waves, interspersed with deep gulps of air, and was trying to push the doctor away with one hand, in the other hand she was still clutching a filthy plastic doll whose clothing was also torn. Dr. Chukwu gave the child a shot to relieve her pain and anxiety and they finally persuaded the mother that the surgery was needed to save her daughter. The poor woman's face was coated with grief and tearstains. Her eyes were almost swollen shut from crying, but she finally calmed down and the little girl was sent for surgery. Justina wanted to stay with the mother and comfort her, but Dr. Chukwu told her in his firm but gentle way that there were many more people needing help.

The rest of the day was a blur with barely a chance to even get a drink or use the bathroom. It seemed that the entire city was there in the hospital. Not only were they treating the patients who had been trapped in various collapsed buildings, they were seeing the patients rescued from the destroyed hospitals. Many were already in the hospital for other problems and then they were trapped. Those patients were especially difficult and Justina was amazed that the doctor could keep going, one after another, the way he did.

It was late in the afternoon when a plump young nurse came into their examination room to tell Justina that Victor was there. She suddenly realized how long she had been there, but there was so much more to do. Dr. Chukwu told her it was fine to leave—she had been helping nonstop for hours—but she felt that if he was going to stay she could too. Her father, surprisingly, didn't argue with her once they agreed that the doctor would get her back to the hotel that night. Victor did go and find her a sandwich and brought it to her, knowing she probably hadn't eaten.

During the drive back to her hotel, Dr. Chukwu told her he was very pleased with the day. He admitted that he hadn't expected her to be able to hang in there so long—it was a very difficult day with so many tragic situations, one after another. She suspected that what he really meant was that he didn't expect a politician's daughter to be very useful, but she appreciated that he didn't put it that way. She was proud that she had stuck it out, despite the sadness in her heart and the horrific images in her head.

When she got to her room, she discovered a bottle of sparkling water and a tray of snacks from Victor. As she looked in the mirror and hardly recognized herself. Her hair was hanging in loose straggles, rather than the neat ponytail she had worn in the morning, and her clothes were wrinkled and streaked with blood and grime from comforting patients and families. She had no makeup left on her face and her eyes were bloodshot, but she looked at herself with satisfaction, feeling that she had done a good day's work.

She called her father's room, too tired to talk much, and went to bed as soon as she had eaten her snacks. That night she didn't have any bad dreams at all

CHAPTER THIRTY TWO

The next day began early for Daniel who had slept hard all night. When Marcos woke him, he discovered that his whole body was aching from the previous day's work. He hadn't really noticed the physical aspect of what he was doing—the mental and emotional intensity had really been at the forefront of his attention with his focus on finding survivors. As he rolled out of bed he realized that he felt like he had been run over by one of the dump trucks used to haul away debris. Marcos, of course, was ready to go—a ball of energy.

"Come on man, get your lazy butt out of bed!" he teased, armed with a cup of coffee for Daniel.

"I'm up, I'm up," he groaned, accepting the coffee gratefully. "Right now I wish I was more of an athlete like you, maybe I wouldn't feel like I've been ridden hard and put away wet!"

"Yeah, man, chicks dig it," Marcos bragged with a laugh, flexing his muscles. "Now get your pants on, Maria is cooking us some *huevos* and I am starved!"

They wasted no time eating the huge breakfast that Maria had prepared and then headed out for another day at the hospital site. They knew that the chance of finding survivors reduced dramatically each day. The banter from breakfast quickly dissolved into silence as they neared the site and saw the crowd of people who were still gathered around the remains of the hospital, hoping for loved ones to appear. The atmosphere had an even greater feeling of desperation than the day before; people had posted notices on any available standing wall, trying to locate family members.

There were a number of search and rescue teams already at work, climbing the piles of rubble with dogs to locate additional survivors, while others formed a human chain to methodically remove the chunks of steel and concrete. They passed the chunks of debris down the row to create new piles that would be scooped up and hauled off. As Daniel and Marcos looked around to figure out where to go, they heard a loud whistle and a torrent of shouting.

"Those guys think they found some people," Marcos translated for Daniel and they joined a flurry of other men who rushed to help. One of the dogs was barking and pawing at the pile of rubble and everyone quickly starting grabbing at pieces of concrete, rebar, and steel and throwing them aside. Within a few minutes they discovered an opening into a partially collapsed room, although they couldn't immediately see any survivors or bodies. As they cleared the opening further, they heard faint crying and one of the men immediately located the source. The baby was miraculously unhurt. He was lying under a steel beam, which had apparently fallen in such a way that it prevented other debris from crushing the infant. The baby was still wrapped in a blue flannel blanket. He was maybe two or three months old and cried weakly as he was pulled out of the rubble and quickly taken down to the medics.

Next to the baby was the body of a young woman, fatally crushed under the same steel beam that had protected the baby. There was a moment of silence as the team realized that the woman was likely the mother of the baby. They worked to free her from the beam and her body was taken to join the hundreds of others who had not survived.

Daniel and Marcos, with several others, went to work on opening up the inside of the collapsed hospital unit, hoping to find additional pockets of survivors. They found several more bodies and the team worked to unearth them and get them out of the building. It was looking like there weren't going to be any more survivors when one of the men shouted. Marcos hurried over to help. Daniel could see that they had opened up a little cubbyhole and it sounded like they had found a child. It turned out to be a little girl and a woman who appeared to be a nurse, both alive but badly injured. Marcos and another man carried the survivors out. The remaining men dug deeper into the newly revealed earthquake cavern with renewed energy and hope.

As Daniel resumed his efforts to pull apart a pile of crumbling debris, he suddenly heard a low rumbling that was seemingly all around him. At first he thought was one of the dump trucks or tractors that had been coming to haul away the mountains of hospital remains. As the roaring sound got louder and the debris started to fall around him, he quickly realized what was happening. The other men shouted urgently and scrambled to get out of the hole they were in, ducking falling pieces of concrete and steel.

Daniel was the furthest back in the opening and he panicked for a split second, realizing that he might not be able to get out because there were huge chunks of debris falling between him and the opening. His mind flashed to those seemingly irrelevant earthquake-training drills he did as a kid in school, "If there is an earthquake, get under your desk!" He looked around and saw a huge steel beam lying diagonally behind him and quickly ducked under it, hoping it would shield him in the same way the baby had been protected. The roaring tremor lasted less than a minute, but to Daniel it seemed like an eternity as he crouched helplessly under the beam, covering his head with his arms to ward off falling pieces of the ceiling.

As the rumbling and shaking subsided, Daniel could clearly hear shouts outside, so he knew that the opening was not completely sealed off—although he couldn't see much of anything because of all the dust that was filling the air and coating everything. He was going to start digging out when he heard a muffled cough and realized that the tremor had opened up the area behind him. He started digging through the rubble in the direction of the cough and called out, "Hello. . .hello, where are you?" He was rewarded with a weak cry that guided where to dig. The first thing he saw was a red tennis shoe and a skinny brown leg protruding out from under a twisted pile of rebar. He dug frantically until he found the owner of the shoe—a frail looking boy of about seven or eight with badly torn denim shorts and a tattered red t-shirt that was streaked with blood and filth. He had a bad cut on his arm, probably from the rebar, but Daniel didn't see any major injury—at least not on the surface.

"Hey, it's okay, I got you," Daniel said, wishing his high-school Spanish came to him more readily. As Daniel got closer he was able to see the boy better. His face was caked with dust except for his huge dark eyes that seemed sunken and terrified. The boy struggled to move his body from under the debris, but his arm was pinned.

"Shh, shh, it's okay, be still," Daniel said, knowing the child couldn't understand him, but feeling the need to talk to him anyhow. He pulled the pieces of rebar carefully off the boy, not wanting to cut him with the jagged edges that poked out at odd angles. The pieces of rebar were not particularly heavy, but they were bent and twisted, tangled between each other, making it slow and difficult work to remove them. Daniel worked doggedly as the boy watched him intently, occasionally coughing but otherwise quiet.

"*Como te llamas?*" Daniel asked, recalling some basic Spanish and trying to distract the hurt child. As the boy started to answer he coughed and licked his dry, cracked lips. Finally he said "Jose, *mi llamo* Jose," and coughed again. "Okay, Jose, *mi llamo* Daniel. We are almost done." Daniel realized the child was probably dehydrated and getting him to talk was maybe not helpful, so he focused instead on the last few stubborn pieces of rebar that were lodged under a large chunk of concrete. Jose whimpered as the last piece came free, pulling his leg into an odd angle as it did so. Daniel looked and didn't see any injury to the leg, so he leaned down and wrapped his arms around the Jose's skinny body, pulling him loose.

"Come on, Jose, we are going to get out of here now," Daniel promised, putting the boy headfirst over his shoulder so he could have one arm free to open a path to the entrance of the cave they were in.

Getting out of the hole was slow going with the new piles of debris making it difficult to walk. Daniel found himself basically climbing up a small mountain of rubble, trying to hold Jose against his body so he wouldn't get any more cuts or scrapes.

The entrance was almost totally blocked, although there was enough of an opening for Daniel to push the pieces of concrete out of the way. In a few minutes they were out and Daniel climbed out into the daylight, blinking at the sunlight, which seemed so bright after the thick haze of dust inside the building's remains. "Daniel, *mi amigo!*"

He immediately heard Marcos' voice, calling to him. Marcos met him halfway up the pile of rubble that Daniel was navigating with Jose's thin arms wrapped around his neck, holding tightly.

"Oh man, I thought you were trapped in there! We were just coming up to try to dig you out! And you found a boy," he added excitedly. "Come on, let's get a medic to look at him." Marcos held out his arms for Jose, but the child grabbed Daniel harder, burying his head in Daniel's neck.

"You have a new best friend, I see," he said with a laugh and added, "is he hurt? I can't see anything bad."

"I don't think so. He has a cut and he is weak," Daniel replied as they crossed from the pile of rubble to the area where the aid station and medics were located.

"Okay, let me go find a medic, they are very busy after the last tremor, and I will find some water for him. Stay here." Marcos instructed before heading off.

Daniel sat on the ground and reached for Jose's arms. "Okay, big guy, let go so we can look at you, *por favore?*" The child relaxed his grip and Daniel was able to pull the child onto his lap to get a better look at him. Jose's face and hair were an almost uniform shade of grey because he was so completely coated with gritty dust. Daniel shifted the boy to take a look at the gash on his arm and started working at peeling off the part of his shirt that was stuck to the wound and caked with dried blood.

"Here, let me help," a familiar voice said and Daniel looked up to see Victor Gonzalez standing over him. He opened his mouth to respond, but nothing came out, he was speechless with surprise. Victor looked as impeccable as ever in a beautiful navy suit and expensive sunglasses and Daniel looked around to make sense of it. He quickly noted two shiny black cars that had parked nearby and several other men and women in suits as well as a cameraman standing beside the car.

Victor squatted down, producing a bottle of water. "Here, he needs this," he said, letting the boy drink. As Jose drank, Victor slowed him from gulping too quickly. Then he looked over toward the group by the car and called to them in rapid Spanish. Immediately a woman came over with another bottle of water.

"Gracias," Victor said to her dismissively and returned his attention to Jose.

"We need to get this shirt off him and clean this wound," Victor said and he pulled off his jacket. Laying it on the ground, he told Daniel, "Lay him here on his side."

Victor spoke calmly to Jose, giving him additional sips of water. "Hold his arm," Victor instructed as he worked the shirt off the wound. As he pulled it free, it started bleeding again and Jose cried out, looking at Daniel as if for help.

"It's okay, buddy," Daniel said, stroking the child's head soothingly with his other hand.

Victor pulled a neatly folded white linen handkerchief out of his pocket and poured some of the water onto it. He began gently cleaning the cut on Jose's arm, talking to him quietly as he did so. Once it was wiped off, Daniel realized the gash was much worse than he thought. Jose was crying quietly, although there were no tears coming from his eyes, and the wound was bleeding copiously.

Victor looked up at a couple of boys who were standing nearby and watching. He gave them an order in rapid Spanish and the boys ran off, returning almost immediately with a half-used roll of bandages. Daniel watched silently as Victor bandaged the wound as efficiently as any of the Red Cross workers Daniel had witnessed so far.

"He needs stitches—this bandage isn't enough," Victor told Daniel. "You might need a couple stitches as well," he said, nodding to Daniel's leg.

Daniel hadn't even noticed the cut on his own leg, just above the ankle, where a piece of steel or rebar must have cut him on the way out of the demolished hospital unit. Victor folded the handkerchief over to the clean side and handed it to Daniel. "We need to get to the hospital. Can you carry him? He seems attached to you."

"Yes, of course," Daniel agreed and he reached out to Jose, who immediately wrapped his arms around Daniel's neck and hung on him. He picked up Victor's jacket, now filthy, and held it out to him.

Victor shook his head. "Put it around him. He needs it more than I do."

Daniel wrapped the jacket around Jose who was engulfed by the navy fabric—only his head and skinny legs peeking out. Daniel followed Victor to the car and realized the cameraman had been filming them, which gave him a really weird feeling. Victor spoke to him in Spanish and the guy turned the camera off. Then Victor spoke to a young man standing at the driver's side door of the first car who was apparently the driver. He quickly opened the back door and Victor motioned for Daniel to get in. Victor spent a moment talking to the group he had arrived with and then climbed in the car.

Daniel was at a loss for words. Finally he asked, "What were you doing there at the hospital wreckage? I was so surprised to see you there."

"Yes, I'm sure you were and I was equally surprised. One of my colleagues pointed you out, coming out of that pile of rubble after the tremor. They could not believe me when I said, I know that guy!" Victor laughed. "I am working with the Senator and the Mexican Ambassador. We were there to see one of the disaster sites where survivors are still being found. Everyone, of course, is worried about a hospital. How did you end up here?"

"My engineering professor is originally from Mexico City, so he was able to get the school to fund a group to come here and help rebuild. Of course, rebuilding doesn't start while people are still trapped. This is only my second day—I have never seen anything this horrible. It is such a tragedy." Daniel looked down at Jose who had fallen asleep already, curled up at Daniel's side. He wondered if Jose would have any family left alive, and how they could ever be found.

"Yes, it is a tragedy. I wish I could say I have never seen something like this—it is never easy," he said, taking off his sunglasses and rubbing his eyes.

"You seemed to know exactly what to do for Jose back there. I never saw a medic or nurse do any better," Daniel said. "Not that I am an expert," he hastened to add. "Where did you learn that?" Daniel couldn't get over his surprise at how Victor had taken over and managed the situation so expertly. His opinion of Victor as a selfish politician was shaken much like the hospital unit had been during the tremor.

Victor smiled sadly. "There are many things I have done in my life, Daniel. That is a long story for another day. Let's just say that I was not born in a suit. I have seen and done many things that do not get discussed at cocktail parties."

Daniel nodded, not sure how to respond to that, and shifted Jose whose weight was making Daniel's arm go numb. Victor cleared his throat and took a deep breath. "Daniel," he said. "I have something to say to you. It is not easy for me, but I have to say it. I was very unfair to you. I made assumptions about you, which is something I try to never do. But when it comes to my daughter I do not always behave rationally. I want you to know that I am sorry for that. Justina told me I was wrong and it only made me angrier. I don't know about all the things in your life, but I see you are trying to work hard and do right in the world. Despite what you might think of me, I don't like to give speeches, but I had to tell you that."

Victor leaned back in his seat, putting his sunglasses back on, and Daniel sensed that the subject was closed. He could see that Victor was a very proud man and hated to admit being wrong. Daniel was feeling a bit overwhelmed again. Victor had this way of leaving him unsure of what to say. The man had always intimidated him, but now he found himself admiring Victor and wondering what path he had traveled to become this powerful presence.

"Thank you, sir. I understand why you wouldn't think I was good enough for Justina. I get that. It's okay."

Victor nodded without saying anything more until they got to the hospital.

CHAPTER THIRTY THREE

J ustina's day had an even more hectic beginning than the day
before. People were getting sick from contaminated water and
they had an even bigger group of patients crowding the little hospital than ever. The scene outside was mayhem, with people still
congregating all around the area trying to find family and loved
ones, posting pictures and notes on any vertical surface, and many
more clumping around the entrance of the hospital as they tried
to get in for medical care . The police could not control the scene
with so many needing to go in for treatment and others trying to
get in to look for people they could not find. The cacophony of
voices shouting and crying and car horns blaring on top of ambulance sirens was overwhelming to the senses. Justina felt over-
loaded before she even got in the door.

The patients in the morning weren't in such critical condition
as the ones the day before. It seemed that the number of survivors
being brought it had dwindled, but the patients now had medical
issues relating to contaminated water or health problems made
worse by lack of medication. Many people were living in makeshift

shelters and didn't have the medicines they had been using before the earthquake, so their conditions were starting to deteriorate. Although their problems were generally less severe, there were many of them. They almost had a revolving door of patients being quickly evaluated, their condition explained, and prescriptions given. Justina was relieved that the Red Cross and others had sent a shipment of medications—otherwise the hospital would never have been able to meet the demand.

They were well into the morning when they heard from a nurse that there had been a tremor again in the city. They hadn't felt it, but knew it would probably mean another influx of injuries. Dr. Chukwu looked at Justina and shook his head when he heard the news. "If you need a drink or a snack, you had best go now. We may have a long day ahead of us," he advised her while giving the young woman they were seeing a prescription for insulin.

After a short break, the next batch of injuries began to pour in. Apparently the tremor hadn't been very severe, but it was enough to bring down a couple of additional buildings that were already rendered unstable and shake loose debris that hit some people and caused less severe injuries. They were finishing up a young man who had a minor head injury when a very young nurse came into the room. "I am looking for Justina?" she said in Spanish, not sure she was in the right place.

"Yes, I am Justina. What do you need?" Justina couldn't imagine why this nurse would be looking for her.

"A man named Victor Gonzalez is looking for you. He said it is important that you come. That's all I know. He is at the front entrance." With that the nurse scurried off, back to her own duties.

Justina looked to Dr. Chukwu who nodded and said, "Go ahead, we are done here. Just let me know if you need to leave for some reason, so I can get someone else to help."

"I hope everything is okay," she fretted. She couldn't imagine her father coming there in the middle of the day unless something had happened. She knew he was going to see some of the sites, she hoped he wasn't hurt in the tremor.

In the lobby people were lying on the floor, sitting against the walls, standing in clusters—all talking, crying, and praying. As she got toward the entrance, she saw her father before he saw her and she looked to see if he was hurt. The only thing she could see was that his jacket was off and it looked like there might be a little blood on his sleeve. And then she saw Daniel, and the shock almost sent her over backwards.

He was almost unrecognizable, he was covered in dust and blood like all the patients she had seen, but she would recognize his curly blonde head anywhere. He was holding a little boy who was clinging to him. He had his head down, talking to the little boy, who was crying and had a bandage wrapped around his arm that was seeping blood. Just seeing Daniel overwhelmed her and she felt tears coming to her eyes almost instantly.

"Daniel!" she called out. He looked up and the shock on his face quickly turned into a huge grin.

"Oh my God! Justina!" Daniel looked from her to Victor who reached out with a smile to take Jose. Daniel held out his arms and she pushed through the people to wrap her arms around him, burying her face in his filthy shirt. She found herself crying from the sheer shock and emotion of seeing him. She couldn't imagine how he had gotten there, but she didn't care how—just so long as he was there.

Daniel was asking her father why she was there in Mexico City and she heard her father's quiet response, but none of it really registered except that Daniel was there and her father was there in this madhouse hospital with her. And so was a little boy. She finally remembered that and dislodged herself from Daniel to look at the boy in her father's arms who was, by now, bleeding onto Victor's shirt.

"Oh my God," she murmured, realizing the situation.

Victor reached over and stroked her hair, smiling. "Are we just going to stand here or are you going to find us a doctor for Jose here?" he asked. Justina nodded, smiling, with tears still fresh in her eyes.

"Of course, right this way," she said and led them off to find the doctor with Daniels hand held tightly in hers.

ACKNOWLEDGEMENTS

The people who I worked with and got to know during my time in New York truly affected me, and are the reason I felt compelled to tell the story of Sandy and the neighborhoods where I lived and worked. It was because of those people that I felt so saddened to leave my job at St. John's Episcopal Hospital and why I felt the horror of Sandy so strongly. In addition, I would be remiss not to acknowledge my support at home, those who encouraged me and also left me alone when I needed time to work on this book: my mother, Velma Lee, and my son, Dmitry Walberg, who is now starting his own book. I also have to mention my appreciation for Hector Porras, my very best friend who helped me through many rough times and kept me sane (kind of)!

From St. John's, I need to offer special thanks to Rev. Dr. Cecily Broderick y Guerra, otherwise known as 'Mother B'. Your input was invaluable, and I will never forget the drive around the Rockaways to find Daniel's house! You are a wonderful friend and an amazing woman.

Last, but certainly not least, I appreciate all the help from Kevin Anderson and Associates, for their wonderful editing work, in addition to creating the cover and coaching me through a process that has certainly been like nothing I have been through before. It has been an incredible journey for me!

EPILOGUE

I wrote this book to help tell the story of what happened to a couple of neighborhoods, and a hospital, during Hurricane Sandy. I will acknowledge that certain details were altered for purposes of telling the story; for instance, the Gonzalez house would most likely have not survived so unscathed, based on where it is located. The majority of the details relating to Sandy, however, do reflect the reality of those neighborhoods and St. John's Episcopal Hospital.

Hurricane Sandy was a life-altering event for many people along the east coast, particularly New York and New Jersey. Many people lost their homes and belongings, and some even lost their lives. Homes were uninhabitable due to the mold and contamination, and people couldn't restore power until the electrical systems were rebuilt. A lot of people left and didn't come back, as happens with many disasters of this scale. People who rented did not get compensation for their lost belongings, which in many cases included everything on the first floor. Renters insurance doesn't cover flood damage. Many people were able to patch together a financial recovery through FEMA money, insurance money, and money from other local sources, but many did not.

It was discovered much later that insurance companies were putting roadblocks in place to avoid paying the claims of Sandy victims, even going to far as altering engineering reports. FEMA reported this early this year, and it was investigated and reported by 60 Minutes. Nearly three years later, hundreds of storm victims are now suing their insurance companies to get the money owed under their policies.

Long Beach today is back to being a vibrant and bustling beach town. Sandy was still a defining event for the people there, though, and is still very present in their minds and in their homes, as not all homes have been completely restored. Businesses are back, and those that never returned were replaced. The beautiful and well-known boardwalk has been rebuilt, and the beach is again crowded.

Far Rockaway has come back to a lesser degree. The boardwalk there is still not completely rebuilt, and there seems to be a greater number of residents who never returned.

St. John's Episcopal Hospital, where I worked until shortly before Sandy, has been a financially struggling facility since before the storm, and continues those struggles today. St. John's was not eligible for much money from FEMA, since it did not sustain much 'actual' damage. Many of the people St. John's cared for during the storm and the period after were there because they had nowhere else to go. The hospital serves a very poor and vulnerable population, and there are no other hospitals nearby, so this facility provides a very important service to the community. The census, or number of beds filled, has been down since Sandy, and it is likely that this is due at least in large part to the number of residents that left and never returned. This issue adds to the financial challenges of an already-strapped organization.

Finally, the earthquake in Mexico City, although fictitious in terms of timing, was based on an actual event that occurred in 1985.

I wrote this story to tell what happened with Sandy, but also to highlight the strength of people in overcoming challenges and helping their communities. In both Hurricane Sandy and the Mexico City earthquake, the communities came together to take care of the victims and to help rebuild. Although disasters such as this are horrific, they provide tremendous examples of the human spirit and of people coming together and helping each other, without regard to race or culture.

I hope you enjoyed this book. Please visit my website at susan-walberg.com for additional notes on this story as well as information on upcoming projects.

Thank you.

AUTHOR BIO

Susan Walberg was born and raised in Seattle, Washington, where she received her Bachelors of Arts degree in Psychology from the University of Washington. Susan's education also includes a Masters in Public Administration from Seattle University and a Juris Doctorate from Seattle University School of Law. Susan worked in Seattle for a large health system as the Regulatory Attorney before moving to Maryland in 2007. Susan has continued working in the health care field as a Compliance Officer and now as a consultant. She also spent over a year living in Long Beach, New York, and working at St. John's Episcopal Hospital in Far Rockaway, New York, which was the inspiration for this novel. Susan now lives in Laurel, Maryland, with her mother and a variety of pets.